TOO
RICH
FOR A
BRIDE

A Novel

MONA
HODGSON

Author of *Two Brides Too Many*

WATERBROOK
PRESS

Too Rich for a Bride
Published by WaterBrook Press
12265 Oracle Boulevard, Suite 200
Colorado Springs, Colorado 80921

All Scripture quotations or paraphrases are taken from the King James Version.

The characters and events in this book are fictional, and any resemblance to actual persons or events is coincidental.

ISBN 978-0-307-45892-6
ISBN 978-0-307-45893-3 (electronic)

Copyright © 2010 by Mona Hodgson

Published in association with the literary agency of Janet Kobobel Grant, Books & Such, 52 Mission Circle, Suite 122, PMB 170, Santa Rosa, CA 95409-5370.

Published in the United States by WaterBrook Multnomah, an imprint of the Crown Publishing Group, a division of Random House Inc., New York.

WaterBrook and its deer colophon are registered trademarks of Random House Inc.

The Library of Congress Cataloging-in-Publication Data
Hodgson, Mona Gansberg, 1954–
  Too rich for a bride : a novel / Mona Hodgson. — 1st ed.
    p. cm.
  ISBN 978-0-307-45892-6 — ISBN 978-0-307-45893-3 (electronic) 1. Businesswomen—Fiction. 2. Sisters—Fiction. 3. Cripple Creek (Colo.)—Fiction. 4. Colorado—History—1876-1950—Fiction. I. Title.
  PS3608.O474T66 2011
  813'.6—dc22
                                          2011005869

Printed in the United States of America
2011—First Edition

10 9 8 7 6 5 4 3 2 1

For two sisters…
my daughters: Amy Eardensohn and Sara Hodgson

But thanks be to God, which
giveth us the victory through
our Lord Jesus Christ.

1 CORINTHIANS 15:57

ONE

Portland, Maine
18 September 1896

Ida Sinclair didn't know where her ambition would take her, only that she possessed a liberal measure of it. That was why the Merton School of Business was the perfect place for her. And why she sat in the front row of the classroom. She didn't want to miss any bit of information or instruction that could move her closer to success.

Gazing from the calculations on the blackboard to the guest lecturer's dark eyes, offset by traces of silver at his hairline, Ida waited for Mr. Bradley Ditmer to finish his point about customer relations and then raised her hand.

"Miss Sinclair, you have another question?"

Ida moistened her lips. "Yes. I'd like to know how one goes about securing financing to launch a busi—"

A roar of deep laughter startled her and she turned to glare at the source—a gangly, beak-nosed young man in the row beside hers.

"I wouldn't worry too much about financing, missy," he said. "Learn how to make a good pot of coffee and keep a file cabinet organized, and maybe I'll hire you to work in my company."

More laughter swept across the room until the professor made his way to the mouthy student's desk. Mr. Ditmer's footsteps stilled all other noise.

"Mr. Burn—"

"Burkett."

"You are a child to indulge in such hubris. Kindly keep it to yourself."

Ida felt the same burn she'd become accustomed to since her first day in class. Her fellow students didn't approve of her plans and aspirations. Even the women. But she also felt somewhat vindicated by Mr. Ditmer's gallant stand against such boorish rantings.

The professor cleared his throat. "To answer your question, Miss Sinclair, bankers, private investors, and those on the stock exchange could provide necessary funding for a business." He sauntered back to the front of the room then turned to face her. "However, no investor is wont to throw away money on frivolous pursuits. Each business proposal is weighed individually by its likelihood of success."

"Thank you, sir." Ida sealed her mouth shut against the numerous questions his answer raised.

She was still recording her thoughts and ideas in her notebook when Mr. Ditmer dismissed the class, making her the last to head for the door.

"Miss Sinclair?" Mr. Ditmer's clear tone resonated off the empty desks in the room.

Ida stilled her steps a few feet from the classroom door and turned to face her instructor. A pleasant view, to be sure. The man was no Teddy Roosevelt, but he exuded the same commanding presence and compelling confidence.

She glanced down at the reticule she held in one hand and her satchel in the other, then looked back at the first row of desks. She saw no evidence to indicate she'd left anything behind. So what did Mr. Ditmer want?

He walked toward her, then stopped at a respectable distance. "I wondered if I might have a word with you."

Ida nodded while her mind raced after an explanation. She had asked a lot of questions during class this morning, but she didn't detect any irritation in his gaze. "Is there a problem, Mr. Ditmer? I didn't intend any disruption, sir. It's just that I find the topic of business ethics intriguing."

"Your questions posed no disruption, Miss Sinclair. On the contrary." A smile revealed perfectly straight teeth. "I, for one, appreciate your participation and find your interest and questions thought-provoking. Even rewarding. Discussions on business ethics can be—as a rule—a mite drab."

If her instructor wasn't set on scolding her for an overactive curiosity, then what *did* he want to talk to her about?

"Miss Sinclair, you have your sights set on success in what has been dubbed a man's world." It wasn't a question.

Although he didn't seem the least bit intimidated or put off by her unconventional aspirations, she squared her shoulders anyway. She was prepared to defend her determination to him or anyone else who might question her entrance into the world of business. "Yes, sir, I do."

"Then I'd like to discuss some possibilities with you."

Ida shifted her weight to one foot, hoping the act would slow her pulse and make her appear more relaxed than she felt. Bradley Ditmer owned a large clothiers chain in New York City. She'd love nothing more than to discuss business with him, especially if their conversation held any promise for her future livelihood.

She glanced up at the clock atop a bookcase. Thirty-five minutes after twelve. Only twenty-five minutes remained of her lunch break between classes and her work in the school's main office.

Unfortunately, she had no wiggle room in her schedule today, and such a discussion could require every minute of her remaining break, and then some. Her employer was out of the office until Monday, and he counted on her to see to the mound of work he'd left for her, including interviewing two prospective students. Still, this was *the* Mr. Bradley Ditmer, one of New York's foremost commerce tycoons standing before her, interested in her business ambitions.

"You want to talk with me about my future in the world of business?" she asked.

"If you're amenable to it."

"Yes." She'd allowed herself to sound far too anxious. "I'd be most interested in hearing what you have to say."

"I have a luncheon appointment. And I know you have a job to attend to." He pushed a silver-tinted strand of hair from his temple much the way her father did, only Father's was more salt and pepper than gray. "We could chat after you're finished with your afternoon's work."

A meeting after work would make for a long day, and perhaps mean she wouldn't get home until after dark, but Mr. Ditmer was very knowledgeable and influential. Father would want her to pursue her dream, and knowing she had a bright and secure future ahead of her would be a comfort to him.

"We can discuss job possibilities over coffee." His eyebrows arched into a question mark.

"Coffee sounds lovely."

"Very well, then. I'll brew a fresh pot in my office at five o'clock."

In his office. Ida fussed with the wrap draped over her shoulders. Of course he'd want to meet with her in his office. It made sense that he'd keep his list of contacts there—all of his business resources. She brought her bags together in front of her. It wasn't as if she hadn't been in his office before.

She'd delivered files and telephone messages to him there. The twinge of apprehension niggling at her stomach was senseless. She was behaving like a nervous schoolgirl, something a woman with her "sights set on success" couldn't afford to do.

Ida offered him a tight nod and took quick steps out the door, closing it behind her. She pulled her mother's pendant watch from her reticule and glanced at its face. Only fifteen minutes left of her break, barely enough time to scoot down the hall to the washroom and then unlock the office door by one o'clock.

At the end of four hours of filing, typing, and bookkeeping, Ida retrieved her belongings from under her desk and put on her wrap.

Mr. Ditmer, as the guest lecturer for the final month of school, had an office at the end of the empty corridor. Ida's low-top shoes drummed against the parquet flooring as she made her way around the corner and past three quiet classrooms. She drew in a fortifying breath as she approached his office.

Mr. Bradley Ditmer had taken notice of her business acuity. Her father and her sisters Kat and Nell expected her to move to Cripple Creek, Colorado, next month following her graduation, but surely they'd understand that she couldn't turn down a lucrative job in New York City. That'd be plain foolish.

After admiring the shine on the brass nameplate—Bradley P. Ditmer III, Industrialist and Adjunct Professor—she knocked lightly on his office door.

"Do come in."

She did, and was met with the rich aroma of freshly brewed coffee. Her instructor stood behind an oak desk, his suit jacket draped over a brass hook behind him. He motioned for her to be seated in one of the two high-back leather chairs that faced his tidy desk.

Ida left her bags by the door and sat down, watching him pour the steaming liquid into two cups at a buffet in the corner. She'd expected him to ask her to make the coffee, or at least to pour it. Instead, he was serving her. And given his calm response to her many and varied questions in class, he seemed perfectly capable of picturing a woman's role in business as something more than a kitchen aide and secretary.

"Cream? Sugar?" He returned the pot to the hot plate on the buffet and turned toward her.

"No, thank you."

He crossed the room and handed her a full cup on a saucer. "One cup of coffee, undiluted." He smiled. "I should've guessed you liked your coffee full-strength. You seem to be one who appreciates the straightforward and direct approach."

"Thank you." Ida set the saucer on the desk and loosened her wrap so that it hung at her sides.

"My apologies. This office is on the warm side. Why don't I take your wrap and hang it with my coat?"

She lifted the shawl over her head, mindful of the cup in front of her, and handed it to him.

While he draped her wrap over a hook and then returned to the buffet, Ida lifted her cup from the desk and let the steam moisten her face. She carefully took a sip, enjoying the coffee's rich warmth on her throat.

"It's a Brazilian blend." Mr. Ditmer carried his cup over and sat down, but not behind his desk as she'd expected. Instead he perched on the chair beside her and took a big gulp of hot coffee.

She enjoyed another swallow of hers while wondering what direction this conversation would take, and how.

"So, what did you do this afternoon?" he asked.

She set her cup on the desk. "I interviewed a prospective student. A second didn't show up. Most of my work involved typing and filing."

An eyebrow raised, he set his cup back into the saucer. "Sounds like humdrum busywork to me. A mite mundane, I'd say, for someone with your sharp intellect."

His candor surprised her, and a blush burned her cheeks. "It's surely not what I aspire to do." She paused, uncomfortable in the silence. Taking a deep breath, she continued. "And what about you? You have a successful retail chain in New York City, and yet you're here in Portland, teaching."

"Everyone needs a change now and again." He glanced around the office. "Besides, I'm careful to employ people I can trust to run the operations in my absence. It's good for them to have the opportunity."

Sitting a little straighter, Ida forced herself not to squirm. Might she soon be one of his trusted employees?

"During our class discussions the past two weeks," Mr. Ditmer said, "you've mentioned your father living and working in France."

"As you said in your lecture earlier this week, sometimes it's best not to set your roots too deep because it's necessary to go where the opportunities are. That was the case with my father. His position overseeing locomotive engineers here in Portland was eliminated, but he was given the opportunity to instruct and oversee European design engineers in Paris." Growing weary of the sound of her own voice, Ida lifted the cup to her mouth. She was doing all the talking. "I doubt you called this meeting to discuss my father."

"No, but…" He leaned forward, his hands on his knees. "Do you intend to join him in France?"

"I have no plans to go to Paris, sir." *New York, on the other hand…*

"*Sir* is a bit stuffy for business colleagues. And, speaking of stuffy—"
He slid his vest off and laid it over the back of his chair. "Please call me
Bradley. May I call you Ida?"

"That'd be fine." Of course it was fine. Even though he was her instructor and would be for another two weeks, he did seem more of an associate
right now.

"And what about Portland, Ida? Are you set on remaining here?"

"Not at all. I don't expect to, or want to." She kept the Cripple Creek
family plan to herself.

"That's good news." He peered at her from over the brim of his cup. His
gaze held a cordiality she hadn't noticed earlier. "You'll be finished with
your course work in just a few weeks. I don't know how you'd feel about
moving to New York City—"

"I like New York City." Never mind that she had never been there.

He smiled and set his cup in its saucer on the desk. "Good. I might have
an opening in my buying division."

He was offering her a job. Ida opened her mouth to say the buying division sounded like an interesting prospect, but quickly closed her mouth
when her instructor took the cup and saucer from her hand. He set them on
the desk, a little too close to his, dinging the sides of the plates.

They hadn't finished their coffee. Or their conversation, had they? She
expected to hear more about the opening in his company.

Ida's throat went dry before she could question him. A thick silence
layered the room as Mr. Ditmer clasped her hands and stood, pulling her up
with him. Then his lips sealed hers shut and his hands began to travel her
rigid frame.

Ida jerked her arms upward, dislodging his hands from her backside.
She pulled away from him, her backward momentum stayed by the massive
desk behind her. She swallowed hard against the acid burning her throat.

Ditmer shrugged. "You said you had your sights set on the business world."

"I do." She glanced past him, at the door.

"If that's truly the case, then you should know the only way a young single woman would be able to achieve your goal is to become a companion to someone who can make it happen."

"A *companion*?" The word soured her tongue and she swallowed hard.

"A mistress, if you will. I can answer all of your questions and pay you very well for your"—he raised a thick eyebrow—"personal services." A smirk darkened his face and he raised a finger to her cheek.

Ida slapped him. The stinging in her hand travelled up her arm as she spun away from his reach, jamming her toe on the ornate desk leg.

"You're wrong," she spit, then scooped up her things and slammed the door shut behind her.

She would prove him wrong.

Twenty-five minutes later, Ida was yanking the pins from her hat when her youngest sister burst into the entryway.

Vivian's five-foot, four-inch stature and brown doe eyes made her look much younger than her nearly eighteen years. Sandy blond curls dangled from a knot on the crown of her head and bounced above her slight shoulders as she pulled an envelope out of the pocket on her yellow gingham apron. "It's a letter from Nell."

Ida felt her spirits lift. News from Nell would help distract her.

"We're glad you're finally home." Her aunt Alma glided into the entryway. Her braids, pinned in a circlet above her ears, formed a strawberry blond halo. "It's parlor time."

In the parlor, Ida sank into the oversized brocade chair. After positioning a velvet pillow behind her, she let her tired shoulders and back relax against the cushioned support. Sassy, Vivian's Siamese cat, stirred beneath a rosewood table in the corner, her slumber disrupted. The cat stretched and then sidled up against Ida's leg. When Ida bent over to give the feline a back rub, she noticed the scuff marks left on the pointed tip of her shoe, telltale signs of her run-in with Mr. Ditmer's desk—and Mr. Ditmer.

She'd been an eager idealist.

Not anymore.

Once Vivian and Aunt Alma were seated on the circular sofa, Sassy leapt onto Vivian's lap and curled into a ball. Vivian pulled a piece of onionskin stationery from the envelope with dramatic flair and cleared her throat before she began reading.

Nell had written about a new claw-foot tub Judson had added to their modest house, along with electric lights. She told them more about the landlady at the boardinghouse, and then she spent at least two long paragraphs describing the new and improved face of Cripple Creek. She wrote about the brick-and-sandstone town beginning to bulge at its seams, filling most every lot in the center of town and sprawling far up into the foothills. The wealth of gold being discovered attracted people from all over the country. Investors. Stockbrokers. Attorneys. Bankers. Railroad men. Entrepreneurs of all sorts, including someone who had recently opened an opera house and a businesswoman named Mollie O'Bryan, who was causing quite a hullabaloo.

A thriving city that offered comforts and culture. A place where Ida could learn the underpinnings of business and prosper with the city. A city other than New York or Portland.

Vivian held up the letter, her pinky finger pointed outward.

Ida, as the result of Judson's work as an accountant, he knows many folks in business. Bankers. Investors. Brokers. He says you could have a solid job here in no time.

But Ida barely heard the last few sentences. Her mind had been racing from the moment she'd heard that there was a *businesswoman* in Cripple Creek. Ida knew she'd rather work for a woman. Working for a successful woman would be icing on the cake.

Ida rose from the chair. "Mollie O'Bryan," she said, garnering stares from her sister and her aunt.

Vivian dipped her chin and raised a brow. "I haven't finished reading yet." She motioned for Ida to sit back down, which she did.

I hope you are well and you enjoyed the summer.

I miss you terribly. I know Kat does also. She said she'll write again this week.

I'll close for now. Judson is due home from the mine, and I have oatmeal cookies baking in the oven.

Forever your sister, with love,

Nell

Vivian folded the letter and slid it back into the envelope on her lap, then glanced up at Ida as if she expected an explanation for Ida's outburst.

"I've finished school early," Ida said. "So it works out that I can leave for Cripple Creek this next week."

Unlike her sisters, she wasn't going to Colorado for love or marriage. She had no intention of letting anything or anyone stand in the way of her ambitions. And she would succeed without the kind of compromise that men like Bradley Ditmer expected from her.

Two

Cripple Creek, Colorado
22 September 1896

ucker Raines shouldered his leather bag and stepped off the platform onto the dusty road in front of the Midland Terminal Railway Depot in Cripple Creek. The streets weren't that much different from those in Stockton—wide, packed dirt teeming with people, animals, and wagons. But the overpowering sounds of new construction were different. His mother had written him about the fires that had raged through the town in April, the devastation and subsequent renovation. Until her last letter, she hadn't mentioned his father was ill.

Tucker pushed the felt hat back on his head. He wasn't ready for this, and judging by his folks' absence at the station, he surmised the feeling was mutual. He shouldn't have come. But what kind of a son would he be if he hadn't responded to his mother's request?

He tugged her letter out of his jacket pocket. He wasn't sure he had the will to face what the near future held, but he'd at least take the first steps. He shifted his hat to block the glaring sunlight and then reread his mother's directions to their home.

Left on Third Street off Bennett Avenue—the main road through
town.

Right on Warren Avenue.

Left on Second Street. Second cabin on the left.

He set off on Bennett Avenue, looking for Third Street. It'd been more
than a year since his father had sold the icehouse in Stockton and left California for Cripple Creek. Tucker had never been to Colorado before, but
given Cripple Creek's elevation—nearly ten thousand feet—he hadn't expected such sultry weather, especially in the second half of September. He
peeled off his canvas coat and stuffed it into his bag.

Tucker saw a pine boardwalk where the first line of new brick and stone
buildings began, many of them completed. Most, however, were still in
various stages of construction. Considering the misshapen bulk of his bag,
he decided it best to forfeit the wooden footpath and remain on the road,
where he was less likely to block the way.

The sharp trill of laughter drew his attention to the gaggle of women
who poured out of a mercantile and stepped into his path. They were all
dressed for moonlight entertaining. Stilling his steps, he waved them by.
The last one stopped directly in front of him, her blond hair swept to one
side and her green eyes wide.

She studied his leather bag. "Looks like you could use a little direction,
mister. And"—her brow raised, she fluttered her eyelids like hummingbird
wings—"I'd be real tickled if you were going my way." She swayed her
bustled hips.

"I am if you're headed for a camp meeting, ma'am." He wasn't, but if
wishes counted for anything, he would be.

The young woman's raspy giggle quickly changed to a snort. She slapped her chest above her low neckline. "Tagged me a traveling preacher, did I?"

"You did, ma'am." He lifted his hat from the crown. "Tucker Raines."

"I'm Felicia," she said, slowly and softly, pronouncing her name *Feel-easy-a*. "Preacher, you ever need some real touchy-feely lovin', you come see me." She tilted her head to the left, toward the corner where the others had turned. "You can find me on Myers Avenue." After a brief curtsy, she followed the crowd of women down the side street now edged with men.

When Tucker didn't see any respectable-looking women out and about, he concluded Tuesday was Cripple Creek's morning for the *other* women to do their shopping.

He saw the sign for Third Street and turned left, where Felicia had rounded the corner. He'd just dodged a one-horse carriage and was stepping around a fresh deposit when a voice as deep as a cavern called out his name. "Mr. Raines?"

Tucker turned around. He saw the two massive draft horses first. A man big enough to match the voice waved from his seat atop an enclosed wagon with a familiar business name printed on its side: Raines Ice Company. A boy peeked out around the man as he addressed Tucker again.

"You Mr. Tucker Raines, sir?"

"I'm Tucker." He'd seen full-grown bears smaller than this man.

"Otis Bernard, sir." The man stepped down from the wagon and extended a beefy hand the color of coal.

Tucker shook his hand. Even at six feet tall, Tucker felt like shrubbery beside an oak tree. The left side of Otis's face drooped from his eye down to a permanent frown, sparking Tucker's curiosity, but he was mindful not to stare.

Otis glanced up at the boy still seated in the wagon. "That's my oldest son, Abraham. He's been helping out with deliveries since your pa took sick."

The boy removed his straw hat and dipped his chin in a greeting. He looked about ten and shared his father's build, muscular in the upper body.

"I'm pleased to meet you both," Tucker said.

"Pleased to meet you too, sir." Abraham returned his hat to his head and curled his right arm to show a hillock of a bicep muscle through his plaid shirt. "I can lift twenty pounds without even breaking a sweat." His dark eyes twinkled like midnight stars. "Know why?"

Tucker had an idea, but he shook his head anyway. That was what he had wanted folks to do when he was that age.

"Because it is ice cold." Snickering, Abraham slapped his pant leg.

Tucker chuckled. Otis joined him, pride in his son lighting his face.

Tucker gave the boy a thumbs-up. "That's a good one."

"I'm afraid you're in for it, Mr. Tucker. Only time this boy don't tell jokes is when he's with a fever." Otis lifted Tucker's leather bag off the ground and swung it up behind the seat on top of the ice wagon as if the bag were full of dried leaves. "Your mama sent us to fetch you. Hop in on the other side of Abraham, and we'll get you there."

Tucker wanted to ask why the boy wasn't in school, but he knew there weren't many schools, even in the West, that allowed Negros to attend with white children. He also wanted to know why his own mother hadn't met him at the depot. Either his father didn't know of the visit or he was too ill to be left alone.

Swallowing his unspoken questions, Tucker walked to the other side of the wagon and climbed up into the seat beside Abraham. "I liked your joke."

"Thank you, sir. I wanna write jokes for vaudeville comedians like Dan

Leno someday. I heard some men talkin' about him in the grocery. They said he's so funny, he could make a lion laugh."

Tucker admired his ambition and didn't doubt the lad could do it, given a little age and polish. "I'd say you're off to a good start."

"Mama says practice makes perfect, as long as I don't practice them all on her."

A lopsided grin spread across Otis's face as he gently flicked the reins and clucked his tongue, pulling the horses around and back up to Bennett Avenue.

"My directions say my folks live off Second Street," Tucker said, wondering where they were headed.

Otis's crooked smile disappeared. "They're not home, sir."

"Tucker. Please call me Tucker." He'd come all this way, and they were out of town?

"Your pa's in the hospital." Otis slowed his speech, harmonizing with the cadence of the horses as they pulled the wagon up the hill on the other side of Bennett Avenue.

"For how long?"

"Been in a few days now. Since last Thursday."

"My mother's letter said he'd been having spells. She asked me to come, but she didn't offer any details."

"Heard he's to go home this afternoon," Otis said. "We were delivering ice the start of August when he had a bad coughing spell."

"Seven weeks ago?"

Otis nodded. "Your father wouldn't claim it, but he'd been draggin'… not really himself since last winter."

Tucker felt a knot form in his stomach.

A large brick building was under construction on the next block. Otis guided the horses around the corner. "That there is the new hospital the

Sisters of Mercy are building." He raised his voice over the din of stonemasons slapping bricks together.

"Last week your pa took to coughing blood." Abraham spit out the last word, his eyes wide. "I saw it."

Tucker looked over at Otis, trying to mask the fear that threatened to topple him. "Blood? He's coughing up blood?" He didn't know much about medical affairs, but he'd met his share of consumption widows at camp meetings.

Otis returned Tucker's gaze and despite the light of the midday sun, Otis's eyes darkened. "It's not good, Mr. Tucker." He paused and patted his boy's knee.

"He can't work anymore?"

"No sir."

An elderly man wearing loose-fitting trousers and a wide-brimmed straw hat waved at them from outside The King's Chinese Laundry.

"Be back by with your ice before lunch, Mr. Jing-Quo." Otis waved, and then looked at Tucker. "He and his wife have an icebox in their place up top."

But Tucker's thoughts were elsewhere. *If not for this man, there would be no Raines Ice Company.* Tucker had liked him from the start, but that affinity was fast becoming an admiration.

Tucker himself knew nothing about his father's business here in Cripple Creek. While he hesitated to show that ignorance to Otis, his need to know was greater than his desire to appear knowledgeable. Had to be, for his mother's sake. He'd asked her plenty of questions about the business in his letters, but she preferred to talk about the town's rebirth and the way the majestic mountains heralded the seasons. Anything but the situation with Tucker and his father, or the business.

"How many wagons and horses does he have?" Tucker asked.

Otis glanced at the two workhorses pulling the wagon. "Titan and Trojan is the only horses, Mr. Tucker. And this is the only wagon."

"And the icehouse?"

Otis shook his head. "He had big plans, but…" His voice drifted off, as did his gaze. He lifted his floppy canvas hat and dabbed at the beads of sweat on his high forehead with a red bandanna. "That's why me and Abraham was late. We pick up a load of ice from the depot three or four days a week. Then we deliver it. Sometimes we leave some in the wagon overnight for impatient folks who want their ice first thing in the morning." He stopped the horses in front of a clapboard house. "This here's the Sisters of Mercy's hospital till they get that new one open come spring."

Tucker jumped to the ground. Before he could reach for his bag, Abraham hoisted it off the top of the wagon and handed it down to him.

"Thank you." Tucker hung his bag from his shoulder.

"Mr. Tucker, you know what the block of ice—"

"Not now, son," Otis said.

"Yes sir." Abraham turned his attention back to Tucker. "I'll save that joke for next time."

"And I might even come up with one of my own."

As far as Tucker was concerned, the boy's wide smile was worth more than a hillside full of gold.

"You'll find your pa in the hallway to the left," Otis said. "His ward's at the end. He's in the last bed."

"Thanks, Otis." Tucker touched the brim of his hat and nodded at the man who looked daunting but was proving to be the opposite. "You too, Abraham. Thanks for the work you're both doing."

"Proud to do it, Mr. Tucker." Otis poised the reins. "I'll bring the wagon back soon as it's empty so you can drive your people home."

Tucker nodded and waved. As Otis drove the wagon around the corner, Tucker took slow steps up to the door.

His people. Remorse stabbed Tucker in the chest. The best part of his people wasn't here. He'd left her in Stockton.

Honour thy father and thy mother.

That was why he'd come to Colorado. As he walked into the hospital toward an uncertain future, he prayed his resolve to honor his parents would be strong enough to sustain him. At the first corner, he turned left. A nurse in a uniform pushed a wheelchair past him. A white-haired nun in full habit huddled against a wall with a wailing young woman who held a child in her arms.

A disharmony of coughs drew Tucker to the end of the hallway and to the last door on the right. Breathing another prayer, he stepped through the open door. Worn privacy panels the color of dusty roads separated the beds. Groans and muffled conversation filled the ward. Listening for a familiar voice, he quieted his steps as he approached the back of the room. He stopped at the foot of the last bed on the left.

His father lay still, a light blanket tucked at his sides, outlining his shrunken frame. His mother sat in a chair beside the bed, her body bent forward and her knitting needles clicking through a ball of orange yarn.

Suddenly, her hands stilled and she straightened, her gaze taking Tucker in, from his dusty boots to his face, settling on the preacher's hat he held in his hand. Tears flooded her eyes as she stood and dropped her knitting on the chair.

His father's eyes popped open. A glare hardened his sallow features, his face ashen and his eyes sunken. "What are *you* doin' here?"

Tucker lifted his shoulders and let them drop.

"I asked him to come." Tucker had never before witnessed the strength in his mother's voice and the set of her jaw.

"I told you no."

"I need my son." She rushed to embrace Tucker, snagging the curtain and nearly ripping it from its frame. Tucker caught her as she stumbled, and she wrapped her arms around his neck.

"Well, I don't need him here. I don't want him here." His father's voice escalated. A series of deep, gurgling coughs rent the stale air and resonated in Tucker's core.

Something had to be done to stop the spasms. Tucker released his mother and rushed to the bedside, reaching for his father, but he was met with a flailing hand, slapping his arm away even in the throes of a coughing fit.

God, help us. His father did need him here, even if he would never admit it.

The nun he'd seen in the hallway scuttled in. "Mr. Raines, it sounds as though you could use another steam treatment before we send you home this afternoon." She tucked a stray feather of white hair under her headpiece, and looked at Tucker over the top of her wire-rimmed spectacles. "This might be a good time for you and Mrs. Raines to help yourself to a cup of coffee in the kitchen."

Tucker nodded, comforted by the warm sensitivity he heard in the nun's soft brogue. He took his mother's elbow and guided her out of the room.

The long table in the sisters' dining room sat empty. Tucker set two full coffee cups at one end and pulled out a chair for his mother. The strength he'd seen in her moments earlier seemed to have evaporated.

He knew the feeling. He sat beside her. Thirsty, he lifted the cup of hot brew to his lips. Never mind that the coffee was bitter, as long as the liquid coated his insides with warmth.

"I'm sorry." His mother sniffled. Her shoulders hunched more than he remembered. "I shouldn't have asked you to come, but I didn't know what else to do."

He set down his cup and squeezed her hand. "You did the right thing, Mother." He hoped he was right, but the fact that his mere presence had stirred his father into a coughing fit didn't bode well.

"He can't help himself. He just hasn't been right since..." Her face twisted into a frown and she wrapped her hands around the steaming cup in front of her. "How is Willow?"

Tucker glanced up at the crucifix that hung on the wall at the other end of the long plank table and breathed in the reminder. What Christ did on the cross was enough, regardless of how he felt. "She was about the same when I saw her last Wednesday."

Her elbows on the table, his mother put her face in her hands and began to weep.

Tucker pulled a handkerchief from his trouser pocket and handed it to her. "I asked them to send the reports to me here."

Shuddering, she blotted her face. "You'll stay?"

"For as long as I'm needed."

Footsteps drew their attention to the doorway and the man who approached them. Tucker stood.

His mother wiped her eyes and straightened. "Tucker, this is Dr. Morgan Cutshaw. He's tending to your father."

"Doctor." Tucker shook hands with him, noting the doctor was a couple of inches shorter than he was. Like Sam. "I'm Tucker Raines."

Dr. Cutshaw pulled out a chair and sat on the other side of Tucker's mother.

"Can we take him home?" The strength had returned to his mother's voice.

"Yes. Sister Coleman is seeing to the paperwork now." He looked at Tucker, then at Mrs. Raines. "The results of my consults came back."

"It's tuberculosis, isn't it?" she asked.

"Yes ma'am. Active tuberculosis disease." Dr. Cutshaw's voice was tender, full of compassion. "I'm sorry, Mrs. Raines, but there's really nothing more we can do for him here."

Tucker enfolded his mother's quaking hand in his. "Did you tell my father?"

The doctor nodded. "I just spoke with him."

"How did he take it?"

His mother wiped a tear from her cheek. "He likely took the news like a man who thought he was invincible."

Another nod from the doctor.

"Thank you." Tucker tightened his grip on his mother's hand. "There has to be something we can do."

"I've telephoned the Glockner Sanitorium down in Colorado Springs. The doctors there specialize in caring for tuberculosis patients."

Caring for. Tucker didn't know if his mother had detected the specific wording, but he had. Tuberculosis at this stage had no cure, no proven treatment. If his father stayed here, he would only worsen and his mother would grow all the more frail watching him diminish and suffer.

Tucker didn't wish that on either of them. They'd been through enough. He couldn't stand by and do nothing. At the sanitorium his father would receive the care he needed and his mother would be close enough to see him, but also have her sister, Aunt Rosemary, who lived in Colorado Springs, for support.

Dr. Cutshaw shifted his attention to Tucker's mother. "They can have a room ready for him in about a week—next Monday."

"Will he be up to traveling by then?" She slipped her hands around her coffee cup again.

"If he has good rest in the meantime, he should be able to tolerate the train ride."

"What do you think, Tucker?"

Was that why she'd summoned him, to make the decisions? He looked at Dr. Cutshaw.

"We've drained the fluid off his lungs. The bleeding has stopped for now. But I can't say for how long."

Tucker met his mother's fragile gaze. "We need to do what's best for Father. And for you. I believe that's the sanitorium."

She nodded.

Dr. Cutshaw stood. "I'll call them back and reserve a space for him."

As Tucker watched the doctor leave, he wondered how he would pay for his father's care. He'd taken a sabbatical from preaching to come here, and his father had only one ice wagon for deliveries. How was that even enough to put food on their table, let alone pay Otis and cover the cost of Willow's care?

❧

Three hours later, Tucker carried a tea tray into his father's sparsely furnished bedroom in his parents' cabin. Lemons would be hard-pressed to match the sourness in his father's expression. He sat propped up in bed on a nest of pillows, his eyes narrowed.

"You can stay," he said through gritted teeth.

"Thank you." Tucker set the tray over his father's lap and spooned honey into the cup.

"For your mother's sake."

Tucker nodded. "The doctor said peppermint tea with honey will help keep your throat calm."

"You'll sleep in the barn."

Tucker clanged the spoon against the edge of the cup.

Honour thy father.

Apparently, his father believed he should pay penance, even though no amount of atonement would bring Sam back.

Or Willow.

Swallowing his frustration with a bitter bite of regret, Tucker turned and walked out of the room.

THREE

Colorado Springs, Colorado
28 September 1896

The shrill call of the train's whistle sent a fresh pulse of adrenaline into Ida's aching legs. Tightening her grip on her reticule and satchel, she rushed out the depot door of the Midland Terminal Railroad and across the platform to board the train in Colorado Springs.

"Last call." The conductor hung from the grab bar of the rear passenger car. "All aboard!"

The engineer released the brakes, adding a deafening whooshing sound to her pounding heartbeat. Steam belched from beneath the car, blowing her duster and dampening her dress.

Ida grabbed the railing and propelled herself up the steps as the train began moving. Inside the car, the conductor motioned her toward the back of the train and a seat at the window—the only one available in the car. Holding her bags out in front of her with one hand, Ida reached with her other to grasp the back of each seat as she passed to brace herself against the rocking motion of the train.

When she arrived at the second-to-last row, she couldn't help letting out an audible gasp. A portly man slouched in the aisle seat, his eyes shut and his double chin propped against his chest. His rumpled shirt and tousled gray hair spoke to a serious neglect of personal hygiene.

Although he was a far cry from her preference for a seatmate, she saw no choice in the matter. Ida nestled her satchel on the pipe-framed shelf above the seats and laid her coat on top. The young couple sitting across from the man and the only empty seat were huddled together.

"Pardon me," Ida said.

They tucked their legs, allowing her passage to her window seat. As she passed, the tang of whiskey soured her stomach. The man reeked of it—which explained his capacity to sleep in this jostling conveyance.

Ida squeezed into the small space beside the man and held her reticule in her lap. How would she bear the next two hours? Hopefully he would disembark at an earlier stop.

She'd planned to arrive at the train platform early that morning for the last leg of her trip from Maine to Cripple Creek. She'd even spent the night at a hotel within walking distance of the depot to assure her timeliness. But who would have expected that the rains last night would have formed ponds in the roadway disguised as mere puddles? She'd headed straight for the washroom at the depot to change into dry clothing, not a task she could tend to quickly when soaked clear through her petticoat.

Ida's head began to ache, and she pressed her fingers to her temples, trying to assuage it. She drew in a deep breath she hoped would cleanse her of the frustration. She was aboard now and seated. And although she found the seat lacking on many levels, it had to be more comfortable than the baggage car—her only other option. Besides, her sisters waited for her on the other end. This would be a mere tick on the clock in comparison to the near week's worth of traveling to get to this point. She could do this.

If she kept herself occupied. Fortunately, she'd come prepared to do just that. Ida pulled out the envelope wedged against the inside edge of her reticule. Vivian had slipped the mysterious packet into Ida's hand before she boarded the train in Portland and told her to save the surprise for an especially tedious stretch. This was it.

Ida opened the flap and removed a colorful, folded page obviously taken from a magazine. Unfurling the telltale newspaper-sized sheet, she recognized it as part of an issue of *Harper's Bazar*. Vivian, the fashion connoisseur in the family, occasionally picked up a copy of the magazine.

Ida studied the sheet, which only held advertisements for Pears Soap and soiree fashions. Was Vivian implying she needed a more efficient soap or fresh fashions for her new life as a businesswoman? No, such subtlety was not one of her little sister's traits.

She flipped the page over and found the answer. The surprise had nothing to do with advertisements and fashions and everything to do with the first article: "Women Out West" by Kat Sinclair Cutshaw.

Ida's mouth dropped open. Drawing encouragement from her sister's accomplishment, she began to read.

Kat had written about her introduction to the West, filling in a few of the blanks left in the two letters she'd sent home. And she quoted Hattie Adams, the landlady at the boardinghouse where Kat and Nell stayed before their double wedding. "Strength and wisdom are *not* the same thing. And a wise woman knows her limits."

The quote swirled through Ida's thoughts like the autumn wind stirring leaves outside the train window. Strength would most certainly be required to accomplish what she intended. Bradley Ditmer had proven few men took women in business seriously.

Brushing her fingers over her lips, she still felt the sour remnants of his stolen kiss. Now that she'd had miles and miles of time to think, it was possible the experience could be a blessing in disguise. The actual business world, and in a booming mining town no less, was sure to be all the more challenging, and she'd best be on guard. She needed to be both wise and strong.

The thought had barely formed when the train began to descend a steep hill. As the cars caught up to each other and banged their hitches together, her inebriated neighbor jerked himself upright and blinked, then leaned back, shutting his eyes again. In the process, he encroached on her already cramped space.

Ida shifted closer to the window. Fresh air and solid ground couldn't claim her soon enough. A week's worth of breathing in the acrid stench of burning coal presented enough of a challenge to her senses. The past several minutes, body odor and alcohol had mixed with it to create a repulsive combination.

The man's snores and snorts provided an offbeat to the *clickety-clack* of the train wheels and the staccato huffing of the locomotive. But the man's snores or smell wasn't what troubled her most. The narrowing of her small space had her teeth clenched and her blood about to boil. She returned the magazine page to the envelope and began fanning herself with it.

She needed to keep her mind occupied. Her future in business was sure to do the trick.

Twisting the latch on her reticule, she opened it and pulled out the wire from Mollie O'Bryan, then stuffed the *Harper's Bazar* packet back into its proper place.

Ida unfolded the note she'd received at Aunt Alma's home in Portland the day before she'd boarded the train. The Cripple Creek businesswoman's message instantly redirected her attention.

Received your telegram stop

Could use competent help stop

You look good on paper stop

We can talk stop

My office Wednesday thirty September stop

Three pm stop

She wouldn't have looked so good on paper if Mr. Alan Merton, her former boss, had his way. But she did, thanks to some fast talking and the director's concern she would spread "her exaggerations" about the guest lecturer and cause "undue harm" to the school. While their compromise wasn't fully fair to her, she had found it acceptable. He had awarded her the certificate as if she'd completed the last two weeks of the course and written a letter of recommendation based upon her attendance record and work up until the day Mr. Ditmer tried to have his way with her.

As the train snaked around a mountain, Ida's neighbor slumped against her shoulder, fanning the flames of her headache. The wire in her hand fluttered to the floor.

"Sir." Ida raised her arm, pushing against his.

The man only snuffled, his hibernation undisturbed.

She'd paid for a whole seat. This was unacceptable. Bracing herself against the window with one hand, she shoved him, letting his arm fall to his lap. "Mister!"

The man jerked and flailed his arms, and then stared at her, his wide eyes looking like a map with a route penciled in red. "Huh?" He pointed his unsteady finger at her. "You, madam, are one pushy broad."

Ida huffed. "Pushy? You haven't seen pushy yet." She paused, taking in a breath of stale air. "You, sir, are—"

"Changing seats."

The understated male voice quieted Ida, and she looked up. A dark figure had appeared in the aisle. Surely a brawny angel had come to her rescue, as she hadn't heard anyone approaching.

The gentleman laid one hand on the drunk's shoulder. With the other, he pushed back the bowler on his head and smiled. "Ma'am."

She raised her chin. "You're relocating this man?"

He nodded, his hazel eyes full of understanding and compassion.

"Thank you." Not that she needed to be rescued, exactly, but she'd endured quite enough distress this day and gladly welcomed the man's help—though she kept a careful watch for any strings attached to his consideration.

Her incorrigible neighbor gazed at the other man, blinking as if he could send a message by Morse code. "You, sir, need to strike a deal and calm these waters."

"I'll see about that, Baxter. But first, I'm moving you to a window seat with less turbulence. Where you'll be able to sleep undisturbed." Her knight in a pinstripe suit grinned at her, and then helped the man he'd referred to as Baxter to his feet and guided him up the aisle, away from her.

Already, the ache in her head began to subside. Ida glanced at the floor where the telegram lay. She extended her leg and drew the paper back with the toe of her boot. She'd bent forward to retrieve Miss O'Bryan's message when she heard her new hero returning to the seat beside her.

"I would have gotten that for you," he said.

"You've already done more than your fair share of good deeds by relieving me of that man."

"Happy to help, ma'am. Colin Wagner at your service." He removed his bowler. "And you'll be happy to know I'm not a leaner. Nor do I drool."

A smile came despite her. "I'm glad to hear that, Mr. Wagner." She held his gaze, searching his eyes for any hint of ulterior motive in his kindness or in his humor.

"And you are?" he asked.

"I'm Ida Sinclair."

"Pleased to meet you, Miss Sinclair." He returned his hat to his head.

"You know that man?" She looked toward the seat where Baxter was now collapsed against the window.

"We're both from Cripple Creek. I'm a legal counselor there. What brings you to Colorado, Miss Sinclair?"

"I've recently completed course work in a business college." She tucked the telegram into her reticule. "I have an employment interview with a businesswoman in Cripple Creek—Miss Mollie O'Bryan."

"Miss O'Bryan is one of my steady clients." Mr. Wagner rubbed his smooth chin. "You certainly possess the poise and spunk Miss Mollie would admire."

"Thank you."

"I doubt you'll need it, but I'd be happy to put in a good word for you. That is, if you'd like me to."

Ida focused on a swirl of soot on her sleeve.

"Without any obligation on your part, Miss Sinclair."

"I'd appreciate that, Mr. Wagner."

Colin Wagner began a conversation with the older gentleman across the aisle, likely unaware that he'd redeemed the last leg of her trip.

FOUR

*N*ell smoothed a plaid cloth over the maple table, then set a quart-sized Mason jar of daises in the center of it. She put five stoneware plates and settings in place, and then stood back to inspect her kitchen. No sooner had Judson left for the mine that morning than she had put her hand to sweeping and cleaning. The nickel trim on the stove her husband bought her last month shone like a mirror. The polished pine flooring gleamed in the slivers of light that spilled in through the paned-glass window.

Kat and Morgan came to supper every other week. On the off weeks, she and Judson went to their home. They didn't normally meet on the first day of the workweek, but today was no ordinary Monday. Ida arrived in Cripple Creek today, and a celebration was in order.

Since Nell had moved into Judson's home, she'd added yellow calico curtains to the two windows in the main room and the window in their bedchamber. She'd also added the True Lover's Knot quilt her aunt had made for her to their bed. Her gaze lingered there while memories sent a wave of warmth up her neck and into her face.

Judson was a good man. Tender and passionate. Fine qualities for a husband. And for a father. She was a blessed woman, and she so longed to bless her husband with a child.

Nell squared her house slippers with the edge of the quilt and nudged the photo frame on the side table straight. She was pulling the curtain panels back to see if Kat was on her way yet when she felt that familiar searing ache low in her abdomen. Sighing, she sank onto the bed. She'd said a prayer and hoped things would be different this month.

Help me be patient, Lord.

"Nell, are you here?"

Kat had arrived.

"I'll be right there." Nell pulled her mantle from the maple wardrobe and joined her sister in the main room.

Kat stood near the stove, wearing her duster. "I was beginning to think you'd gone off without me."

"On sisters' day?" Nell smoothed the rug at the entry one last time as she followed Kat out the door. "I was making sure everything is ready for when we get back from Hattie's."

"Morgan's surgical rooms aren't that spotless." Kat giggled, and Nell swatted her arm.

As they walked past the school yard, a gusty autumn breeze pulled bright crimson leaves from oak branches and sent them twisting and twirling through the chilled air.

"Our autumn acrobats are right on time." Kat held out her gloved hands as if she intended to catch one. "Soon we'll be eating our fill of apple pie and pumpkin bread."

As they walked down the hill toward the depot, Nell stared toward the mountain pass like she had gawked at the fireplace on Christmas Eve as a little girl. This time she waited for her oldest sister.

"Do you think Ida will like living here? Our adjustment to Cripple Creek was quite abrupt, with no one to meet us, then the fire. And it's not at all like Maine." Kat waved at a woman passing by in a wagon.

"I expect she will. Judson said there are plenty of business opportunities to appease her appetite."

"Sounds like he knows her already." Kat winked.

"I think I've been talking about her and Vivian nonstop since I saw Ida's wire about her early arrival."

"Seems to be the way with us Sinclair sisters."

Nell watched a raven soar on an air current. "I know why we had to come early, but I can't figure out Ida's change of plans." A sharp whistle sounded and the train cleared the cut, slowing for the last grade down the hill. Nell enfolded Kat's gloved hand in hers. "Sounds like I'll know her reasons soon enough. She's on the last stretch."

Kat raised a brow, her brown eyes pensive. "I remember it well."

"It seemed the longest."

"Not as endless as our wait here outside the depot."

"She's expecting Sinclair sisters, not a man, so she'll be fine." Nell giggled.

The sisters stepped up onto the depot platform just as the train rounded the last corner on its approach into Cripple Creek. As the locomotive slowed to a stop, they could see Ida's face at the window. When their eyes met hers, Nell and Kat both let out squeals of joy, causing those around them to stop and stare.

❧

Ida wished she could shed her soiled duster before she reunited with her sisters. However, given the pressing crowd, she counted it good enough that she'd found space to pull her coat and satchel from the shelf above her before she finally stepped out onto the deck. She accepted her hero's hand and he guided her to the ground.

"Thank you again for your help, Mr. Wagner." She hooked a pesky tendril of hair behind her ear. "With my sloshy seatmate and seeing me off the train."

"My pleasure, Miss Sinclair." He tapped the rim of his bowler. "I'll have that talk with Mollie O'Bryan, and I'll see you again soon."

While he walked away, Ida scanned the platform to relocate her sisters now that she was on solid ground. Kat and Nell stood not even six feet away, their feet planted and their mouths hanging open.

After they greeted one another with warm hugs, Nell took Ida's satchel from her and lifted a questioning brow. "You traveled with Mr. Wagner?"

"It feels like winter out here." Ida glanced down at her soot-covered duster. "I need to remove this thing and put my coat on." After Nell helped her do just that, Ida led the way toward the depot.

"Don't play coy with us, Ida Mae." Kat caught up to her, wagging her finger. "Mr. Colin Wagner is a single man, and he helped you off the train."

"And spoke to you in hushed tones." The dreaminess Ida saw in Nell's blue eyes matched that of her voice.

Persistence was a Sinclair family habit. Still, the less said, the better. "You already know him, so you must also know he is an attorney here in town."

"He said he'll see you soon." Kat's chin jutted out in a teasing smile. "You're already making social arrangements?"

"Business. He meant he'll see me soon at Mollie O'Bryan's office, if I get the job."

"All business?" Nell batted thick blond lashes.

Ida huffed. "Yes. But it's good to know we still have an incurable romantic or two in the family." She tilted her head and raised a brow. "Now tell me, are my brothers-in-law really good enough to be related to me?"

Kat's laugh sounded like thunderclaps and Nell's like a trickling brook. Both were music to Ida's ears.

They talked nineteen to the dozen all the way into the depot washroom. Letters provide sketches, but sisters take pleasure in the details. Ida told them the story of her soggy seatmate and Mr. Wagner coming to her rescue…anything to steer them clear of the shameful incident with Mr. Bradley Ditmer.

After Ida arranged for the porter to deliver her trunk to Hattie's, she was ready to see the town she'd been hearing so much about. She was reaching for the depot door when it burst open from the outside.

A gust of wind caught the brim of her hat and yanked it free from its pins. She wasn't quick enough to keep the hat from tumbling off her head, but she managed to catch it before it flew any further than arm's length. She didn't have such luck, however, with the pearl-headed hatpin that landed like a dart into the toe of a dirty work boot.

The man attached to the hatpin filled the doorway, and his brown eyes were the size of her aunt's hot cakes. He scrubbed his neatly trimmed beard, then bent and retrieved the pin. As he stood, he held it out to her. "I apologize, ma'am."

And so he should. This was his fault.

Ida finger-combed her mussed hair back from her face, aware he was watching her. She felt a wave of warmth burn her cheeks despite the chilled air from the open door.

"Tucker, dear?" A thin-faced woman peeked around the man. "Your father—"

"Yes." He glanced out the door and then back at Ida. "Would you mind holding the door for a moment?"

Ida stepped forward to do so. She watched him reach out to a man who leaned on a hand-carved walking stick and looked as if he'd been sucking on persimmons. The younger man cradled the gentleman's elbow and assisted him over the threshold. Then he extended his hand to the thin-faced, fragile-looking woman and helped her up the step as well.

She'd stood in their way, embarrassed that she had been so concerned about a little gust of wind. "I should've been the one to apologize," Ida said.

He looked back at her and nodded, his smile warming his cocoa-brown eyes.

On her way out the door, Kat handed another wayward pin to Ida, then glanced toward the ticket counter and the brown-eyed man. "Business?"

Giggling, the three of them set off for the boardinghouse, hand in hand.

∽◉∾

Tucker took long strides from the depot to the ice car. Otis had dropped him and his folks off before driving the wagon around to the loading dock for the ice pickup. By the time Tucker arrived, Otis and Abraham had already loaded a full layer of ice into the back of the wagon, and while Abraham spread straw over the first layer, Otis slid another three-hundred-pound block on top of it.

He looked up at Tucker. "Didn't expect you till after the train hooted on its way out of town."

Tucker pulled his wool gloves out of his coat pockets. "My father said he'd rather I tend to the work needing to be done." He jammed his fingers into the gloves.

"I'm sorry."

Sorry his father was sick? Sorry he'd left Willow and the work of his heart in California? Or sorry his father blamed him for the drowning and held him responsible for everything that had happened since then? Tucker chose not to ask. He simply nodded, grateful for Otis and his loyalty to the family. Raines Ice Company wouldn't have survived at all without his steadfast work ethic and brawny build.

"He never mentioned having children." Otis's tone held the same flatness Tucker felt. "Your mama told me about you. Said you're a preacher." He glanced at the flat-topped, wide-brimmed hat Tucker wore.

"I am. I mostly speak at camp meetings." Tucker shifted his weight to the other boot—the one punctured by the hatpin. "That is, I did until I left California to come here."

"You miss it? Preaching?"

Tucker turned and sat on the edge of the wagon. "I was eighteen—five years ago—when I placed my faith in Jesus Christ. My curiosity and my 'gift of gab,' as one of my seminary professors called it, shifted to focus heavily on Scripture and spiritual things. Some people call it 'religion.' I call it 'relationship beliefs.'"

"I expect your pa wanted you to go into the ice business."

Tucker nodded. If that had been their only roadblock, he probably would've found a way through it.

"I have that joke for you, Mr. Tucker," Abraham said as he climbed out of the wagon.

"He may not be of a mind for one right now, son."

Tucker met his friend's gaze. "The Good Book says there is a time to mourn and a time to laugh. I think now might be a good time for laughter."

"Does that mean I can tell my joke?" Abraham's dark eyes twinkled like polished jewels.

Otis nodded and Abraham straightened to his full height. The boy cleared his throat. "What did the ice say to the lake?"

Tucker glanced at Otis, who shrugged.

"Freeze. I got you covered."

Tucker pictured a block of ice wearing a gun belt and started chuckling. Within seconds all three of them were laughing and drawing the attention of the dock workers around them. When they'd settled down, Otis grunted as he hoisted another block onto the wagon. "What'll you do about the ice company?"

"It's all my parents have, but it's not enough to pay the bills. The pittance I've been able to earn as a preacher isn't enough to support the whole family." Tucker hopped down from the wagon and into the railcar. "I don't know what I should do."

"This town's gettin' to be a regular city. Lots more businesses." Otis wiped his brow with his red bandanna. "More folks with money for iceboxes movin' in. With just one wagon, we're only supplying about ten businesses a day—a lot of them the same ones. If we could grow the business—"

"We'd need more wagons and horses. More men."

"I could drive a wagon, Mr. Tucker."

Tucker had no doubt that Abraham could do so as well as most men and leave the customers charmed while he was at it. "One day, but it's still a little early for that." He returned his attention to Otis. "We'd also need an icehouse to store enough ice for the city's year-round needs. That's the only way we can keep the ice company alive."

Tucker scraped the tongs along the edges of a block of ice until he had a good grip. Then he slid the block out of the ice car and into the wagon.

Otis stuffed his red bandanna in his back pocket. "And what about iceboxes?"

"You could sell lots of 'em to the rich folks." Abraham drew a generous circle with his arms.

"I like the way you two think. Hopefully, the banker will too. I'll talk to one this week about a loan." Tucker slid another block out of the rail car, and Otis hoisted it into place.

Icehouse. Seminary. Appointment as a circuit preacher at camp meetings. Now it seemed he'd come full circle...back to the life he'd walked away from. And the duration of this detour depended upon the banker.

FIVE

Ida's new landlady walked into the parlor, carrying a tray laden with cups and goodies. Ida scooted forward on the sofa and pushed a worn Bible to one side of the sofa table, clearing a space large enough for the silver platter.

Nell rose from a Queen Anne chair and filled the four cups with hot cocoa. Ida lifted her cup and inhaled the aromatic steam. The creamy chocolate smelled rich enough to carry away the cares of her day, along with the myriad of offensive smells that had accompanied them.

Hattie passed out dessert plates, each with a stack of shortbread cookies on it, then settled back onto the sofa beside Ida. "Your sisters asked me to reserve a room for you for mid-October."

Ida nodded. "Yes, and you have a lovely place here, Miss Hattie."

"Thank you. My George and I worked very hard on it."

"I especially like the square grand piano." Ida sipped her cocoa, letting its warmth soothe her travel-weary body.

"She's storing the piano for Morgan until our house is finished," Kat said.

"September's not even over yet, and here you are." Miss Hattie peered at Ida over the top of her cup.

"Yes ma'am." Ida glanced at the flocked wallpaper on the far wall.

"Kat said you've been attending business school and would complete your course at the beginning of October."

"I completed my schooling earlier than expected." Ida took a big gulp of the chocolate drink.

"It was because of a man, wasn't it, dear?" Miss Hattie twisted to face Ida. "I can see it in your eyes."

Ida blinked. This woman's tenacity would shame the most diligent of worker ants. Ida set her saucer on the table and rose from the sofa. She walked over to the fireplace, looking for warmth, but the snaps and pops only competed with the barrage of questions that had been unleashed by her evasion.

"Is Hattie right?" Kat had followed her and now stood beside her. "Did you leave early because of a man?"

Ida needed to tell them the truth. They cared about her. They'd believe her, if anyone would. "Yes, I left early because of a man—a very improper man. A guest professor." Tears stung Ida's eyes. She detested the quiver she heard in her voice, a sign of weakness. How could she have been so trusting? So naive? "He began… He kissed me, then offered me a job in New York if I would agree to be his…companion. He said that was the only way I'd find success in the business world—that women couldn't make it on their own."

"You must have been mortified." Kat held both of Ida's hands and squeezed them, her eyes full of compassion.

"What did you do?" Nell sat rigid on the edge of her chair.

"I slapped him. Told him he was wrong, and then ran out of the room."

"Good for you. We women have to stand up for ourselves." Hattie clucked her tongue. "For the life of me, I don't understand why men can't keep their lips to themselves. Until we ask for them, anyway."

"You said he was a guest professor. Did you report him to the school's director?" Kat led her back to the sofa.

"I did." Ida sat down and Hattie patted her knee much the way she imagined her mother would. "The professor is a powerful businessman and a childhood friend of Mr. Merton, the school's director, but I convinced him to give me a certificate of completion and a glowing letter of recommendation."

"That's what I love about you Sinclair girls." Miss Hattie shook her fist in the air. "You might get knocked down, but you get right back on the horse."

Ida bit back a giggle and gave the hand on her knee a squeeze. "Thank you, Miss Hattie."

The sound of wagon wheels churning the rocks on the road drew Miss Hattie to the window. She pulled the curtain back and stood on her tiptoes, her face pressed against the glass. "It's the ice wagon and Otis with a man I don't know. You girls will have to excuse me."

When the three of them nodded, the older woman rushed out of the parlor.

The faith and support Ida saw in her sisters' eyes made her believe this was where she belonged. Hopefully, Mollie O'Bryan would agree.

Tucker removed his hat and wiped his brow with his coat sleeve while Otis parked the wagon in front of a yellow, two-story clapboard house. Hattie's Boardinghouse was their last stop for the day. His body was tired, but his mind raced with possibilities, thanks to Otis, and he was anxious to get back to the house and put them to paper.

If he could secure a bank loan to expand the business to three wagons delivering ice every day, they could make enough to pay six men and cover the costs of the care his father and Willow required.

Tucker hadn't received a report since he'd left Stockton, but he had to hope Willow wouldn't always require care. He had to believe one day soon, the Lord would heal her heart and he'd be able to bring her to Colorado for a visit. He wanted to show her these magnificent mountains.

Tucker bounded to the back of the wagon and grabbed the ice tongs before Abraham could. He smiled. "I'll carry this block. I wouldn't want your muscles to grow bigger than mine."

Abraham, his laugh as heartwarming as his smile, secured the reins to the hitching rail while Tucker clasped a twenty-pound block of ice and followed Otis to the back porch. Abraham then scuttled ahead of them, trailing a new joke behind him like smoke following a flame. Tucker smiled, remembering the boy's joke about not breaking a sweat under the weight of the ice.

A generously proportioned woman wearing a shawl over a housedress stood in the doorway and waved them inside.

Tucker shifted the block of ice to look down at his boots. The tops were dirt encrusted. The fact hadn't bothered him much until the young woman at the depot dropped a hatpin into one of them. She'd stared at it, then up at him as if he were a vagabond.

"Don't you worry about your boots none. I have something for that." The woman of the house pointed to a shiny brass-and-bristle fixture just outside the door. "Abraham, I do declare that you stand taller every week."

Abraham shook her hand, then ran his boots through the contraption. "Yes ma'am. And I'm funnier too."

Her cheeks puffed out as she bit back a giggle. "I think you might be right."

Smiling, Otis removed his canvas hat. "Good afternoon, Miss Hattie."

After shaking hands with the woman, he scuffed his worn shoes through the brush and stepped into the kitchen.

Tucker followed his friend's example. "Ma'am," he said, ducking his head in a hands-free greeting. The kitchen's bakery aroma caused his stomach to growl as the door clicked shut behind him.

Otis pulled the top off the wooden icebox, and Tucker picked a straggling piece of straw from the block and then set it inside. "Mr. Tucker, this is Miss...Mrs. Adams."

Tucker set the ice tongs on the lid and removed his hat before accepting the woman's hearty handshake. "I'm pleased to meet you, Mrs. Adams."

"I'm a widow. Please call me Miss Hattie. We're pretty informal around here."

"Informal suits me just fine, Miss Hattie. I'm Tucker Raines, but please call me Tucker."

Miss Hattie's eyes widened. "You're Will Raines's son?" She pressed her lips together and shook her head. "Well, if that man isn't full of secrets. Your father delivered ice to me for months and months. Why, I've known him for a year, and I didn't know he had a son."

Apparently, no one this side of Stockton knows.

"Oh." The woman's sudden frown said he'd done a poor job of keeping the pain's shadow from clouding his face.

His dark eyes full of compassion, Otis gave Tucker a sideways glance.

"My father is a private man," Tucker said to Miss Hattie. "Doesn't talk about family matters much."

If ever.

Even when he thinks he's going off to die.

"I'm sorry about your father's illness." She pulled a strand of silver hair from her face with bent fingers. "I heard he had to go to the sanitorium. And your mother?"

"Thank you. My mother's staying with her sister in Colorado Springs."

"Did you bring a wife with you to Cripple Creek?"

"I never married, ma'am. I'm a traveling preacher."

One eyebrow stretched toward her hairline, deepening the wrinkles on her forehead. "I see."

"Miss Hattie, you ready to hear my new joke?" Abraham squirmed impatiently in front of the woman.

"Is it short?"

"Real short." He held his hands out about an inch apart.

"Then fire away."

Abraham tapped the narrow brim of his felt hat. "What did the hat say to the hair?"

Light danced in Miss Hattie's silver-gray eyes as she glanced first at Otis, then at Tucker. When they remained silent, she shrugged. "I give up, Abraham. What did the hat say to the hair?"

"Top that!" Giggling, Abraham waved his hat, then plopped it back on his head.

Tucker and Otis had both heard the joke that morning, but the woman's carefree laughter was contagious, and so was Abraham's cheery nature. He and Otis both joined in.

"Funnier every week is right, Abraham. I have something for you and your brothers." Miss Hattie reached into her apron pocket and pulled out a handful of Tootsie Rolls. "The newest treat to come out of New York City. You'll see they each receive one?"

"I will, ma'am." He displayed them on his open hand. "But there's six candies and only four of us boys."

Only four boys? Tucker had entertained the thought of having a family of his own. That was no longer an option. Not considering his responsibilities to his parents and his sister, and the traveling he did from one camp meeting to another.

"I suppose your folks will have to eat the other two chocolates." Miss Hattie smiled at Otis.

"We'll surely do that, Miss Hattie. Thank you. For now, son, you best stuff them into your shirt pocket till we get home." Otis turned to Abraham and tipped his head, gesturing toward Miss Hattie.

The boy obliged and gave the woman a tight squeeze. "Thank you lots, Miss Hattie."

"You're welcome." She faced Tucker. "Otis and Abraham always save my delivery for last. And now it's time for some hot cocoa." Miss Hattie pulled three mugs from a shelf.

Tucker would rather hurry home and prepare a business plan for the banker, but the woman did have a certain charm about her and visiting with her seemed part of Otis's routine.

Abraham took a mug from the woman and glanced from the cupboard top to the small round table in the corner. "She always has shortbread cookies ready for us on Mondays. Where are they, Miss Hattie?"

"The platter is in the parlor...with the three young women I left waiting for us." She gazed at Tucker, her brow raised. "I'd like you to meet them."

"Is Miss Faith one of them?" Abraham removed his hat and looked back at Tucker. "Miss Faith lives here. She comes to the Gulch and teaches us on Saturday afternoons."

"Miss Faith is not home yet. She must still be at the school." The landlady shifted her attention back to Tucker. "One of the young women is married to an accountant at the Mary McKinney Mine. Another is married to Dr. Morgan Cutshaw."

"I met Dr. Cutshaw at the hospital. He's the doctor who treated my father."

"Then you must come in and visit long enough to get warmed up."

Tucker could tell the woman wasn't accustomed to taking no for an answer, and he didn't want to be the first to introduce such a concept.

Miss Hattie sauntered out of the kitchen. Wisps of dark gray hair rode the high collar on her housedress. The landlady fairly swished across the dining room, down the hallway, and through an open doorway.

Hat in hand, Tucker followed her into the parlor. He expected to see fine furnishings, but that wasn't what attracted his attention. The three young women she'd wanted him to meet were those he'd encountered that morning at the depot. The one with the floppy topper and the projectile hatpin sat on the sofa, looking anything but mussed as she related a story to the others.

Miss Hattie stopped at the end of the sofa, holding the mugs together in front of her chest as if they were lovebirds. "Pardon me, ladies."

The hatpin woman quieted and looked up. As soon as she saw him, her face blushed redder than a cardinal. She rose from the sofa and smoothed her skirt.

The other two women stood across from her with amusement etched in their tight smiles.

"Let's see…where do I begin?" Miss Hattie tapped her fleshy chin. "Mrs. Cutshaw, Mrs. Archer, you've met Otis Bernard and Abraham."

The four of them exchanged nods and greetings. Then Miss Hattie turned back toward the sofa. "This is their sister, Miss Ida Sinclair." She set the mugs on the sofa table. "Ida, these are my friends, Mr. Otis Bernard and his oldest son, Abraham."

"I'm pleased to meet you, Mr. Bernard, Abraham." Ida then walked toward Tucker. "I thought you left on the train."

"No ma'am. My parents were the ones making the trip."

"You've already met my young women?" Miss Hattie asked, her brows arching.

"Not formally, ma'am."

"We, uh, saw one another at the depot this morning." The woman she'd called Ida touched the brim of her hat just above her ear.

"Oh." Miss Hattie glanced down at his boots, then back up at him. "I overheard something about a hatpin incident. You're the one who—"

"Yes ma'am." He spoke to her, but it was Ida who held his attention.

"I'd say proper introductions are in order." She set the mugs on the table. "Mr. Tucker Raines, these are the Sinclair sisters—Mrs. Judson Archer, Mrs. Morgan Cutshaw, and Miss Ida Sinclair."

High cheekbones and pronounced chins, times three. "It's my pleasure, ladies." He met Ida's gaze. "I'm pleased to see that you were able to reattach your hat."

She nodded, and then, apparently aware of him staring at her bobbing hat, abruptly grew still. "Perhaps I could have done a more thorough job of pinning it."

"These fine gentlemen are joining us for a little refreshment." Hattie sat on the sofa, leaving space on one side for Ida and Abraham, and on the other for Tucker and Otis. When the other women sat down, Tucker and Otis did the same.

Abraham, however, remained standing before them like a showman. "Miss Sinclair, did your hatpin really fall and stick in Mr. Tucker's boot?"

"It did indeed, Abraham."

"I tell jokes. Would you like to hear one?"

Her half nod was all the encouragement the boy required.

"What did the hatpin say to the big toe?"

Ida glanced over at Tucker, her lips pursed as if she were about to burst into laughter. She looked up at Abraham and shrugged her narrow shoulders.

"I'm stuck on you."

Amidst a wave of giggles, Otis motioned for his son to sit down. "I think that's more than enough jokes for one day."

While Abraham seated himself beside Ida, Hattie poured hot cocoa into the mugs and handed them out. "Kat, dear, Tucker told me your Morgan is the doctor who treated his father."

"Then I'm sure he received the best care." Her brown eyes shimmering, Mrs. Cutshaw leaned forward in her chair. "I've worked with Morgan some."

Miss Hattie lowered her cup. "Actually, that's a fun story too. They met in a birthing room."

Abraham giggled. The doctor's wife blushed. And the heat rising up Tucker's neck told him he had too.

Ida leaned forward on the sofa, looking at him. "My sister had gone in to help a stranger, and he assumed she was a midwife."

Sister.

The word made Tucker's heart ache for Willow. For all she'd lost. The children she and Sam would never have.

A smile tilted Mrs. Cutshaw's mouth to one side. "He's a fine doctor."

Tucker recognized the lilt in her voice, the shimmer of pride in her eyes, the buoyancy in her movements. She was obviously a happy newlywed. He remembered Willow having the same glow about her after she and Sam had married nearly four years ago. Suddenly, the air left the room and he jumped to his feet. "I can't stay, Miss Hattie."

Her cup rattled in its saucer. "But you didn't even—"

"I'm sorry. You must excuse me, ladies." He glanced at the sisters without really looking at the two across from him. He still couldn't bear to witness the joy his actions had cost Willow.

Ida was the first to stand. "Of course."

"Another time?" Concern darkened Miss Hattie's eyes to a gray blue.

He nodded and left the room, hoping there would be another time but dreading the explanation that next meeting would require.

SIX

*T*uesday afternoon, Ida carried two teacups to Kat's table and sat in the chair that faced the one glass window. Last night she had enjoyed a family dinner at Nell and Judson's modest home. Then this morning her sisters had given her a tour of the town. She'd never seen so many evocatively attired, brash-mannered females. But then, she'd never been out West before. Now she knew Tuesday was the morning designated for the *other women* to do their shopping.

The morning also included seeing Kat and Morgan's new home, still under construction, and the telegraph office, where she'd sent a wire to Aunt Alma and her sister Vivian to let them know of her safe arrival. Ida, Kat, and Nell enjoyed lunch with Morgan and a couple of the Sisters of Mercy in the hospital dining room, and then Nell parted company with them to go tend to a widow's children.

Ida had been torn between needing a rest and wanting to see Kat's infamous miner's shanty. After vowing to tend to her own need for peace and quiet that evening, she had agreed to make the trek up the hill to see the Cutshaws' temporary nest. Now she'd glimpsed both sisters' new lives here, and tomorrow she would take long strides into her own.

Kat set a plate of cinnamon-topped oatmeal cookies on the table in front of Ida, then sank into the chair across from her.

Nodding, Ida lifted the cup to her mouth, breathing in the memorable scent of peppermint—their mother's favorite. "This was a good idea."

"I couldn't send you off without spending a few more minutes with you." Kat tucked a strand of auburn hair behind her ear, then drizzled a stream of honey into her cup and stirred it. "I didn't think I would... I was sure I wouldn't, actually, but I like having a man in my life."

Ida glanced around the one-room cabin. Lace curtains hung at the window. The True Lover's Knot patterned quilt Aunt Alma made for Kat was spread across the bed. And a man's razor and strop lay on the washstand in the corner. Ida might have that one day, but for now marriage wasn't in her plans.

"Morgan seems good for you. Marriage suits—"

"And what about you?"

She hadn't expected this from Kat. Nell had always been the hopeless romantic in the family.

"You don't want love in your life?" Kat had never pressed her about such matters.

Ida studied a gouge in the plank flooring near the door. "I have my sisters. You three provide enough love for me."

Kat laid her hand on Ida's. "It's not the same, Sis."

"I know that." She might never have experienced romantic love before, but she'd seen enough of it in the people around her to know love could be distracting. Something she couldn't abide. Not now.

Ida took another sip of tea. "Did I tell you how proud I am of you—writing for *Harper's Bazar*?"

"You told me last night over veal and sweet potatoes." Kat's smirk formed soft ripples at the corners of her mouth. "I think what you plan to do is pretty exciting myself. Not many of us would want to brave the world of business. The world of businessmen, I should say."

"It may be a challenge, but I think I'm ready for it. Right now, I'd best go. I'm sure you have writing to do." Ida rose from her chair and carried her empty cup to the cupboard. "Thanks for the tour and the tea." She pulled her wrap from the peg by the door and slipped into it.

"I do have an article to finish." Kat retrieved Ida's reticule from a side table and handed it to her. "I'll see you tomorrow after your interview. Nell and I will be at Hattie's at four o'clock."

"I should be back by then."

Kat walked out to the porch with her and pulled her into a hug.

After the warm embrace, Ida took the gravel path to the road. The weariness of the past two days tugged at her eyes as she walked to the corner on Pikes Peak Avenue, then down Florissant. She needed a little solitude— time to untangle her thoughts. A leisurely stroll to the creek would help her do just that.

Riding in on the train, she'd seen a strand of water weaving across the bottom of town. She headed that direction, and it looked as though First Street could get her there. Crossing Bennett Avenue in late afternoon proved a challenge, but Cripple Creek seemed to buzz with activity at all times of the day and night.

Once she had crossed seedy Myers Avenue and broken free from the chaos in the center of town, Ida slowed her steps to enjoy the more artistic aspects of her surroundings. The panoramic mountains that encircled the valley rose up like green and golden yellow feathers on a Sioux chief's head- dress. Father had indeed chosen a breathtaking place for his daughters to relocate, and this had been the perfect time of year for her to come— autumn. Winter wasn't far off, but in the meantime, she'd enjoy the patches of sunflowers and the earthy scent of fallen leaves and drying grass.

Ida continued down First Street until she caught sight of a burbling creek through the brush. She followed the dirt path toward the water's edge, hoping to find a rock she could rest on for a spell of tranquility. Before she reached the water, she heard twigs snap and boots crunching on gravel upstream.

Perhaps coming down here alone hadn't been her best idea. She'd just turned back toward town when a motley apparition of a man stepped out of the brush in front of her.

"Well, I'll be...one of the ladies done come to see us."

"Only one?" Two other beastly-looking men emerged from the undergrowth behind her.

"I only came to see the creek." Her words squeaked out on ragged breaths.

"Well, then"—the man clamped his hand around Ida's forearm and spun her back around—"I say we be good hosts and show it to ya." Her head swam in the nauseating stink of his breath.

"Let me go!" Ida pounded her fists into his chest. When his grip tightened, she blindly tried to stomp his foot.

Holding her as she squirmed, he called her insulting names that made her skin crawl almost as much as his touch did. He pushed her through the brush and into a clearing cluttered with bedding, hard hats, picks, and shovels.

Ida kicked his shins and dug at his ears with her fingernails. He snarled like a wounded badger and covered his ears, freeing her arm from his grip. Seizing the opportunity, Ida turned and ran toward town. The men's sneers and retorts propelled her up the path. She heard at least two running after her for a few moments, but the sound soon fell away. Perhaps the heartbeat pounding in her ears had only drowned out their pursuing footfalls. She needed to press on.

As Ida came up over the rise, she tripped and landed face first in a surprisingly deep, offensively odorous puddle left by the recent rains.

Shivering from the cold water, she lifted her head to wipe her face with her sleeve. A snort startled her, and she looked up into the large snout of a drooling mule.

"That's Sal, ma'am. And we'd be right pleased to help you."

Ida looked past the mule at a wiry man with unruly gray hair.

"No, thank you." She·rose to her knees and studied him and his mule. Picks, shovels, and every sort of tool hung from the man's animal. *Another miner.*

He spit a brown streak into the dirt behind him. "You need to know we're not all the same, ma'am. When I saw you runnin', I figured you come across those no-accounts down at the creek. Thought you could use a friend 'bout now."

She could do with a friend, but…

He reached out his hand, giving her a chance to grasp it. Given her circumstances, she could fight him off if necessary once she was out of this mire. And the sooner, the better.

The miner gently lifted Ida out of the muddy mess. What a frightful sight she must be. She took some comfort in the fact that she didn't know many people here yet, and those she did know were mostly family.

"Name's Boney Hughes." He pulled a canteen from Sal's side and removed the cork. Then he pulled a clean handkerchief from his shirt pocket. "You can rinse your face, if you like."

Ida poured water onto the handkerchief and blotted her face. "Thank you, Mr. Hughes."

The man winced. "Mr. Hughes would be my daddy, if he were alive. Folks 'round here call me Boney."

His stare made her even more uncomfortable than she already was in her wet clothes. She needed to stop shaking.

"You look a lot like two sisters I know," he said.

"You know my sisters?" Ida regretted the condescension she heard in her voice, but Boney didn't seem the least bit offended by it.

"That's it—you're a Sinclair. You've got Kat's darker hair. Nell's blue eyes. And the same high cheekbones."

"Yes, Miss Ida Sinclair."

They moved to the side of the road to let a wagon by. When Ida looked up, she felt a sudden additional humiliation, as if this all hadn't been enough. The wagon was emblazoned with Raines Ice Company and was being driven by Tucker Raines.

Could this day get any worse?

"Miss Sinclair, is that you?" Tucker leapt off the seat of the wagon, approaching them with a bluster she'd only seen before a fistfight. "What is going on here? What is this man—"

Ida raised her hand, waving the soiled kerchief. "Mr. Boney Hughes, I'd like you to meet Mr. Tucker Raines."

Tucker stopped short, but maintained his fighting posture, his jaw tight. He regarded her muddy appearance.

"I did this on my own coming up from the creek," Ida said, waving a hand over her dress. "Mr. Boney here assisted me."

Relaxing his clenched fists, Tucker looked at her with skepticism etched in the creases in his forehead. "You went down to the camp?"

"I didn't mean to. I just wanted some peace and quiet, and I like water."

Tucker looked at Boney, the intensity gone from his brown eyes. "No personal offense intended, Mr. Hughes."

"Call me Boney." He shook Tucker's hand. "None taken."

Ida shivered, and Tucker glanced back at his wagon. "You need to get out of those wet clothes."

"Pardon me?"

Mr. Boney chuckled while Tucker shook his head. "I meant we need to see you home so you can change into dry clothing."

For a woman who intended to avoid entanglements with men, she was doing a poor job of it.

"My wagon would make short work of getting you to the boarding-house." Tucker regarded her muddied hat brim, then her mud-soaked boots before continuing. "Besides, it'd be much more pleasant than walking up the hill looking and feeling like...that."

Good point. Ida pushed a wavy strand of hair back from her face. "I accept your offer for a ride. Thank you." She turned back to Boney. "And thank you for your help." He'd been right—men weren't all the same.

"My pleasure, little lady." Boney removed his short-billed canvas hat and slapped it against his leg, creating a cloud of dust around him.

Tucker cupped her elbow and helped her up onto the wagon seat.

She hated being dirty...and indebted to a lawyer, a crusty miner, and now an ice man. But showing up at Hattie's with a man at her side would be the worst. Her landlady's reputation as a matchmaker worried her.

So much for her determination to not give the woman any bait for fishing.

Tucker swung up to his perch on the ice wagon. Ida Sinclair sat on the far edge of the seat, straight-backed and proper, staring straight ahead. She obviously wasn't going to allow the indignities of lecherous miners, a mud bath, and climbing onto an ice wagon in such shape to soil her spirit. While Miss Sinclair closed her eyes and drew in a deep breath, his respect for her grew roots and so did his desire to protect her. Sensing that would be impossible, he snapped the reins and clicked his tongue, signaling the horses forward.

As the wagon lurched up Bennett Avenue, he wanted to tell her she'd been foolish to take such a risk going to the creek—a woman alone. But she'd come from Maine with no concept of the personal danger that awaited her here in the West.

"Miss Sinclair, you are no longer in the genteel society of Maine." The late afternoon activity of carts, mules, and pedestrians on the street commanded Tucker's attention as he continued. "You need to be mindful of the fact that here in Cripple Creek there are a whole lot more men than there are women. Fact is"—he held his hand up, his fingers spread—"I can count on one hand the, uh, respectable single women in town and still have fingers left."

His speech had no sooner run the course of his breath when regret tied a knot in his chest. She had discovered all of that for herself, and didn't require a lecture from him. Expecting her to tell him so, he braced himself for her well-deserved wrath and looked her direction.

Instead, her lips sealed, Miss Sinclair worried the hem of her mud-encrusted cape. The tears streaming down her face caught his breath and wrenched his heart. A scolding for stating the obvious would have been easier to withstand.

"I'm sorry," he said, guiding the horses up Third Street. "I didn't mean to make you cry."

She sniffled and shook her head. "It's not your fault. You were right—I was foolish."

Had he actually said that? "You're new here. You didn't know they camp down there." Tucker shifted the reins to his left hand. He pulled a handkerchief from his coat pocket and held it out to her. "You're safe now," he said.

Nodding, she accepted the handkerchief and blotted the muddy rivulets on her face.

"I'll have you home soon."

"Miss Hattie will think I've been wallowing with pigs."

He formed a fist around the reins just thinking about those pigs.

"Next time you want some peace and quiet by the water, consider sitting at the stretch of creek on my father's property. Down Second Street off of Warren Avenue. Second cabin on the left. I put a bench down there for just that purpose. No miners." He pulled up on the reins in front of the yellow boardinghouse and brought the wagon to a stop. "I'll help you down."

Silent, she slid the handle of her reticule over her wrist and gathered her soiled skirt with her left hand. "That won't be necessary."

Tucker hurried around the back of the wagon anyway, just in time to watch Miss Sinclair's foot slip off the bottom step, her boot still coated with slick mud. Her hand held fast to the grab bar as her feet dangled inches from the ground.

Her forehead pressed against the wood siding, and a sigh of resignation escaped her lips. "If you insist on helping me down, Mr. Raines," she said, her words muffled, "I suppose I could oblige you."

Swallowing his laughter, Tucker planted his hands on her waist. He lifted her off the wagon and set her on the ground. He'd helped his sister from a wagon many times, but holding on to Miss Sinclair weakened his knees. And as he released her, he found himself hoping to see her again soon...at the bench by the creek.

SEVEN

*T*uesday evening a steady rain tapped on the cabin's tin roof in
rhythm with Kat's flow of words. She added the period to her last
sentence, capped her jar of ink, and smiled down at her fifth article for
Harper's Bazar.

Although *Harper's Bazar* was predominately a fashion magazine, in her
column Kat wrote stories about real women in the West. This month she'd
written about a young woman in Victor who had lost her sister and brother-
in-law to disease and had taken in her five nieces and nephews. Writing for
such a prestigious magazine still seemed like a dream to Kat.

However, life with the man who stood at the washstand in the corner
was the most unbelievable dream. Morgan caught her gazing at him and
gave her one of his dimpled smiles that made her grateful she was seated.
The man had an uncanny ability to sweep her off her feet with one tender
glance. Although she looked forward to the completion of their new home
and having more elbow room, she would miss the closeness this one-room
cabin afforded them.

Morgan set his razor next to the basin. "You couldn't help yourself,
could you?" He took slow, exaggerated steps toward her. "You just had to
write another story about your charming husband, didn't you?"

Kat giggled. The man was impossible. He'd heard all about her trip to Victor and the interview.

Impossibly irresistible.

Morgan sat across the table and laced his fingers with hers. "Do you plan to write a story about Ida?"

"Perhaps. Or a story about Mollie O'Bryan. A western businesswoman would no doubt be of interest to my readers."

"You know I'm partial to industrious women of independent means." He winked. "But I fear your sister may not know what she's getting into."

"Working for Miss O'Bryan?"

He nodded. "And the men who dominate the mining and investment companies here."

"She's the 'big sister,' remember? I think she'll keep those fellows in line and do just fine. Besides, if she does run into any bullies, she has at least one noble brother-in-law who can offer her counsel."

He drew her hand to his lips and kissed it. "Mrs. Cutshaw, I do believe you have me right where you want me."

"Ready to lose at a game of checkers, are you?"

"I'll do my best"—he pushed his chair back and stood—"but I may not be able to stop myself."

Kat smiled. She was already a winner, and this man the prize.

"We'll see. I'll put these things back in my trunk while you get the board." Kat stacked her writing materials and rose from her chair. She'd taken only a few steps when the room began to spin and her insides started to convulse.

Morgan rushed to her side and handed her a tin bowl. Fortunately, she didn't have to use it. When the gagging subsided, Kat straightened and drew in a deep breath.

Her husband, looking as pained as if he'd just smashed his finger, guided her back to the chair at the kitchen table and knelt in front of her. "Feeling better?"

She gave him a slow nod. She felt better, but she didn't know how long it would last. Her body had been at odds with her since the moment she'd raised her head off the pillow that morning.

"Did you eat something that didn't agree with you?" Morgan asked.

"You've eaten what I've eaten." Kat shrugged. "Nell and I spent much of the day giving Ida a walking tour of town, and then she was here with me this afternoon. Too much excitement, I suppose."

The creases in his brow told her he wasn't convinced. "Have you noticed any other changes?"

"It was nothing. Really." She raised herself from the chair to prove it. "I feel much better now."

He stood beside her, his hands open as if he expected to have to catch her.

Now that she thought about it, she had made more trips to the outhouse the past couple of days. And she'd felt like a newborn calf on wobbly legs today.

Newborn calf.

Kat's mind raced, trying to remember. The last one began the day before she'd received the August issue of *Harper's Bazar* with her third story printed in it. That was August 10. This was September 29.

She pressed her hands to her abdomen.

"You missed it?" Morgan's voice had suddenly gone flat.

She nodded. He'd been through this before.

"You've been feeling a little queasy for the past few days?"

She nodded again.

"More frequent visits to the room outside?"

Another nod.

Tears pooled in his green eyes. "Our house may be ready none too soon."

Her eyes were wet too. A baby should've been wonderful news. A pregnancy would've been cause for celebration for Nell. But Judson had never lost a wife and unborn son in childbirth.

"I'm sorry," she whispered.

"Don't be silly." Morgan laced his fingers in hers and drew her hand to his lips. "A baby is good news, Kat."

She wanted to believe him. But more than anything, she hoped he believed it.

Eight

ucker lifted the pitchfork from a nail in the wall of the hayloft where his father stored sheaves of hay and straw. He breathed in the earthy scents of leather, hay, wet horses, and manure, feeling more at home out here in the barn than he did in his father's house. How was it that he reached hundreds of strangers for Christ every year in camp meetings but couldn't so much as nudge his own father?

Or help Willow?

He'd asked why time and again, and God hadn't been forthcoming with so much as a hint.

Tucker jabbed the pitchfork into the haystack. "Here you go, fellas." He tossed a meal of hay down into the stalls for Trojan and Titan.

He'd been so certain God had called him to the ministry. He felt most at peace when he was preaching. He glanced down at the ice wagon.

Had God changed His mind?

Tucker descended the ladder from the loft and looked around. The barn was no bigger than necessary to house two ice wagons, five or six horses, and a small tack room where his father kept extra ice hooks, picks, and saws.

Although Tucker didn't much like his current circumstances, he knew he had to do all he could to save the business and see to his parents' needs.

And to Willow's.

His responsibilities meant convincing the banker that the Raines Ice Company was a good investment; that if he had the funds to build the business, he was capable of doing so. He'd stopped by the First National Bank on the way to the depot that morning and set up an appointment for three thirty that afternoon. In the meantime, he'd write his Wednesday letter to Willow and then head to the post office. Two weeks had passed since his meeting with Willow's attendant, so a report could arrive in today's mail.

The prospect spurred him into action. He retrieved his five-pound block of ice from the wagon and let the canvas flaps close.

"See you later, fellas." Tucker shut the barn doors on his way out and walked the twenty-foot path to the square-cut log cabin. His father's property consisted of the modest dwelling, the barn, and an outhouse on an acre with a creek running through the back of it.

Tucker climbed the two steps up to the back door and stomped his muddy boots on the rag rug just inside the kitchen. He crossed to the small icebox and set the block of ice in the top of it.

Until eleven days ago when he boarded the train in Stockton, he'd been living in a parsonage. He had his own room in the basement, but spent most of his free time with the Hutchinson family of six who lived upstairs. Before that, while attending seminary in San Francisco, he'd shared a rented room with three other students, and he'd spent his first six nights in Cripple Creek sleeping in the hayloft with the horses and a crusty barn owl for company.

Now he had the whole house to himself and didn't much like it. Too quiet and settled, with a coldness that had nothing to do with the room temperature.

Tucker set the ice tongs by the door and moved into the sitting area. The knotty pine side tables were devoid of any family photos. The day the fishermen found Willow in the river was the day his father found having children too much of a burden.

Embarrassment. Shame. Grief. Loathing. All were gripping reactions to the sorrow dividing his family. Tucker understood that reality and yet was powerless to change it.

After Tucker added a lump of coal to the parlor stove, he went to the smaller of two bedchambers. He lifted his leather bag onto the bed and unbuckled the straps. He'd removed his clothing and hung it in the wardrobe Monday evening, but he hadn't touched the few whatnots he'd packed. This was as good a time as any.

Tucker pulled out his writing box and carried it to his mother's plank table. He opened the lid to the box and lifted the picture frame off the stationery. He studied the watercolor portrait as he did every Wednesday. In it, Willow's green eyes sparkled like polished emeralds in a full-face smile. His finger traced the image of her, pencil and sketch pad in hand, while his heart remembered happier days when they went to the river together. He and Sam fished while his sister sat on the grassy banks drawing whatever struck her fancy.

That was before his father had her committed to the Stockton State Mental Asylum.

During his most recent visit, just before he left for Colorado, an attendant had led Willow to the front porch. Tucker followed them out. He and his sister sat in white rocking chairs with a stone pot of red geraniums on the table between them. It may as well have been a six-foot tall stone fence.

"Willow, I received a letter from Mother yesterday." Pausing, he studied her for even the slightest hint of a response. Nothing. Not so much as a blink. Her doctor had told him to use her name often and to mention the names of the people she loved. They all hoped using Willow's name frequently might trigger a pleasant memory that could one day bring her back. So far, nothing he or anyone else had tried was working. Water therapy. Music. Work. Art.

Nothing.

Willow, her hands folded in her lap, had stared out at the lush garden, her rocker still. Tucker watched a gilded butterfly flit from one sunflower to another just beyond them. Before the tragedy, his sister would've recited the specifics of its species for him. Now the butterfly fluttered in her line of vision seemingly unrecognized. How could she look out at the world, and not see it? Not respond to any of it?

Tucker set the photo on the table and twisted the cap off the inkwell. Breathing a prayer for guidance, he dipped the quill in the ink and began this week's one-sided conversation with his beloved older sister.

NINE

*I*da stood in front of the full-length mirror in her upstairs room at Hattie's Boardinghouse. In a slow twirl, she checked for any unruly threads or twisted seams in her clothing. She'd chosen a blue serge skirt and embroidered jacket for this afternoon's meeting with Mollie O'Bryan. Vivian had suggested the dress while helping her pack for the move out West. Her youngest sister insisted the outfit would reflect business savvy without masking her femininity. If only Vivian possessed as much common sense as she did fashion sense. Ida hoped Aunt Alma was keeping a close watch on her.

Satisfied with her overall appearance, Ida returned to the wardrobe for the finishing touches. She pulled the mushroom-style hat with yellow silk roses off the top of the cabinet and carried it to the dressing table.

She sank onto the cushioned bench and reached for the jam jar where she kept her hatpins. She could scarcely look at her pins the past two days without thinking of the ice man—Tucker Raines. She let herself enjoy the memory of their first meeting as a smile tugged at her mouth.

He delivered ice to the boardinghouse wearing a preacher's hat. His father was sick and sour. His mother looked and sounded frail. One minute, he came across as lighthearted with a clock-stopping grin. The next, dark storm clouds rolled in from out of the blue. Like Monday afternoon at Miss

Hattie's. Then there was the memory of yesterday afternoon and him escorting her muddy self back to the boardinghouse.

Ida wove a pin through the back of her hat. Why was she spending so much time thinking about him? The ice man was a curiosity, that was all. Certainly not someone she'd have business with, so she'd have to live without knowing the rest of his story. She had her own story to live anyway—a tale of inspiring success.

Once she'd fastened the hat to her head, she glanced at the stack of notebooks on her bedside table. She'd spent the better part of the morning reviewing her class notes. Proper correspondence formats. Bookkeeping methods. Telephone etiquette.

Confident she'd done all she could to prepare for her interview, Ida left the books where they sat and descended the narrow staircase. Halfway down, she found herself swaying to the tune of the sentimental ballad coming from the parlor. One of the three two-minute cylinders Miss Hattie had for her Edison Home Phonograph. Already, Ida had heard all three songs multiple times. When she achieved a modicum of success working with Mollie O'Bryan, she'd spend fifty cents and buy the woman a fourth cylinder.

Miss Hattie waltzed out of the parlor wearing a cropped tent dress. She met Ida at the bottom of the stairs, her warm smile creating soft folds at her ears. "You look nice, dear. And quite professional."

"Thank you." Ida tugged at the embroidered cuffs of her jacket.

"Since you are ready for your interview more than an hour early, might you have a few minutes to spare before you leave the house?"

Ida couldn't afford to be late, but she had plenty of time, and this was her home until she'd achieved enough success to have her own built. "Yes, I'd like that. Let's sit for a few minutes."

The landlady captured her hand and pulled her toward the parlor.

"You've been so busy since you arrived in town that we've hardly had a moment to ourselves for a visit."

Hattie sat on one end of the sofa. Ida chose the wingback chair across from her and set her reticule on the sofa table between them.

"You met your brothers-in-law Monday night. What did you think of them?" Miss Hattie asked.

"I found them both quite likeable. Morgan still has a lot of the Boston way about him, while Judson is much less reserved but just as charming."

"Did your sisters tell you I helped things along with both couples?"

"They did." Ida didn't need or want that kind of help. "Judson seemed very attentive to Nell. And Morgan and Kat appear to have a spark that suits them. I'd say my sisters have done very well for themselves."

"You will too, dear."

Clearly, the woman required a more direct approach. "I don't want what my sisters have, Miss Hattie."

"You want success in business."

"Yes, I do. That's why I'm here." She met the woman's attentive gaze. "Not to seek out a husband."

"Who says you won't have both?" Miss Hattie cocked a salt-and-pepper eyebrow above a thinly disguised grin. "You and the young Mr. Raines seemed to have a bit of a spark yourselves Monday afternoon."

"I'd hardly call dropping a hatpin in his boot a spark." She was only curious about him. Concerned about him was even more precise. She and her sisters were all alarmed by his abrupt flight from the parlor.

Her landlady had an endearing and motherly way about her, and since Ida's own mother had passed many years ago, Hattie's warmth felt good. Especially now, as she started her new life in Colorado. The matchmaking, however, she couldn't and wouldn't tolerate.

"Ida, dear, you've only been here a couple of days, but I can already see you are bright and well studied, conscientious and professional. I'm sure Miss O'Bryan will see those qualities too."

"I wish I knew more about the stock market and the mining business. I've heard she's become quite involved in them."

"That she has." Miss Hattie looked down and fiddled with a button on her skirt.

Ida subdued a sigh and met her landlady's gaze. "You don't approve of Miss O'Bryan's business dealings?"

"I don't really know the woman past hello."

"But you have reservations?"

"She sat at my table at the Women for the Betterment of Cripple Creek luncheon last month. I gathered Mollie may have her ducks lined up too tightly."

Ducks?

"It's something my mama would say." Miss Hattie glanced at the ceiling as if she might glimpse heaven there. "It meant I needed to leave room for God to work out His own plans."

"I see." Ida chose to keep her own adage to herself—*God helps those who help themselves.* She hadn't talked to God more than once a day, if that often, since her mother died. Had never really conversed with Him the way her mother had. But they'd read the book of Proverbs often enough in their family Bible readings for her to know that God didn't favor sluggards.

Miss Hattie glanced at the mantel clock. "You best be on your way, dear." She walked with Ida to the front door and opened it.

Ida looped the handle of her reticule over her left arm and stepped outside. Though she didn't see a cloud in the sky, she knew last night's pounding rain had replaced the dust on the roads with a mud thicker than porridge.

Hattie waved at her from the front porch. "I'll be praying for you, dear."

Ida returned the woman's wave and smiled. *"I'll be praying for you, dear."* Something her mother would've said.

At the corner, Ida turned down Third Street. She dodged a puddle and hoped her landlady prayed she'd find a way to avoid the mud and keep herself clean. At the bottom of the hill, she turned west on Bennett Avenue. Yesterday on their walking tour, Nell had pointed out Miss O'Bryan's stenography firm, near the corner of First Street and Bennett Avenue.

Outside the narrow brick building, Ida pulled her mother's pendant watch from her reticule and checked the time again. Miss O'Bryan's wire stated a three o'clock appointment, and being anything but early wasn't in Ida's nature. She pulled the door open and stepped inside at ten minutes before three.

The room was well-appointed, though devoid of people. Three burgundy armchairs sat empty at one side of the door. Two oak desks filled the center of the office while matching bookcases stood against the wall.

Muffled voices drew Ida's attention to a closed door at the back of the room. She read the brass nameplate: Mollie O'Bryan. While she couldn't hear what was being said, she did distinguish two voices—a woman's and a man's. Miss O'Bryan must have been with a client.

Ida admired the framed oil painting that hung over the armchairs and then sat down.

"You don't think I'm smart enough to smell a rat?" The woman had apparently abandoned the notion of using hushed tones.

"I'm only telling you what I heard." The man's voice was steady and calm but loud enough to be audible from Ida's position near the front door. "You don't want to get tangled up in anything—"

"And just what would you have me do about such hearsay?"

Ida glanced. toward the door. Perhaps she should wait outside. She didn't need any strikes against her, and she doubted eavesdropping, unintentional or not, would sit well with Miss O'Bryan.

"It's more than mere speculation, Mollie. He's being investigated for embezzlement."

"He's a paying client who has already retained my services." She paused. "Besides, you know that investigation isn't conviction."

"Give the money back. You can't afford—"

"Right now I can't afford to listen to you. This is a mining town. If I judged everyone's moral character before serving them, I'd have no business."

Ida rose from the chair. She shouldn't be hearing this. But before she could step outside, the side door was flung open and she let out an audible gasp, like the one that had escaped her at the depot. A flawed tendency. She wasn't being coddled by the comforts of Maine anymore, and it was time she learn to expect the unexpected. Especially since the unexpected seemed the standard here in Colorado.

The woman charging out of the office wore her auburn hair back in a tight chignon. However, it wasn't the woman who captured Ida's attention but the man standing in the doorway with a coat draped over his arm: Colin Wagner, her hero from the train.

Ida took slow steps toward the woman, who looked about her age—maybe a year or two older than her nearly twenty-two years. "Ma'am—"

"Miss Sinclair." The gentleman's warm smile did nothing to take the chill out of the scowl shadowing Miss O'Bryan's face.

Ida gave him a tight nod. "Mr. Wagner."

He smiled, then returned his attention to Miss O'Bryan. "Mollie, this is Miss Ida Sinclair."

She'd intruded. At the very least, she'd caught her potential employer in a foul mood. "If this isn't a good time, ma'am, I can come back later."

"Call me Miss O'Bryan." Miss O'Bryan's features softened as she regarded Mr. Wagner with a sideways glance. "We have Mr. Wagner to thank for my lack of readiness for your arrival."

"I didn't mind waiting." Ida would have gone on doing so if it would have spared her this unpleasantness.

"Colin here"—the woman waved his general direction—"is my legal counsel."

He shrugged into his tweed coat. "And her friend."

"Yes, well, be that as it may, friendship hardly gives you the right to tell me who I should accept as a client and who I shouldn't."

Ida studied the royal blue Persian rug under her feet, wishing she could disappear beneath it.

"I merely shared information that could help you make an informed decision in regard to a questionable liaison. My obligation as your counsel and even more so as your friend."

Miss O'Bryan's grin helped to dispel the darkness from her face. "Your song and dance could help any politician win an election. Nonetheless, I appreciate your concern." She straightened and her grin disappeared. "But the buck stops here, and I choose to take his bucks. Gladly."

"Just watch yourself with him. I'd hate to see you taken advantage of." Mr. Wagner turned his warm smile toward Ida and brushed the edge of his bowler. "Best of luck to you, Miss Sinclair."

"Thank you."

Miss O'Bryan waved, shooing Mr. Wagner away, and then spun toward her office. Ida followed her. The woman pointed her to a chair in front of her desk and closed the door behind them.

Ida had barely set her reticule on the rug at her feet and sunk into the cushioned armchair when Miss O'Bryan leaned back against the front of her desk. "So, Miss Sinclair, why do you want to work for me?"

Ida swallowed hard against the suffocating space between them. "You're a successful businesswoman."

"And you want to be one."

Ida straightened, clasping her fingers in her lap. "Yes, ma'am, I do." She needed this job, and apparently, she had to prove herself worthy of this woman's mentorship. "Miss O'Bryan, you have a reputation as a business tycoon. You are highly successful in many aspects of enterprise and commerce. I am a capable secretary and assistant with varied office skills. You've seen my resume. You have the letter of recommendation from the director of the school of business."

Pausing for a breath, Ida held the woman's gaze, focusing on the sparkle in her green eyes rather than on her raised brow. "What you don't know is that I am just as set on success as you are, and I won't be thwarted by self-important men who think they know anything and everything better than we do." Ida scooted to the edge of the chair. "I want to work for you because I think you and I could make a good team."

Mollie strolled around her desk and sat in the plush high-back chair. She pulled a folder from a file drawer and slapped it down in front of her. "That, Ida Sinclair, is exactly what I wanted to hear. You're hired."

Ida blew out a breath. "Thank you, Miss O'Bryan. I promise to make the most of this opportunity." She'd fretted over a review of office procedures and protocols for an interview that consisted of a couple of rhetorical questions and her passionate response?

"For now, you and I are it." Mollie glanced at her diamond-studded wristwatch. "If you'll excuse me, I have to leave for an appointment with what Mr. Colin Wagner would call a questionable client." Shaking her head, she pulled a ledger from the top drawer and stood. "You'll start tomorrow morning. Nine o'clock sharp. Work until half past five with a thirty-minute break somewhere in the middle."

Ida rose from her chair and followed her new employer out both doors and into bright sunlight.

"Until tomorrow." Mollie set off at a brisk pace.

Ida didn't bother to stifle her giggle. Figuring out why Miss Mollie O'Bryan might have trouble maintaining an office staff required no stretch of the imagination.

Fortunately for Ida, she wasn't timid. She'd been surprised by the woman's candor, but she could work with it. Truth be known, she found Miss O'Bryan's frankness rather refreshing. She'd learn a lot from her and she wouldn't have to waste a moment wondering what was on her employer's mind.

Neither would anyone else within earshot.

TEN

*T*ucker shifted in the small armchair and realized he had no trouble imagining how a horse might feel being stuffed into a teacup. He'd tried to anticipate the banker's questions and concerns and was prepared to address them.

His mother had managed to pry the financial ledger from his father's hands just two days before they left for Colorado Springs. At her insistence, his father agreed to trust Tucker with all of their "business dealings," which turned out to be a thinly disguised wording for "debts." If he'd known then what he knew now, Tucker wouldn't have accepted the book.

At least that was what he told himself.

Until his stop at the post office this afternoon to mail his letter to Willow, he hadn't known his father was behind on the payments for his sister's care. When Tucker opened the envelope from the asylum, he expected a progress report, hoping for good news. Instead, he'd received a statement and an ultimatum demanding payment for the past three months. He needed to start turning a profit—and soon.

He and Otis had spent most of Monday afternoon talking about the requirements for expanding the business. He'd added a list to the ledger, along with the estimated costs.

This has to work.

Mr. Updike settled into the leather chair on the business side of the mahogany desk. He lifted a folder from the top of a tall stack to his left. The sleeves on his herringbone suit jacket had obviously been tailored for someone with longer arms and a taller torso. When he set the closed file down in front of him, only his fleshy fingers extended beyond the cuffs. He gazed up at Tucker over the top of wire-rimmed spectacles "Mr. Raines, correct?"

"Yes sir." Tucker set his father's ledger on the edge of the desk. "I am Tucker Raines. Again, thank you for adding me to your afternoon schedule today."

"You're new here in Cripple Creek."

It wasn't a question. Tucker saw the rest of the statement etched in the little man's beady eyes. *I didn't know Will Raines had a son.*

"I arrived in town last week, sir. I'm helping my father with the family business. The Raines Ice Company."

Updike nodded. "Why are you here, Mr. Raines?"

"My father is ill. I'll be running the business for him, and I want to expand it."

His revelation of sickness in the family hadn't changed the man's expression in the least.

"Better you running the company than that ugly"—Updike regarded Tucker with a squinted stare and spit the next word—"Negro he had working for him."

Tucker swallowed his ire, but not very deeply. Leaning forward, he rested his forearms on the desk. "Otis Bernard is a fine man and still works for us."

Mr. Updike's lips thinned, and he flipped the folder open. Had the fact that he didn't share the man's prejudice cost Tucker the loan? Cost his father his home?

"With the exponential growth here in Cripple Creek and the surrounding communities, I anticipate greater and greater need for iceboxes and ice deliveries," Tucker said.

Pushing his spectacles up, Updike peered at a page in the folder.

Tucker opened the ledger and pulled out his estimate of growth and his list of needs and expenses. "I brought a list of items that would help us better serve the community's needs. An icehouse and more wagons, more horses, and more men would produce more regular customers. I've prepared an itemized list of our needs and the estimated cost to fulfill them."

"Last winter, your father sat where you're sitting with a similar request."

Tucker held out the list to Mr. Updike. When the older man didn't accept the paper, Tucker drew in a breath and prayed it would serve to shrink his fast-growing frustration. "Sir, I think my estimates here would be enough to do the job. I'm confident that by spring the Raines Ice—"

"I told your father no." Mr. Updike closed the folder and sat back in his chair. "My answer to you is the same."

No longer able to abide the man's smugness, Tucker moved to the edge of the chair. "Mr. Updike, I need to ask you why."

The man with too much sleeve peered up at him over the top of his wire rims. "It's my job to choose who and what would be the best investment for the bank, and I say the Raines Ice Company doesn't qualify. If you'd like to reconsider some of your business practices and then reapply, I might be willing to hear you."

Tucker understood. He scooped the ledger off the desk and rose to his feet. "Thank you for your time."

He couldn't leave the bank too soon. He gave the hunched security guard at the main door a quick nod on his way out to the boardwalk.

He could never fire the man who'd kept his father's business alive. Otis was more a part of the Raines Ice Company than Tucker was.

Now what?

He didn't want to go back to the house. Not yet. He couldn't bear to see his father's worn chair sitting empty in the corner. He'd let him down yet again. He was to blame for Willow's broken heart and for his parents leaving Stockton. Feeling the weight of it all on his shoulders, Tucker stuck the ledger inside his canvas coat, then turned right on Bennett instead of left, headed in the direction of Mount Pisgah.

In a matter of weeks he'd have a bill from the sanitorium in Colorado Springs to add to the ledger. He was a preacher, not a businessman. God had called him to minister to the lost—to people who needed Him. And yet here he was, helplessly attempting to run an anemic ice business.

At Second Street, he stepped off the boardwalk and raised his face to the sun. "What are You doing, God?"

He hadn't realized he'd spoken the prayer audibly until he lowered his gaze and saw Ida Sinclair standing in front of him.

ELEVEN

$\mathcal{M}$r. Raines," Ida said in greeting. The redness coloring Tucker Raines's face gave his brown eyes an autumn hue. Ida enjoyed his coy smile until she remembered Hattie's earlier statement. *"Who says you won't have both? You and the young Mr. Raines seemed to have a bit of a spark yourselves."* Her landlady was given to exaggeration. Showing interest in Tucker or in any other man would be putting the cart before the horse. First, a career. Then she'd decide whether or not to add a man to her plans.

Tucker pinched the crown of his flat-brimmed hat and removed it from his head. "You clean up quite nicely, Miss Sinclair."

Ida felt her cheeks blush. So far, flying hatpins and muddy clothes seemed to characterize her meetings with Tucker. No sparks had been involved. "Thank you. Amazing the difference a day makes."

"All the difference in the world." The monotone she'd heard in Tucker's voice at Miss Hattie's had returned. One minute he was all fists, ready to protect her from a harmless old man, and the next he seemed hidden behind a cloud.

Ida considered walking away, but this man stirred her curiosity. She crossed and uncrossed her arms. "So did He tell you?"

"Who?" Tucker glanced behind him.

"You asked God what He's doing. Did He tell you?"

"Not yet." Perfectly masculine brows hooked over his eyes as he squinted at her. "Unless you're part of an answer."

"Me?" Her voice jumped a full octave. The man was as unpredictable as a summer snowstorm. She believed in God, even talked to Him most every night as a sort of benediction on her day, but she wasn't likely to be anyone's answer to prayer. She couldn't do anything for a man running an ice business for a sick father.

"It'd be nice if He'd at least hint at His purposes."

His purposes. Tucker spoke about God in such a personal manner. No, Tucker Raines was nothing like Bradley Ditmer or the miners. Nothing like Mr. Wagner from the train either. Tucker seemed to carry a trace of vulnerability as comfortably as he did confidence, a combination Ida found intriguing—all the more reason to steer clear of him.

She looked down at his boots as if the act would move her own feet in the opposite direction. The ice man had cleaned his boots since their encounter at the depot.

"I had a meeting at the bank," he said.

"I had a job interview and I—"

"Found employment?"

Feeling the excitement of her new job afresh, Ida smiled and nodded.

"Here I've been babbling while you have cause for celebration." He looked her square in the eye. "You have to let me buy you a cup of coffee."

She didn't exactly gasp, but she did feel her mouth drop open. She glanced up the hill. "I can't. My sisters are expecting me at Miss Hattie's."

"Of course. I understand." His voice was steady without a hint of disappointment. In fact, he looked relieved she'd declined. Perhaps he'd also surprised himself with the invitation. Given Tucker's situation with his folks and returning to run the family business, he no doubt also needed to remain focused.

So they were curious about one another. Curiosity didn't comprise a spark. Soon they'd each go their own ways, entrenched in their efforts to thrive here in Cripple Creek—Colorado's city of opportunity.

"Let me at least walk you up the hill."

As soon as Ida nodded, Tucker set his hat back on his head and presented his arm. He guided her across Bennett Avenue and up Third Street, which soon turned into Hayden. She enjoyed the easiness of his company, but she suddenly realized that agreeing to let Tucker walk her to the boardinghouse hadn't been a wise choice.

Clearing her throat, she stopped at the corner of Golden Avenue. "I appreciate your company, Mr. Raines, but you needn't go out of your way any further."

"Another thirty feet is hardly out of my way."

Ida drew in a deep breath. If the man knew about the master matchmaker and her two elves, he too would be concerned about being seen with her. Not that he would be susceptible or interested, as he obviously had his work cut out for him seeing to family matters. Still, there was no need for either of them to suffer embarrassment because of her sisters' or her landlady's good, but misguided, intentions.

"Very well." His gaze seemed to linger. "Have a good visit with your sisters, and best wishes in your new job."

"Thank you." Ida turned away and walked up the block toward Hattie's. About halfway to the yellow house on the right, she glanced back toward the corner.

A mistake.

Tucker still stood there, watching her. His wave was too warm and his smile too bright. He could easily become a distraction.

She couldn't give him that chance.

Ida focused on the sunflowers that beamed from the planters in front of Hattie's house and climbed the porch steps to the door. When she twisted the doorknob, someone else was doing the same thing on the other side. As soon as she let go, the door opened, and Faith, the schoolteacher who rented a room down the hallway from her, stared up at her.

"I'm sorry. I was trying to help." Faith's small smile was the perfect accompaniment for her soft voice.

"No need to apologize." Something the young woman did far too often. Ida stepped inside, expecting to see her sisters, to hear the phonograph playing in the parlor. "Kat and Nell aren't here yet?"

"Yes. We've been waiting for you in the kitchen."

Ida caught a whiff of something sweet and cinnamon. She sniffed the air as she followed Faith Dunsmuir down the hallway and through the dining room. "Apple pie?"

Faith nodded, setting her midnight-colored ponytail bobbing. "Four apple pies. Miss Hattie can't be still when there's waiting to be done."

"I do love autumn." Ida followed the timid schoolteacher into the kitchen. Kat sat at the table, snapping string beans and dropping them into a kettle, while Nell pulled a pie from the oven and Hattie slid another one in.

Her landlady wiped her hands on her paisley-print apron. "I was beginning to think we might have to go pry you out of the stenography office."

"Miss O'Bryan had someone else with her when I arrived so we were late starting the interview." Ida kept the names of the men to blame for her delay to herself as she crossed the room and sat down between Kat and Faith.

Kat snapped the ends off a bean and dropped it into the kettle. She looked pale, and her eyes a bit dull.

Before Ida could open her mouth to inquire as to her sister's dreary countenance, Kat met her gaze and shook her head ever so slightly as if to say, *Don't ask.*

"How did your interview with Miss O'Bryan go?" Nell set a teapot on the table in front of Ida.

"Well…" After waiting a moment for full effect, Ida clasped her hands. "The job is mine. I start in the morning."

Hattie, Nell, and Faith erupted with congratulations.

"That's good news," Kat said, but she didn't seem able to rise to the others' level of excitement.

"Kat?" Ida reached for her arm. "Are you sick?"

"Oh dear. We can't have that." Hattie wiped her hands on her apron, then laid the back of her hand against Kat's forehead.

"I'm fine." Kat drew in a deep breath and stared at the kettle of raw beans in front of her. "I mean I'm not sick. I am, apparently, quite pregnant."

"Oh my stars!" Hattie clapped as she plopped down into a chair beside Kat. "What wonderful news!"

Ida reached for Kat's hands and squeezed them. "You're going to be a mother, and that makes me an aunt. Hattie's right—that's wonderful news."

Nell nodded, her blue eyes glistening with tears.

A frown claimed Kat's face as she looked across the table at Nell. "I'm sorry." Her mysterious apology came out on a sigh.

Nell splayed her fingers across her mouth and darted out of the room.

Ida stood, watching her sister flee, and then spun back toward Kat. "What was that all about?"

"Nell is the one who wanted a baby."

"And you don't?"

"Of course she does." Miss Hattie rose from her chair. "Babies are a gift from God."

Kat pressed her hand to her abdomen. "I do, but—"

"Morgan's not happy about the baby?" Perhaps her brother-in-law wasn't so likeable after all.

"He says he is, but, you know, Morgan lost a son in childbirth…his wife too." The last words came out on a whisper.

"I'm sorry," Ida said. "I'd forgotten."

"But that scene with Nell wasn't about me. She hasn't conceived yet. And I did."

Whatever was Nell worried about that for? She'd only been married a handful of months, and as far as Ida was concerned, it was better to wait awhile before the added responsibility of a child.

"I should go talk to her." Kat gingerly rose from the wooden chair.

Ida waved her back down. "I'll go."

Kat's eyebrows arched in concern. "Perhaps you shouldn't be the one to talk to her about this. That particular big-sister look in your eye tells me you don't understand her reaction."

"I can be understanding."

"You go on ahead, Ida." Hattie pulled an oak tray from the cupboard. "Kat and I will gather the teacups and bring them into the parlor. I'm sure that's where she's gone."

When Ida arrived in the parlor, Nell stood in front of the mantel, face to face with the clock. "Are you all right?" Ida asked.

Sniffling, Nell nodded and turned toward Ida, swiping at the tears rolling down her blotchy cheeks. "Of all the times not to have a handkerchief with me."

Ida pulled a handkerchief out of the pocket on her skirt and handed it to her. "You have plenty of time to have a baby, Sis."

"I know." Nell drew in a deep, shuddering breath and dabbed her eyes. "I can't believe I ran out of the kitchen like that. You all must think I'm a baby myself."

"Kat understands."

"But you don't understand, do you?" Nell asked.

Ida pressed her lips together and slowly shook her head. She didn't know what it meant to love a man so much that she'd want to set her ambition aside to marry him and have his child. But she didn't have to understand to *be* understanding.

Nell giggled—a sweet sound. "Don't feel bad. I don't either. Judson and I only married four months ago. It's not like we're going to be childless like poor Miss Hattie and her George. She never could bear children."

A gasp and clanging cups drew their attention to the doorway, where Miss Hattie steadied the tea tray in Kat's hands.

Fresh tears flowed down Nell's face. "I didn't mean… What's the matter with me? I'm such a mess."

"Yes, you are, dear." Miss Hattie approached Nell and reached for her hand. "Love and longing can do that to a person. But there's no reason to feel bad about what you said. It's true that God chose to bless George and me with the care of other people's children—most of them grown—rather than with our own." A warm smile lit her silver eyes.

It seemed God had gifted the landlady with an uncanny way of mothering despite her barren womb. Ida took the tray from Kat and carried it across the room.

"Thank you, Miss Hattie." Nell drew the gracious woman into an embrace then faced Kat. "I am the most selfish person on God's green earth. But you have to know that I really am excited to be Auntie Nell."

"I know you are." Kat hugged Nell.

"Are you and Morgan all right?"

"We haven't talked about that part of it yet."

"I've been thinking about that, Kat." Ida set the tray on the sofa table while the others seated themselves. "I may not be qualified to offer marital advice, but—"

"But that's not going to stop you." A smile tipped Kat's mouth to one side.

"You do know me well, don't you?" Ida sat on the sofa beside Kat. "And I know you. You won't rest until you've expressed your feelings. None of us are good at holding in our emotions."

"Ida's right." Her voice strong again, Nell handed Kat a teacup. "Granted, you needn't be as transparent as I am, but if you don't voice your concerns, they'll fester and your health will suffer."

Ida warmed her hands on her cup. She *was* right, wasn't she? She hoped so. She truly wasn't qualified to counsel either of her Cripple Creek sisters on the finer points—or on any points—having to do with marriage.

Business was her ally. Love and marriage, her foe.

Twelve

hursday morning Ida relished the warmth of the sun on her back as she strolled down Third Street toward Bennett Avenue. She'd chosen to wear a burgundy skirt with a white shirtwaist for her first day of work. She'd pinned her hair up in a French twist and donned a new pair of calfskin shoes. She only hoped she was ready in Miss Mollie O'Bryan's way of thinking.

She'd drunk a hefty helping of bicarbonate soda to settle her stomach. Still, bees seemed to buzz about inside her. It would help if she could shut off the memory of yesterday's interview. Of Miss O'Bryan's battle with Colin Wagner. Of her leaning in toward Ida, close enough that Ida could smell the scent of her lavender bath soap, and asking why she wanted to work for her. Ida shook her head to rid herself of the intimidating image. She could do this.

Turning the corner at the Imperial Hotel, she stepped up onto the boardwalk at Bennett Avenue and drew in a deep breath. This morning she was stepping into her future as a businesswoman. This was the day she'd prove the Bradley Ditmers of the world wrong.

At First Street, she pulled her mother's pendant watch from her reticule. It was 8:50. Ten minutes early was her norm. She returned the watch to

its protected place and crossed the street to the narrow brick building two
doors down from the corner.

Moistening her lips, Ida breathed a prayer for grace and wit, then
reached for the doorknob, which didn't give in the least. She'd beat her
employee to work and the door was locked.

Ida turned around just in time to see a familiar man and his mule stop
in front of the building.

Boney Hughes spit a brown streak into the dirt. He waved his worn
canvas hat. "Hello, little lady."

Heat crept up her neck and into her face as she forced a smile and
dipped her chin. "Mr. Hughes."

He clucked his tongue and wagged a crooked finger.

"Mr. Boney." Ida brushed a piece of lint from her cape, remembering
the two hours it took to wash the mud out of it Tuesday evening.

"You cleaned up right nice, Miss."

"Thank you." She glanced down at her new shoes. "My boots didn't
fare as well."

"I'm sure sorry for your troubles." He patted his mule's ears and looked
around as if expecting to see the ice wagon appear out of nowhere as it had
on Tuesday afternoon. "I take it Mr. Raines saw you home all right."

"He did. Thank you again for your help."

"Happy to do it, ma'am. Just wish it hadn't been necessary. Me and Sal
hate to see a lady in distress."

And she detested being one. Even if her rescuers were charming.

As Mollie rounded the corner at First Street, Boney bade her best
wishes, and then he and Sal moseyed up the road.

∽✺∼

After two hours of rapid-fire instruction from the tireless Miss O'Bryan, Ida was grateful her new employer had taken a telephone call in her office. Ida sat at her own desk, surrounded by files and ledgers, a telephone, and a vase full of sharpened pencils, and drew in a long, deep breath, hoping she'd be able to decipher her notes.

"You think you're ready for your first dictation job?" Miss O'Bryan stood in the doorway of her office.

Ida nodded. "I am."

"Good. That was Mr. Blackmer at the Olive Branch Mine on the telephone. I told him you'd be right over for a stenography job."

Ida felt her pulse quicken. This was the opportunity she'd hoped for—learning more about the mining business. She closed the bakery ledger she'd been working on and pulled a fresh steno pad from her desk drawer.

"This is your opportunity to prove yourself." Mollie pointed a finger at her. "Remember what I told you."

Ida's mind raced with all she'd learned in those first two hours.

Mollie giggled. "I suppose I did run off at the mouth a bit."

"You gave me a lot of instruction."

"Listen well and keep good notes on everything you hear." Her eyes narrowed, Mollie gestured as if she were writing. "Those tasty tidbits prove profitable at the Exchange."

Ida pulled her reticule from the drawer and three pencils from the vase. "Is that acceptable?"

Mollie chuckled. "What? Paying attention?"

Ida swallowed a bite of frustration. "I meant using information overheard while we're being paid to take notes."

"You do have a lot to learn." Mollie pulled a sharpened pencil from Ida's desk. "We have a job to do, and we do it. We listen and learn. There's nothing wrong with acting upon what you know. Everyone does it every minute of the day."

She hadn't thought of it in that way. It made good sense. "I'll do my best."

Ida donned her cape, and after a quick wave, she stepped out onto the boardwalk and into her bright future. Miss O'Bryan was right—she did have a lot to learn, and the sarcastic businesswoman was the perfect teacher for her.

THIRTEEN

ctober sunshine streamed through the cabin window, casting ribbons of light across the table—a glorious Saturday afternoon.

So what was her problem? Kat chewed her last bite of corn bread, then reached for Morgan's empty plate. She'd just grasped the blue floral stoneware when her husband seized her hand and laced his fingers through hers.

"You hardly spoke a word during lunch."

"Are you saying I usually talk too much?"

His grin deepened the dimple just to the right of his mouth. "Nice rabbit trail, but I'm not taking it." He glanced at their empty plates, then up at her. Concern furrowed his brow. "Are you feeling all right?"

Kat nodded. "I'm doing fine." She was. Unless Morgan had meant to include worry in his question. For three days, she'd done little but think about what her sisters had said. *"You won't rest until you've expressed your feelings."* Unfortunately, her preoccupation had proven them right. She did need to know how her husband felt about the baby growing inside her. They should talk about it, but dwelling on his past losses couldn't be beneficial for either of them.

"Something is sitting heavy on your mind." Morgan rubbed his forehead, then gazed at her. "I can see it in your eyes."

Kat studied their joined hands. They'd only known one another a matter of months, but already Morgan knew her sighs and smiles and silence by heart. She hadn't wanted to say anything, hoped she wouldn't have to. But his past was bothering her and he deserved to know her true feelings. Their commitment to one another required honesty, but speaking it was another matter.

"Is it the writing?" he asked.

She shook her head, squeezing her eyes shut against the tears filling them. "It's the baby…" Her voice snagged on the last word.

"The baby?" The dimple disappeared and his grip on her hand weakened. "You didn't want to have a baby?"

"I do." Kat moistened her lips. "But you… I saw your face when you realized what was wrong with me the other day…why I felt so poorly."

Morgan lifted her chin and matched her damp gaze. "It didn't mean I'm not happy about the baby. *Our baby*. I was only caught by surprise."

"You're not worried that I'll…that our baby—"

"That fear has paid me a visit, but I choose not to let fear rule my thoughts."

"You make it sound easy to choose not to be afraid."

Morgan slid off the chair and knelt in front of her. "When I decided I could be married again, I surrendered my past and my future to God. You and our family are the new thing God is doing in my life. We can trust Him."

Nodding, Kat vowed to read Isaiah 43 again that evening before crawling into bed. In the meantime, she couldn't take her eyes off the man God had brought through the wilderness, to her. "You're pleased we're having a baby?"

"I'm overjoyed. I can scarcely wait to have a miniature *you* running around our new house."

"A girl? What if it's a boy?" She held her voice steady while her emotions ricocheted off the wall of her heart. "Would you be all right having a boy?"

"Absolutely. But"—his smile gave way to a grimace—"I'd be a little concerned about you."

"Me? I will trust Him too."

"You're saying you could handle having a miniature Morgan underfoot?"

Kat giggled and tapped him on the nose. "I hadn't thought of having a little boy in quite that way, but now that you mention it…" Grinning, she traced his knee-weakening smile with her finger. "It's no wonder I love you so."

"And I, you, Mrs. Cutshaw."

The thrilling sound of her new name still hung in the air as she bent and kissed him. Too bad he had to work this afternoon.

A knock at the door spoiled the moment.

Morgan stood. "I wasn't expecting anyone. Were you?"

Kat grabbed their soiled plates from the table and rose from her chair. "Would I have kissed you like that if I were?"

Morgan fanned himself and grinned. "An unexpected guest with extremely poor timing."

Kat felt her cheeks blush as she carried their dishes to the cupboard, then joined Morgan at the door.

Ida shifted her weight from one foot to the other, listening to the porch boards creak beneath her. She was about to try the tarnished brass knob when the cabin door whooshed open.

Morgan and Kat stood side by side, their eyes wide and their mouths turned up in smiles the size of desktops. "It's your sister," Morgan said.

Why was he stating the obvious? And why was Kat's face carnation pink? They both were behaving as if she'd just caught them with their hands in the cookie… *Newlyweds.* Ida dropped her gaze to a gap between two boards beneath her feet.

"Oh dear." Warmth raced up Ida's neck and over her tensing jaw, promising to make her face a much deeper shade of pink than Kat's. It seemed just weeks ago they were fussing over a checkers tournament in their parlor in Maine. How was it possible that two of her younger sisters were married? "It seems I've chosen a poor time for a visit. I'll go."

"Please stay. We're glad to see you." Sounding sincere, Morgan stepped back from the doorway.

Ida glanced at Kat, who nodded, looking as happy as Ida had ever seen her.

"Morgan's right—we're glad you're here." Kat gripped Ida's mantle and pulled her inside.

When the door clicked shut behind Ida, she looked up at her brother-in-law. "I didn't expect you to be home this afternoon."

"I'm not," Morgan said.

Kat giggled. "He is, but not for long."

"Only long enough to have a cup of coffee with my wife and my new sister-in-law." Morgan reached for Ida's wrap and hung it by the door. "That is, unless you're in a hurry for a private conversation with your sister."

Ida shook her head and stepped fully into the warmth of the room. "Are you sure I'm not intruding?"

"Don't be silly." Kat's voice had a lilt to it. "You're always welcome here."

"But you might want to wear bells next time." Mischief danced in Morgan's eyes while his smile showed the dimple Kat had written about.

Kat swatted his arm. "Quit with that nonsense, Mr. Cutshaw." She looked at Ida, then at the table where a saltcellar and a peppermill framed a vase of daisies on a blue gingham cloth. "We just finished our supper. Have a seat."

Ida seated herself at one end of the table while the couple pulled three blue mugs from the cupboard and filled them with steaming coffee. They seemed so happy. Positively juvenile in their love for one another. A sudden twinge of something that felt like longing tightened Ida's chest.

She squirmed in her chair and scolded herself. She didn't need what her sisters had. She was different, with entirely different plans.

Morgan set the mugs on the table, then pulled a chair out for Kat before he sat down opposite Ida. "Kat told me you started your job last week."

"Thursday." Ida lifted her cup, breathing in the aromatic scent of hot coffee. In the likelihood that Morgan shared Miss Hattie's concerns about her new employer, Ida began forming a list of conversation topics that had nothing to do with her job. *Doctoring in a mining camp. What he missed about Boston. How construction on their new home was progressing.*

"And how do you like working for Mollie O'Bryan?" His question seemed innocuous enough.

"I've only worked for her for two days, but already I've learned more than I did in a month of classes."

Morgan nodded. "That's how I felt working with Doc Hanson my first week here."

"It's a vastly different atmosphere in Cripple Creek," Ida said.

Morgan swallowed a gulp of coffee. "More intense."

"Exactly." Everything about the town felt larger than life—at least, life in Maine. Miners. The other women. And the stockbrokers and investors she was already meeting in her work with Mollie.

Kat returned her cup to the table and straightened, her gaze solemn. "Some people in town don't like Mollie O'Bryan."

Ida wrapped both hands around her cup, letting the warmth in. So it was her own sister who would join Miss Hattie in protesting her job. "I doubt anyone is liked by everyone. And I expect that's especially true of a woman shattering the constricting mold of what a woman can and can't do."

Morgan looked at Kat. "You can certainly relate to that. You're a woman writing stories for *Harper's Bazar*. Stories about business-minded, independent women. That isn't exactly traditional either."

"But I'm not doing it in the business district on Bennett Avenue." Kat rose from her chair and plopped back down. "I'm sorry. I know this job is important to you. I just don't want to see you hurt."

Morgan rested his hand on Kat's but looked at Ida. "Pregnancy can set a woman worrying about those she loves."

"You needn't worry about me. I can take care of myself."

"Well, I may not be qualified to offer you business advice, but..." Kat raised an eyebrow and her lips thinned in a smile.

"But that's not going to stop you." Ida returned her sister's smile.

"Just be careful. That's all I ask. Not everyone approves of Miss O'Bryan's business practices."

"I will." Ida repressed a sigh. She and Mollie seemed the only ones who understood that success required taking risks. Ida could only hope her family would come to understand and accept that as well.

Fourteen

On Sunday, Tucker lifted a stoneware mug to his mouth and breathed in the rich aroma before taking a long gulp of his coffee. An early morning swath of light striped the side of the bare wood planks of the barn. Titan and Trojan grazed in the pasture, their tails lazily swatting flies. A marmot chirped down by the creek. Lowering the position of his feet on the porch railing, Tucker watched a black-billed magpie hop across the golden grasses out behind his folks' house. The peaceful scene fed his soul and defied the chaos of two hours ago.

Just after five o'clock that morning, the sound of splintering wood had woken Tucker. By the time he'd dressed, lit the lantern, and gone outside to investigate, pieces of barrel lay strewn across the yard, mingled with bruised apples and a trail of imposing bear prints. The draft horses snorted and kicked the confines of their stalls, still mad about the intruder. Tucker had fed the bruised leftover apples to the horses and then stacked the scraps of wood in a corner of the barn.

Yesterday, someone from the Blue Front Grocery had delivered a barrel of apples his mother had ordered before she knew she'd be moving to Colorado Springs. Unfortunately, the shipment arrived too late for his mother, but just in time for the ravenous bear.

Tucker swallowed the last of his coffee and set the mug on the wooden table beside the roughhewn rocker. He glanced at the Bible in his lap. The embroidered bookmark his mother had made him lay across the last several verses of 1 Corinthians 15. He'd read the passage at least a hundred times. Five times before every sermon he'd preached on it. Some folks referred to it as the *death passage*. All the talk about corruptible and incorruptible, mortal and immortality. To him, it was a passage for life. *Death is swallowed up in victory. O death, where is thy sting?* Promises he clung to, praying for a glimpse of that victory here and now. Clinging to hope to assuage the loss that *did* sting.

He still missed Sam. But he grieved the absence of his sister even more. In some ways, losing Willow to melancholia cut deeper than physical death. Why couldn't his love for his sister be enough to bring her back?

A raven squawked, and Tucker returned his gaze to the pastoral scene before him. He drew in a deep breath and considered the essence of the closing verses. Again. And he prayed for strength. Again.

I give thanks to God who gives me the victory through my Lord Jesus Christ. I need to remain steadfast.

He'd preached this message just last month during a camp meeting in Bakersfield. Preaching about steadfastness had been the easy part.

Unmoveable, always abounding in the work of the Lord, forasmuch as ye know that your labour is not in vain in the Lord.

His labor in the camp meetings? His labor with Willow? His labor for his father? The last time Tucker preached a sermon on this passage, he'd suggested that man's will is the location for the toughest job yet to be done. Was that the labor God was calling him to in Cripple Creek?

Tucker lowered his feet from the railing and bent over his Bible, head bowed.

The golden aspen leaves quivered in the light breeze while the sun warmed Ida's back. She couldn't have asked for a more glorious morning for her wagon ride with Miss Hattie. Her landlady's mare gently clip-clopped across Golden Avenue to the First Congregational Church. Following the service Ida and her sisters and brothers-in-law would gather in Nell and Judson's home for a traditional Sinclair Sunday-afternoon supper and checkers tournament.

Autumn Sundays definitely topped her list of favorite days, but her first two working for Mollie O'Bryan had come in a close second. Some folks might find her new employer's matter-of-fact tone and rapid recitation of tasks off-putting and intimidating, but Ida found it energizing and her image of the ideal job.

"You seem especially chipper today, dear." Miss Hattie's hair formed a ring of silver around the edges of the ball-crowned chiffon bonnet she wore.

"I *feel* chipper." Ida watched a squirrel scamper up an oak tree alongside the road. "Like a squirrel who has found a tree bursting with acorns, and all she has to do is gather them."

"Poetic too." Hattie pulled on the reins, slowing the horses to let a family on foot cross the street in front of them. Smiling, she returned the man's wave.

"I really do like living here," Ida said, admiring the white steeple that towered out of a red brick building a couple of blocks ahead of them. "I have much to be thankful for."

"We all do, dear. And I'm thankful for you Sinclair sisters." Hattie reached over and tapped Ida's knee. "Each one of you has brought me such joy." Smiling, she guided the wagon into the open lot beside the popular brick church on the corner. Men, women, and children poured out of wagons, dismounted horses, or added to the crowd on foot.

Excitement stirred Ida's stomach as she stepped down from the buggy. She and her sisters had always enjoyed going to the house of the Lord together. For now, she could settle for only two out of three sisters, knowing that Vivian would join them next summer.

Ida glanced around, expecting to see Kat or Nell waiting for her. Instead, she found Mr. Wagner. He stood on the bottom step of the church entrance, wearing a dark gray suit with a shadow check-and-plaid effect. He looked sharp enough to have stepped right off the pages of a Sears, Roebuck & Co. catalogue. He tipped his bowler their direction.

"Miss Sinclair. Mrs. Adams."

"Mr. Wagner. It's good to see you here." Ida meant it. That the man was a churchgoer boded well for his work ethics and her comfort level in working with him. That, and he'd tried to protect Miss O'Bryan from unscrupulous businessmen.

Miss Hattie excused herself to speak with a friend from the Women for the Betterment of Cripple Creek, leaving Ida with Mr. Wagner.

"I heard you procured the job despite my having riled Miss O'Bryan prior to your appointment." His smile lifted the corners of a neatly trimmed mustache. "I hope you don't hold my poor timing against me."

"Not at all." She considered saying more, but she expected to see Kat or Nell at any moment and wanted to keep the conversation short. Ida glanced toward the road.

"Are you looking for someone?" Mr. Wagner asked.

"Yes. I apologize, I'm a bit distracted. I'm watching for my sisters and their husbands."

"If your sisters are the young women who met you at the train on

Monday, one is already seated, and the other is standing just inside the door, greeting parishioners."

"Mrs. Judson Archer would be the greeter." Kat was probably still fighting her nausea.

"I won't keep you from them." He moved out of her path, motioning for her to enter the church ahead of him.

"Thank you." Ida stepped inside the vestibule and blinked hard, trying to adjust to the sudden shift out of sunlight. Nell waved her over to a small gathering, and Ida obliged.

"I saw Hattie alone and wondered if you had changed your mind." Nell's eyes widened as she looked past Ida.

Ida turned and realized Mr. Wagner had followed her and now stood at her side.

Before Ida could say anything or introduce anyone, Tucker Raines turned around. He'd been talking to Faith Dunsmuir, who stood next to Nell and continued to look at the ice man as he addressed Ida.

"Miss Sinclair." Tucker's smile seemed to fade as he regarded the man standing at her side.

Ida swallowed hard against a surprising wave of embarrassment. "Mr. Raines, I'd like you to meet Mr. Wagner. He's an attorney here in Cripple Creek."

While the men shook hands and exchanged pleasantries, Ida hugged Nell.

"Welcome to Cripple Creek, Mr. Raines," Mr. Wagner said, "and welcome to First Congregational." The attorney glanced toward a side door where a balding man stood. "If you'll all excuse me, I need to speak with Reverend Taggart before the service begins." He met Ida's gaze. "Miss Sinclair."

Ida offered him a tight nod then looked back to speak with Tucker, but the ice man was gone.

"He went inside."

Ignoring the matchmaker's smirk that widened Nell's blue eyes, Ida looped arms with her and walked through the double doors at the back of the sanctuary. "'Tis So Sweet to Trust in Jesus" echoed from the piano, and while Ida slid into the seat beside Kat, she thanked God for bringing her to Cripple Creek and the job of her dreams.

"I know how you feel about it." Nell looked away from Judson, toward the stovetop where chicken sizzled in a cast-iron skillet. Her husband had an intensity about him that normally thrilled her, but not today. She stuck a fork in a chicken thigh and turned it over. "Can you just not say anything to her?"

"You don't believe Ida has a right to know what people will think of her? What they'll say?"

Judson had mentioned having an unpleasant run-in or two with Mollie O'Bryan in his work as an accountant for the Mary McKinney Mine, but she hadn't expected it to become an issue that involved Ida.

Nell pulled a stoneware platter from the cupboard and drew in a deep breath. "I don't think a family picnic is the appropriate time for such a serious discussion."

"She's already working in that office. It's just a matter of time—and little of it, I'm sure—before that woman has your sister doing her bidding." He peered out the window that overlooked the picnic setting. "The sooner Ida knows what she's gotten herself into, the better off she'll be."

"You don't know my sister all that well yet. She's not going to do anything she doesn't want to do—or anything that isn't right." Nell moved the skillet to the cooler side of the stove. "Besides, I'm the one who mentioned Miss O'Bryan to her in my letter. It's my fault Ida's working for her in the first place."

"All the more reason to set her straight."

Nell stared at the grease splattered across the stove top. She should have known Judson and Ida would be at odds on this issue. She prayed the inevitable argument wouldn't be here or today.

Kat stepped in through the back door, holding an empty pitcher. "That was the last of the lemonade."

Thankful for the interruption, Nell pointed toward the icebox. "You'll find a second pitcher in there."

"I'll take it out." Judson turned toward the icebox and retrieved the pitcher.

Nell caught his free hand on his way to the door. "Please don't say anything to her."

Judson winked. "Don't worry."

Easier said than done. Especially after seeing that spark in those blue eyes of his.

As soon as the door clicked shut, Kat set the empty pitcher in the dish pail and joined Nell at the stove. "I'm sorry I interrupted you two."

"It's just as well. I'd said all I could." Nell transferred a chicken wing to the platter.

"About Ida?"

Nell nodded. "He has a problem with her working for Mollie O'Bryan. I suppose it's sweet that he's worried about her character and reputation."

Kat pulled her bowl of potato salad from the icebox and set it on the cupboard next to the chicken platter. "I rather like having a brother like that."

"Yes, but if he tries to tell Ida what's best for her, she may not be so gracious."

Kat wrinkled her nose and shook her head. "I don't want to be around for that. I tried talking to her about it when she stopped by the cabin yesterday. "

"Didn't go well?" Nell moved the skillet to a trivet on the countertop.

"She was defensive, but said she'd be careful."

"What Ida needs is a man who can help temper her frenzied drive."

"A man from the First Congregational Church, perhaps?"

Nell giggled and nodded, setting the curls on her forehead bouncing. "Did you see the way he looked at her?"

Kat pulled a serving spoon out of a cabinet drawer and grinned. Golden flecks danced in her brown eyes. "Which *he* are you referring to?"

"I was thinking of Tucker Raines."

Kat set the spoon in the potato salad and lifted the bowl off the countertop. "Mind you, Mr. Wagner can't be counted out either. He has a certain charm about him that Ida seems to appreciate. He's also a deacon and quite involved in the church, and she is bound to come in contact with him through her work."

"Ida won't admit it, but I caught her glancing at both men more than once during the service. Not to mention the scene out in the vestibule when she first arrived."

"It'll be fun to see which one she ends up with." Kat grinned and held the door open for Nell.

"In the meantime, our last picnic before winter is bound to be memorable, if I know my husband and sister." Nell led the way down the back steps and across the leaf-strewn yard to the picnic table situated under a half-naked aspen tree. Judson and Morgan sat across from Ida, bent over a checkerboard. Judson stood to take the platter from Nell.

"Blockade!" Ida bounced upright on the bench, crossing her arms.

"You were right, Kat." Morgan pretended to wipe sweat from his brow. "The eldest Sinclair sister is a formidable opponent."

"Aren't they all?" Judson winked at Nell.

Ida's blue eyes sparkled in the autumn sun. "We have yet to settle the tournament we started in Maine, little sister. Your turn."

"I'd be happy to defend my title after our meal," Nell said, "but we mustn't keep the baby waiting for nourishment any longer."

All attention shifted to Kat.

"The way the baby makes you feel so lightheaded, I'm sure it's a girl. Same effect you have on me." Morgan brushed Kat's cheek with a light kiss.

Judson patted the bench beside him and held out his hand to Nell. She slid in close, enjoying the shiver his warmth sent up her spine. "Let's ask the blessing, shall we?"

They all bowed their heads.

Following the prayer, Judson slid a thigh and a drumstick onto his plate. He held the platter out to Nell and looked up at Morgan. "How are things coming along with the new hospital building?"

"Good, as far as I can tell. Sister Coleman seems happy with the progress. Says we'll have a dedication in the spring." Morgan scooped his fork full of potato salad. "How about your work at the mine? You keeping those ledger books in line?"

"Going good. Not too many problems lately." Judson gulped lemonade, then looked across the table at Ida. "How about your job with Mollie O'Bryan? How do you like working with her?"

Nell nearly choked on a bite of potato salad. She would have elbowed her husband if she thought it could derail the conversation.

Ida swallowed hard and set her fork on her plate. "I'm enjoying it very much."

"That's good." Nell picked up the pitcher. "Anyone care for more lemonade?"

Morgan took it from her. "I could use some. Thanks."

Judson's fork froze in midair, his attention still fixed on Ida. "So you haven't yet discovered what's so objectionable about what your employer does?"

Ida met Judson's gaze, matching his intensity. "Don't tell me you object to a woman having a mind of her own and putting it to work earning her own money?"

Judson planted his forearms on the table and leaned forward. "Miss O'Bryan *earning* money is not the issue."

Nell gulped half a glass of lemonade.

Ida's jaw rocked to the right, then to the left. "You disapprove of the way she earns her money?" She spit out the question. "I can think of several lesser ways for a woman to earn money than running a legitimate stenography firm."

"Even though there are more than a handful of folks at church who believe Miss O'Bryan's business practices are sinful?" Judson didn't budge.

"Oh, please!" Ida pointed her chicken wing at him. "Some folks believe cooking on Sunday is sinful. And yet you allow your wife to do it."

Definitely a memorable picnic. For all the wrong reasons.

Nell cleared her throat. "It is indeed Sunday." She glanced from her husband to her businesswoman sister. "At the very least, we don't discuss business on Sundays."

Her husband and sister both nodded. The blue in their eyes softened, but the set in their jaws did not. Nell knew she hadn't heard the last of this debate.

FIFTEEN

*F*irst thing Monday afternoon, Tucker set a five-pound block of ice into the top of the small icebox in the apartment above The King's Chinese Laundry.

Mr. Jing-Quo tugged at the starched collar on his Mandarin shirt. "You bring in your clothes, Mr. Raines. My wife, she clean them good. Fix buttons and holes too."

Tucker looked at the small woman who stood off to the side. "I'd like that." He smiled, receiving a deep bow from her. He picked a piece of straw off the top of the icebox, then returned his attention to her husband. "I'll bring my laundry by tomorrow. Thank you."

The man gave Tucker a slight nod, his dark eyes averted. "Ready in two days."

Tucker followed him down the stairs, then waved good-bye on his way out of the shop.

Outside, the wind flapped his unbuttoned coat, and he looked up at the gray ceiling of clouds overhead. He pressed his hat back on his head and held it there. The wind didn't pack a chilling punch yet, but it blew strong enough to clatter the wood signs that hung from the storefronts over the boardwalk. Otis waved at him from atop the ice wagon.

Tucker returned Otis's wave and walked to the wagon. He did have a basket of dirty clothes to tend to, and they could surely use some repair. But day by day it became clearer why his father couldn't build the business. Last Thursday, Tucker had accepted a dozen eggs from a young widow with three children. Earlier today he'd accepted squash and greens as payment from an elderly man whose wife was bedridden.

So many people here were starting over after two horrific fires. He needed to find a way to help the needy. But he also needed to pay his own bills and his father's debts. He had to find a way to expand the business to include the moneymakers who had moved into town. Cash customers.

Tucker set the ice tongs in the back of the wagon and climbed up into the seat beside Otis, his first real friend in Colorado. Abraham had stayed home today to help his mother with his brothers.

"Well, what'd Jing-Quo say about the bill?" Otis snapped the reins he held.

"I'm getting my laundry done this week." Tucker picked a blade of straw off his coat sleeve and stuck the tip in his mouth.

Otis gave him one of his lopsided smiles as the Belgian draft horses clip-clopped up Bennett Avenue.

When they turned up Third Street, a gust of wind caught the brim of Tucker's hat, and he quickly pulled it down toward his ears. "The day I bought my train ticket in Stockton, I expected to be here just long enough to make sure my father received the medical care he needed. I didn't expect he and Mother would have to leave their home and livelihood in my guardianship, dependent upon me for financial support. But I can't keep the business going much longer without the loan."

"The bank isn't the only way to raise money." Otis turned onto Golden Avenue, then hooked his thumb in the strap of his overalls. "You could sell stocks in the ice company."

"I'm a preacher. *Was* a preacher. I don't know the first thing about selling stocks. Not sure I want to." But as soon as the words left his mouth, Tucker knew that if selling shares could save the business and his father's home, he needed to figure out the stock market.

Otis slowed the horses in front of Miss Hattie's boardinghouse and regarded Tucker with a raised brow. "Mind you, I don't know a whole lot about stocks myself. I'm not welcome at the Cripple Creek Mining Stock Exchange, but I have a white miner friend. He's takin' a liking to my wife Naomi's Cowboy Potato Loaf, and he's been teachin' me some about the stock market. I find it fascinating. Want to invest in it myself one day."

Tucker didn't know about going that far, but if selling shares would help, he'd consider it.

"I met an attorney at church yesterday. Apparently, he's a good friend of Miss Sinclair's. Talking to him could be a good place to start."

Otis parked the wagon and headed to the back. "And when I see Boney next, I'll ask him about sellin' stock in the business."

"Boney Hughes is your miner friend?" Tucker hopped down from the seat and secured the reins on the hitching rail.

Using the ice tongs, Otis pulled out a twenty-pound block for Miss Hattie. "You know Boney?"

"Met him in town last week." Tucker waved at some neighbor kids while he and Otis went around to the back of the house. "Remember the story I told you about finding a woman muddied after running from the miners at the creek?"

A shadow crossed his friend's dark eyes. He nodded.

"Boney was the miner who helped her."

"Sounds like something Boney would do, all right. He's the one who helped me when a horse stomped my head."

That explained the palsy on the left side of Otis's face, but Boney was still a mystery. "Seems a good friend to have."

Otis had barely set foot on the first porch step when Miss Hattie opened the kitchen door and waved them in. "You fellas have the timing of a cooling summer rain. Just pulled the trays out of the oven." She smiled at each of them in turn and then looked past them.

"Abraham stayed home today." Otis removed his canvas hat. "Naomi wanted his help with the little ones."

"I'll send a plate of cookies home with you."

Tucker felt better the moment he stepped inside. The aroma of freshly baked shortbread cookies called for a deep breath that eased the tension in his shoulders. He opened the top of the icebox for Otis. "Smells mighty good, Miss Hattie."

"And you fellas look good. Been too quiet around here today. I only have two boarders right now. Miss Faith hasn't come home from the school yet, and Miss Ida is off conquering the business world."

Ida Sinclair wasn't there. *Good.* Their previous meetings hadn't gone well. Hatpins and mud. He'd been ready to pummel Boney, not to mention what he'd wanted to do to the real culprits, and then she'd heard him talking to God. He'd surprised them both with an invitation to coffee, which came out sounding more like a plea.

He could find no proper excuse for his feelings yesterday. He'd expected he might see her at church, but seeing her walk in with Mr. Wagner had caught him off guard.

She was an intelligent and lovely woman. It made sense that she'd be attracted to businessmen—and they to her—and the attorney clearly fit that category.

Miss Hattie held a plate of fresh baked cookies out to Tucker. "You were hoping to see Miss Sinclair?"

"Uh."

Otis chuckled, a sparkle replacing the earlier shadow in his eyes. "You're in trouble now, Mr. Tucker." He set the tongs down by the kitchen door and picked up the tray of cups. "Miss Hattie matched up me and Naomi, you know."

He knew. He also knew about the Cutshaws and the Archers.

Tucker raised his hand. "I'm not looking to be matched up with Miss Sinclair, or with anyone else. I'm only in town for a short while." Granted, it'd be longer than he expected, but… "Not long enough for that kind of relationship."

Miss Hattie's smile deepened the lines that framed her mouth. "When we're not looking seems to be the time when God finds the most delight in surprising us."

Tucker hadn't been nervous about matchmaking before, but he was now. He knew about God's surprises and detours, and he'd had enough of them lately. He already had two women depending on him, and he wasn't about to let them down. The first bill for the sanitorium had arrived on Friday, adding to the one from the asylum and a multiplying stack of debts.

Miss Hattie turned and led them to the parlor, where a love song played on the Edison phonograph.

Before Tucker took his place in the chair across from the sofa, he glanced up at the wedding portrait on the mantel of Miss Hattie and her husband, George, regal with his mane of bone-white hair.

Tucker had wanted to be married, to have a family of his own. But the family he already had needed him. They had to be his priority. Providing for them might be all he could ever do for his sister. Even Miss Hattie's best matchmaking efforts would be for naught.

Sixteen

*T*hursday morning, Ida heard the office door open with a squeak, and she looked up from her desk. Her employer floated in, beaming and humming an unrecognizable tune. Her black satin palatine made her look like royalty.

Nearly every morning Miss O'Bryan sashayed down to the stock exchange. This morning she'd done so wearing a taffeta shirtwaist with leg-of-mutton sleeves, a brocade skirt under her hooded cape, and black calfskin shoes. Mollie was the best-dressed woman in Cripple Creek.

"You had a good morning at the Exchange," Ida said in greeting.

"A most delicious time. Like eating dessert first and swallowing the lima beans with a mouthful of Belgian chocolate." Mollie removed her wrap. Its rose-colored satin lining reminded Ida of the Colorado sunsets she'd witnessed on her walks back to the boardinghouse.

One day she would dress the same way—silk, satin, and Italian lace.

Mollie, her mossy green eyes sparkling, hung her palatine on an oak coat tree and planted her hands on the front edge of Ida's desk. "I've been buying one-thousand-share blocks of stock in the Damon Gold Mining Company for five dollars per block."

"That sounds like a good deal, if Damon produces well."

"Tell me"—Mollie straightened and tapped her rounded chin with one finger—"would you consider ten cents per share a good deal?"

Ida did a quick calculation in her head. "That's a profit of ninety-five dollars on one block of a thousand shares. A lot of money."

Mollie squealed like a girl much younger than her twenty-three years. "That's precisely what I did this morning. I sold a thousand of those shares for ten cents each."

"No wonder you're smiling and humming."

"And I intend to do more than that. Even the gray clouds are lovely this morning." Mollie opened her sealskin purse and pulled out two cigars. She held one out to Ida.

Surely puffing on a tobacco stick wasn't a requirement for success. If so, this could be more of a challenge than she'd anticipated. "I don't smoke, but I am happy for you, nonetheless. Congratulations!"

Mollie returned the second cigar to her purse and set the bag on the desk. She looked Ida square in the eye. "You were right—we do make a good team." She peeled the paper band off the cigar and pointed it at Ida. "Your day to turn a handsome profit is coming."

From Mollie's lips to God's ears. At least Ida prayed it was so. Numbers set her mind whirling. Her employer had said she'd *been buying* a thousand shares. She'd bought more than just one block of that stock. The possibilities were dizzying, and Ida drew in a deep breath. As soon as she received her paycheck next Thursday, she'd have Mollie buy stock for her too. Vivian would need financial assistance with her travel and setup expenses once she arrived in Cripple Creek next summer. And Ida would love nothing more than to be able to donate to the widows and orphans' fund Reverend Taggart spoke of in Sunday's service.

Mollie stepped over to the file cabinet. "In the meantime, how are you faring with the promotional materials for the Big Four Gold Mining Company?"

Ida glanced at the proofs on her desk. "I should have them ready for the printer tomorrow."

"That's good news, but you'll need to set them aside for now. I have another job for you."

Ida couldn't imagine ever tiring of her work. Though some tasks were a bit repetitious in nature, they were never routine. She was always juggling, and never just ledgers or mining deeds, but a wide variety of documents—contracts, wills, depositions, stock certificates, and more.

"This morning you'll learn how a prospectus is done," Mollie said. "You know what that is, correct?"

"The document necessary to attract investors to a business."

"Honey for the bears. Designed to grab the attention of the investing public and entice them to buy shares." Mollie floated across the room, the smoke from the freshly lit cigar leaving a trail in the air. With her free hand, she opened a file drawer, pulled out a folder, and handed it to Ida. "This is a sample prospectus. Mr. Wagner will conduct the interview with his client while you record the information and fill in the blanks."

Ida hadn't seen Colin since Sunday and still didn't know what to think of his attentiveness. Now she was going to his office?

A scowl turned down the corner of Mollie's mouth. "Has Mr. Wagner been pestering you about the integrity of our clients?"

"Not at all."

"Well, if he does, you let me know. I'll make a wall mount of him."

Ida stifled a giggle.

"Don't think I won't do it."

Ida didn't doubt that Mollie could. And would.

"In the meantime, he asked that you be at his office at fifteen minutes past ten o'clock this morning. He'll have the forms you need."

Ida looked at the clock hanging above the door: five minutes before ten. She jumped up from her chair.

"It's not even a five-minute walk." Mollie puffed cigar smoke.

"I like to be early." Ida flushed, remembering how she'd arrived early for her interview.

"You get to hear all kinds of scandal that way." Mollie winked. "Least-wise where me and Mr. Wagner are concerned."

Ida pulled her reticule out of the bottom desk drawer. "Thank you for everything. And, again, congratulations on the profit." On her way out the door, she retrieved her wool mantle from the coat tree.

Ida felt like skipping up Bennett Avenue. Instead she concentrated on taking slow, dignified steps befitting a successful businesswoman. Holding her head high, she strolled past a barbershop, a meat market, a dry goods store, a tobacconist's shop, and the creamery.

Her life here in Cripple Creek was better than she could've hoped for. Mollie O'Bryan was the perfect employer—successful and full of surprises. In only one week, Ida had already learned more from Mollie than she'd learned after nearly a year working for Alan Merton. She'd been blessed with a great job, a comfortable place to live, and friends and family nearby. And this was just the beginning of the good life.

If Colin Wagner was pleased with her work this morning and she continued to provide valuable information to Mollie, it wouldn't be long before she had money for brocade dresses and silk palatines of her own. And a fancy house like the one her brother-in-law was building on Carr Avenue. Vivian and the widows and orphans would benefit from her prosperity as well.

Perhaps God was on her side after all.

Ida crossed the street and stopped in front of the sandstone building that stood on the corner. She'd no sooner reached for the door when a white-haired attendant with a thin smile opened it for her.

"May I help you, ma'am?" Smoothing the wings on his mustache, he stepped behind a wooden lectern.

"I am Miss Sinclair. I have an appointment with Mr. Colin Wagner."

The man adjusted the wire-rimmed spectacles on his nose and glanced down at a ledger. "Your name is here. You'll find Mr. Wagner's office on the second floor." He pointed a crooked finger toward a staircase. "Up those steps, first door on the left.

"Thank you, sir."

Ida climbed the mahogany stairs and paused outside the first door on the left to tug on the skirt of her purple floral dress. Satisfied she was ready, Ida opened the door and entered a modestly appointed office with a maple settee and table. Various oil paintings—all containing images of ships or harbors—decorated the walls. A woman with graying brown hair rose from her chair behind a matching maple desk.

Ida could only stare at the closed door behind the woman. Colin's private office. Moisture beaded on her palms and she wished she'd worn gloves.

This was all Bradley Ditmer's doing. She'd never been nervous around men before his stunt. She drew in a deep breath. She'd just have to get over it. Not all men were like that. And if Colin Wagner did prove to be cut from the same cloth as the professor, he wouldn't catch her off guard.

When the secretary cleared her throat, Ida met her gaze. "Did you hear me, miss?"

She hadn't. "I'm Miss Ida Sinclair, here to see—"

"Mr. Wagner is expecting you, Miss Sinclair. Please have a seat, and I'll let him know you've arrived." The woman pinched her cheeks before knocking on the door behind her.

Ida smoothed her moist palms over the front of her dress before seating herself on the settee. She watched Colin Wagner follow his secretary out of his office and walk toward her, wearing another fine suit and a welcoming smile. She stood.

"Miss Sinclair, I appreciate you agreeing to work with me this morning. Here, let me hang up your wrap for you." Ida handed her mantle to him and he placed it on a coat tree.

"Mr. Wagner." Ida glanced at the folder in her hand. "Miss O'Bryan said you needed me to take dictation for a prospectus."

"Yes, thank you." He motioned toward his office. "Miss Vanderhorn has her hands full with routine tasks. I often use Mollie's services for some of the more time-consuming jobs."

Ida stepped into Colin's office. A model ship filled most of one corner of a claw-foot desk and she admired it, remembering the Atlantic Ocean.

"As a boy, I dreamed of sailing the high seas in search of treasure." Colin glanced toward the four-paned window on the back wall. "And though my feet are still firmly planted on the land, I never got the notion out of my system."

"Having lived in Maine all my life, I also feel at home with ships and waves." Ida thought the small talk should calm her nerves, but the mention of waves only made her queasiness more pronounced. She pressed her reticule against her stomach, hoping the pressure would settle her insides some.

"But you're adjusting to life in the West?" Leaving the door open, he took long strides to an oak office chair.

"I am. I actually prefer the full plate of opportunity Cripple Creek offers."

"That it does." He tapped the back of an oak office chair. "Please, make yourself comfortable." Once she was seated, he sank into a leather chair behind his desk. "I trust your work with Mollie is going well."

"Quite well. Thank you."

"We have a few moments before my client arrives." Colin leaned forward, his hands clasped on the desk in front of him. "Would you mind if I asked you a question—one of a more personal nature?"

Ida felt her mouth go dry. Did he plan to interview her since she'd be working with him? She moistened her lips and nodded.

"Mollie and Charles Miller have invited me and a guest to attend a piano concert at the Butte Opera House on Saturday, the twenty-forth of this month."

Ida shifted in the chair. She did want to enjoy some of the culture her new city had to offer, but...

"We're all essentially working together, so I thought you might like to join us."

With the others joining them, the invitation didn't sound anything like courtship, but more of a business outing instead.

Before she could answer, the sound of voices in the front office drew her attention to the doorway, where Miss Vanderhorn stood.

"Mr. Wagner, your ten-thirty appointment is here."

"Thank you." Colin stood, looking at Ida. "We can discuss my invitation after the business at hand."

Ida nodded, preferring a retraction to a discussion. She'd come to town to work, not to socialize with men. Although it probably wouldn't hurt her standing in the business community to be seen with the successful likes of Mr. Wagner, Mollie, and Mr. Miller.

Colin's secretary stepped aside, and Tucker Raines sauntered in wearing slightly worn dungarees and a soft chambray shirt the color of blueberry cobbler.

Perfect. She would take dictation for the man she was trying to avoid in the presence of the man who awaited her acceptance for a social engagement. Ida felt her face flush and raised her chin a notch in greeting. "Mr. Raines."

"Miss Sinclair." He glanced at the flat-topped hat in his hand, then up at Colin. "Am I interrupting something?"

Colin motioned for the ice man to have a seat in the chair beside her. "Miss Sinclair is here to take notes. She will fill out the paperwork for your prospectus."

"I work for Miss Mollie O'Bryan's stenography firm. Mr. Wagner is one of our many clients."

Colin cleared his throat as if he were aware of her distraction. "Shall we get started?"

Nodding, Ida retrieved a small notepad and a sharpened pencil from her reticule.

"Yes, thank you." Tucker pulled a thin stack of loose papers out of a ledger and handed it to Colin. "I need to expand my father's ice delivery business. I want to build an icehouse, purchase two or three more delivery wagons, and add the sale of iceboxes."

Colin studied the papers. "Very ambitious. And smart. Good timing too." As he read the notes, he asked Tucker specific questions, and Ida used shorthand to record the answers. She'd transfer her notations to the proper forms this afternoon.

Tucker straightened. "Mr. Wagner, I have certain obligations that must be squared up immediately. Do you think it will take long to raise capital?"

Ida assumed his father's care was chief among those obligations. Treatment in a sanitorium had to be costly. He'd listed "traveling preacher" as his most recent work, which explained the black, wide-brimmed hat lying on his lap. Her admiration for him grew as she considered all he was doing for his family. He'd given up his chosen work to run his father's business and pay his family's debts.

Colin leaned back in his overstuffed chair. "The capital you raise through the sale of stock is to be used solely as investment in your business, per the plan we are about to set forth in your prospectus. Any nonbusiness debts are your responsibility and would be payable from your profits."

A frown creased Tucker's tanned brow and his shoulders sagged. "But how do I keep from succumbing to my debts in the meantime?"

Ida felt her own shoulders sag. He had turned his life upside down to help his family, and she wanted to help him.

Colin leaned forward, his gaze fixed on Tucker. "What a person does is directed by his own conscience. But what you say about how you spend other peoples' money is very important to the continuation of that income."

Tucker released a long breath, appearing to digest the attorney's ambiguous comments. "I understand." He closed his ledger, and Ida saw the conflict muddy his brown eyes as he stood. "If you don't need anything else from me, I must—"

Colin nodded. "We're finished here for now."

She hated that he had to leave on such a sad note, but she stood anyway and collected all of the necessary paperwork from the desk. "I'll type this up this afternoon and return it here."

"I'll pick up the prospectus when I've finished my deliveries." Tucker extended his hand to Colin, and they shook.

"If you'll stop at Miss Vanderhorn's desk on your way out, she will phone Charles Miller, a broker I trust, to set up an appointment for you."

"I'll do that." Tucker turned to Ida. "Good day, Miss Sinclair. Thank you for your fine work." He looked at Colin, then again at Ida. With a gentle shake of his head, he walked out into the main office.

Ida finished collecting her things and tried to do the same with her thoughts. Hatpins. Shortbread cookies at Miss Hattie's. Muddy wagon rides. Dictation. She and Tucker Raines continued to meet in the most unusual of circumstances. And she had to put an end to the distraction he caused her.

"Miss Sinclair?" Colin said, taking her mantle from the hook and holding it open for her.

Ida quickly slid beneath her wrap and stepped away from him. "My answer is yes. I will gladly join you and the others on the twenty-fourth of October."

She'd add the concert to her social calendar, but her involvement with Mr. Wagner was strictly business.

SEVENTEEN

*K*at stuffed the pencil into the top of her chignon and stared at the first paragraphs of her new article.

Gibberish.

The one-room cabin seemed especially small today. She felt better but still lacked inspiration. Perhaps some fresh air would help.

She hadn't seen Ida since the picnic on Sunday, and it was now Friday. If she timed it right, maybe she could take her sister to lunch during her break.

Kat retrieved the pencil from her hair and returned her writing box to the bookshelf. She closed the flap window and latched it shut, then grabbed her reticule and cape on her way out the door.

Starting down the hill, Kat drew in slow, deep breaths of the crisp autumn air. The rocky peaks surrounding the town all wore winter white caps thanks to last night's storm. She stepped around the puddles left from the heavy rains in their valley.

As Kat neared Mollie O'Bryan's office, she reflected on the Sunday afternoon gathering at Nell's house. Judson's turbulent questioning and Ida's equally tempestuous responses had caused a layer of tension to settle over the gathering like heavy clouds over the Rockies. Judson and Ida had been cordial the rest of the afternoon, but Ida worried her jaw when she was up-set, and she'd spent the remainder of the day doing just that.

Few folks approved of a woman being as involved in business affairs as Mollie O'Bryan was. Most didn't take well to a woman making as much money as a man did. But Kat knew her older sister. Ida would jump in and fulfill her ambitions with gusto, no matter the obstacles, despite any objections.

Kat crossed Bennett Avenue, dodging a mule train bent on cutting the corner.

Mollie O'Bryan's Stenography Firm stood in the block between First and Second Streets. The narrow brick building had a cast-iron storefront and lace curtains in the windows on either side of the door. Kat stepped inside, expecting to see Ida sitting behind her desk.

Instead, Miss O'Bryan sat in Ida's chair, holding a telephone earpiece in one hand and the microphone with the other. Wearing a cream-colored shirtwaist with brown ribbons woven into a lacy bodice, the businesswoman looked more primed for a soiree than for answering telephones and greeting people walking in off the street.

Ida's employer acknowledged Kat with a glance and pointed at three burgundy armchairs near the door.

Kat seated herself and studied the offering of magazines on the table beside her. *The Century Magazine, Munsey's Magazine,* and *Harper's Bazar.* Kat unbuttoned her cape and picked up the October edition of *Munsey's Magazine,* resisting the temptation to admire her pen name in *Harper's Bazar.*

"That's what he dictated to Ida," Miss O'Bryan said into the telephone. "They found a new vein, Charles."

Kat tried to focus on the magazine, but she couldn't avoid overhearing

Miss O'Bryan's side of the conversation. Mollie O'Bryan whispered louder than most people spoke on a moving train.

"Yes, well, you can bet I'm buying plenty before word spreads."

Before word spreads. Was Mollie O'Bryan making her money off early information? That had to be what Judson meant. Kat felt her face flush. Was the woman using Ida to gather this information?

"Don't be so chary. Of course she's reliable. Ida stands to profit too." Miss O'Bryan regarded Kat, who tried to look engrossed in the magazine. "Gotta run. I'll talk to you later." She hung up the listening piece and looked at Kat. "How may I help you?"

Kat stood. Smoothing her skirt, she walked toward the desk. "I'm Kat Cutshaw."

"Ida's sister." Mollie glanced at the side table as if she'd seen Kat's article in *Harper's,* or that Ida had pointed it out to her. "The magazine writer."

"Yes ma'am."

Miss O'Bryan wore her hair parted low on the left side and pulled back in waves. "I haven't had time to read the article you wrote, but it looked interesting enough."

Unsure how to answer such a statement, Kat smiled and looked up at the clock above the door. "I'd hoped to find Ida here before she left for lunch."

"She's taking dictation over at Colin Wagner's office. She'll be done by noon."

That was ten minutes from now.

"Tell her I said she could have an hour for lunch today," Miss O'Bryan added.

"I will. Thank you."

Twenty minutes later, Kat sat across from Ida at a corner table in the Third Street Café.

"I'm glad you thought of this." Ida unfolded the napkin in front of her and slid it onto her lap.

"I am too. I knew I'd see you on Sunday, but I didn't want to wait that long."

Ida tugged at the cuffs on her dark blue jacket. "How are you feeling?"

"Better, mostly. Midday seems my best time." Kat removed her napkin from the table.

Ida looked out the window. "Do you think we'll have more rain today?"

The last time Kat could remember having such a polite conversation with Ida was on their carriage ride to the train depot in Portland. She and Nell were leaving for Cripple Creek, and Ida discussed anything and everything except the good-byes that loomed before them. Kat lifted her water glass. "Are you afraid I'm going to talk about Colin Wagner or Tucker Raines? Or are you more concerned that I'll bring up Judson's questions?"

"Yes." A dare mingled with a warning in Ida's steely blue eyes.

Kat looked away and sipped her water, as much for fortification as to quench her thirst. She met her sister's gaze. "Lest I be called unpredictable, I say we talk about men. My man, actually. Morgan is giving a piano concert at the Butte Opera House later this month."

Ida sighed. "Saturday, the twenty-fourth of October?"

"You already know about it?"

"I didn't know he was the featured pianist, but, yes, I know about the concert. I plan to attend with a group of colleagues."

"Colin Wagner?"

"Along with Mollie and Mr. Miller."

"Then we'll see you there. Hattie, Nell, and Judson are going too."

Ida peered at her over the top of her teacup. "You agree with him, don't you?"

Kat straightened the fork in her place setting. "Some people don't agree with the way Mollie obtains information." She paused. "When I arrived at your office, I overheard Mollie talking on the telephone to a man she called Charles. It sounded like she was buying stock based upon what you'd learned from a client."

"Very likely." Ida raised her napkin and dabbed her mouth. "We have a job to do, and we do it. We listen and learn. There's nothing wrong with acting upon what you know. That's what you're doing right now. You overheard Mollie's conversation and you're passing on the information."

Kat leaned forward and spoke just above a whisper. "Ida, you and I both know there's more to your work than that. Not everyone buying and selling stocks has your advantage."

Ida looked out the window again, worrying her jaw. "Perhaps we should talk about my niece or nephew."

Kat wanted to protect Ida from making a mistake, from possible heartache, but that wasn't her role as a younger sister. She sighed and pondered an agreeable change of subject. "Do you have any ideas for baby names?"

"The name *Ida* will soon be available. It seems my work with Mollie has brought me a new name—*Mud*."

When Ida began laughing, Kat's giggle deepened. If laughter could delay the inevitable storm that surrounded her sister's involvement with Mollie O'Bryan, Kat was all for it.

Eighteen

ucker made the post office his first stop in town Wednesday morning. He handed his letter to the balding postmaster and accepted an envelope in return.

Not another bill, please.

Tucker's gaze fixed on the return address. Surely the asylum wouldn't send a second statement this soon after the first. Willow's attendant must have sent a report. His pulse quickening, he slid his finger beneath the seal.

In the two years since his father had given up on Willow and decided to have her hospitalized, Tucker's prayers had changed. They had shifted from confident requests for a swift and complete healing to fragile pleas for even the slightest hint of hope. Breathing that prayer again, Tucker stood at the end of the post office counter and pulled out a single sheet of stationery.

Dear Mr. Raines,

    We understand why you had to go, but we do miss your visits. Wednesdays aren't the same without hearing you sing to your sister and speak to her as if she would reply.

No one missed his visits more than he did. Even though Willow didn't respond to his presence, he at least felt like he was doing something. Here, away from her completely, he felt helpless.

We all commend you for the faithful chain of letters you've sent to Willow.

A chain of letters. That was all he had to offer her. If he'd been a good brother, he would've saved her husband.

Tucker drew in a deep breath, praying for the strength to read the words he'd heard week after week: *no engaged change.*

Mr. Raines, I am pleased to provide you with news of a change in your sister's condition. A small change to be sure, but a step forward nonetheless.

Yesterday after I read your most recent letter to Willow, I witnessed a response from her. Willow smiled, and a few words rang out.

Tears stung Tucker's eyes, and he blinked to clear his vision so he could continue reading. Willow had smiled. She'd even spoken. He leaned forward, resting his arms on the counter.

You wrote to her about Colorado. The mountains and the aspens and the people you were meeting. You wrote about taking her to see Colorado when she's recovered.

Tucker remembered his words well. He'd told her he could see her, sketch pad in hand, not knowing what to draw first.

I'd just finished reading your name in the close of the letter, when
Willow pointed her finger at me and said, "The Peak. Tell Tucker."

Blinking did nothing to stay Tucker's tears. They rolled down his face
and he pulled a handkerchief out of his pocket.

Mind you, this was a slight and single occurrence, but your
sister did react. The doctors view it as a sign she is ready to begin
reconnection.

Tucker felt hope lifting the burden from his shoulders and softening the
tension in his jaw. Willow was beginning to respond. "*The Peak. Tell Tucker.*"
He finally had something to add to the last words he'd heard her say.

"Thank You, Lord," he whispered.

"Mr. Raines?" The familiar voice sent warmth up his spine. Tucker
turned to look into the face of a woman he'd last seen in Colin Wagner's
office, a clear object of interest for the attorney. Her brow wrinkled and her
jaw shifted left, then right. She wasn't pleased to see him, and he didn't
blame her. She'd heard him reveal the mess he was in with his father's business and then practically beg Mr. Wagner for money.

"Miss Sinclair. Hello."

"You received the completed prospectus from Mr. Wagner?"

"Yes. Thank you again for your help. Mr. Miller has it. Now I wait for
investors."

"I'm sure plenty of people will snatch up the ice company's stock, especially given Cripple Creek's considerable growth."

"I hope you're correct."

She smoothed the collar on her purple floral dress. "I seem quite adept
at arriving just in time for your discussions with the Lord."

"That, you do." He felt his face flush, remembering the last time Ida had walked up on one of his prayers. He'd extended a sudden invitation to join him for coffee, which she'd just as quickly refused. No wonder, given her interest in Mr. Wagner.

"Do you make a habit of vocal and public conversations with Him?"

"Not always."

"Not that I mind." She glanced at the letter he held. "You've received good news in the mail?"

"Yes, very good news."

She loosed the top button on the wool mantle that draped her narrow shoulders and looked at him, waiting.

"My sister is showing some slight improvement." Tucker folded the letter and slid it into the envelope.

"I didn't realize you had siblings."

"Just one older sister."

"And she's been ill?"

He nodded, wondering how much to tell her. He felt comfortable talking to Miss Ida Sinclair, but he'd already shared too many personal details, especially as she seemed interested in another man.

"Where does she live?" Ida asked.

"I had to leave her in California. Her name is Willow. Willow Grace."

"What a beautiful name." Ida pulled two envelopes out of her bag. "You've met Kat and Nell, but I have a third sister. Vivian is still in Portland, Maine with my aunt, finishing her schooling. My father lives in Paris." She waved the envelopes she held. "Writing letters to them just isn't the same as being with them."

Tucker felt his shoulders tense. "I should return to Stockton."

Ida's brow furrowed. "Rushing to her would be my first instinct as well."

"First instinct." It *was* his first instinct. But what was there to think about? Returning to Willow made perfect sense. She was starting to reconnect. She'd finally answered back. He couldn't stay here. Not when she needed him.

"I could make a difference there. Here, I'm just cooling my heels. I've done all I can." He'd failed at the bank, met with the attorney and then a broker. None seemed too encouraging, and without the proper funds, his hands were tied.

"I understand wanting to be with your sister." Ida held his gaze. "But it sounds as if she's getting better without you there."

She was right. Perhaps his presence had been a hindrance rather than a help. Tucker slid the envelope into his coat pocket.

Ida looked down, color flushing her cheeks. "Oh my, that didn't come out right. My sisters always tell me I need to spend more time thinking before I speak." She fanned herself. "I meant to say that what you're doing here is of great significance to your parents."

"I'm delivering ice all week and eating shortbread cookies on Mondays at Miss Hattie's. That's about it."

"Taking over your father's business so he can receive the care he needs and have your mother with him is a noble task in and of itself."

He wouldn't call it *noble,* but the fact was his father hadn't acknowledged him as a son for two years, and for months he'd been to the asylum every week and Willow hadn't shown any improvement. And now that he was gone, she had.

His mouth went dry and his gut knotted. "You think not having me around is better for her?" The words came out in jerks and shudders, like wagon wheels trying to maneuver a rutted road.

"I didn't say that." Ida's blue eyes narrowed. "But my father says missing someone you love can be like a burr in your union suit—a real motivator."

Tucker chuckled. "Hadn't thought of absence in quite that way."

An endearing, nervous giggle escaped her perfectly formed lips as she apparently realized the intimate nature of her statement. "I best tend to my business here and let you go. I'm glad your sister...Willow is feeling better."

"Thank you."

"I was also glad to hear that things are more amiable between you and God." Smiling, Ida stepped toward the center of the counter, where the postmaster sorted envelopes into various bins.

Tucker waved his hat in an awkward good-bye. Had she perceived his desire to try again for a cup of coffee with her?

Just as well she'd dismissed him. The attorney was clearly a better match for her intellect and ambition. And Tucker wasn't looking for a social relationship.

Not the romantic kind anyway. His life was complicated enough.

NINETEEN

*I*da stared at the dollar bills in her hands. She'd completed her first two weeks working for Mollie O'Bryan. When Ida took the job, her employer said Ida would earn a dollar a day. That seemed fair enough. She was, after all, new to the business. But the amount she held in her hand added to up to significantly more than a dollar per day.

Looking up from her desk, Ida watched Mollie pull her palatine off the coat tree. "Thank you. You were very generous."

"You, Miss Ida Sinclair, are a peculiar mix of lofty ambition, dogged determination, and uncommon gratitude."

The young business owner could've been describing herself as far as Ida was concerned.

She opened the bottom drawer of her desk and pulled out her reticule. Her strong work ethic had obviously paid off. She held enough money in her hand to pay Hattie for the first month's rent and incidentals and still have a sufficient amount to invest in some stock.

Mollie pointed a manicured finger at her. "Your hard work earned you a percentage of the profits because of your thorough notations."

Ida knew better than to question good fortune, but she'd simply done as she'd been asked—to listen and share what she'd learned. The same thing she'd always done as Kat, Nell, and Vivian's big sister—paid attention and acted in the best interests of those she cared about. If that bothered Judson and Kat, then so be it. Worrying about what others thought was their problem, not hers.

So why did she suddenly wonder what the ice man who cared deeply for his ailing sister thought about her business involvements?

"We girls have to stick together. The others who've worked for me didn't seem to understand that, but you do. I like to reward people who are loyal." Mollie lifted Ida's mantle off a hook and held it out to her. "Shall we? The stock exchange awaits us."

"Today?"

Mollie nodded.

Feeling as if she were floating on air, Ida settled her cape over her shoulders. It wasn't a silk palatine, but as she stepped out the door and onto the boardwalk, her wrap did feel a bit like a royal robe and she a princess.

As she walked up Bennett Avenue with Mollie at her side, she couldn't stop smiling. She felt more like a colleague and friend to the wealthy young woman than merely a loyal employee. She didn't know many other women, if any, who would encourage other women, let alone share their secrets to success with them, rather than treating them like competition. Mollie O'Bryan was a rare breed among businesswomen. And misjudged by many.

Halfway to the imposing brick building that housed the stock exchange, a man walking toward them bent his considerable girth to talk in hushed tones to the petite woman beside him. The woman met Ida's gaze and huffed. Her nose in the air, she moved farther away from Ida than was necessary as they passed.

Ida glanced over her shoulder. "What was that about?"

Mollie cupped Ida's elbow, pressing her forward. "Being a schoolteacher, a writer, a nurse, even a cook running her own eatery is perfectly acceptable for a woman here." Squaring her shoulders, Mollie stopped in front of the

Cripple Creek Mining Stock Exchange. "In the world of mines and investments, not only is a smart and prosperous woman intolerable, she's seen as a heathen by many. A threat to their manhood by others. Charles Miller and Colin Wagner being exceptions to that rule."

The minute Ida stepped inside the red brick building, she imagined she knew what a jolt of electricity might feel like. The room buzzed with an energy unlike any she'd ever experienced. Men in suits with pipes hanging from their mouths clustered in front of Charles Miller, Mollie's business partner and friend. White chalk notes and symbols completely covered the blackboard. Every mining company she'd heard of and some other town businesses were listed, including the Raines Ice Company. Mr. Miller called out the bidding at an auctioneer's pace. A tall man who looked like he'd blow away in a windstorm scratched numbers on the board and erased them just as quickly to make room for new bids. Tobacco smoke and chalk dust hung in the air, along with unbridled anticipation.

The word *exhilarating* sprang to Ida's mind.

Mollie hooked her finger under Ida's chin. "Best close your mouth before you cage a dragonfly in there."

Ida spotted Boney Hughes off to one side, unshaven and wearing coveralls. Smiling, the old miner brushed the brim of his equally dressed-down canvas hat. She gave him a courteous nod, then returned her attention to the business at hand, though she was perplexed by his presence in such chic company.

A short gentleman approached Mollie. Removing a pipe from his mouth, he studied the two of them, his thick brow narrowing. "Not enough you're in the club, Miss O'Bryan? You had to bring in reinforcements?"

"Mr. Eugene Updike, I'd like to introduce Miss Ida Sinclair. She works with me." Mollie's voice was soft, but her eyes were not. "You know Miss Sinclair's brother-in-law, Dr. Morgan Cutshaw."

He tucked the tip of his pipe into the corner of his mouth. "Is that so, Miss Sinclair?"

Ida nodded.

"Unfortunately, from the looks of things, it appears you won't do any better job of minding your own business than Miss O'Bryan does." His expression held no hint of an attempt at humor.

Ida felt herself become the big sister in the school yard reacting to the bully who'd just hassled one of her sisters. "Scoff if you must, Mr. Updike, but we'll take your money just the same." She held her hand out flat in front of the man.

Glaring at her, he crossed his arms. "Welcome to the snake pit, Miss Sinclair. Sounds to me like you'll fit right in."

As he turned and stomped to his seat, Ida's insides recoiled. She'd hissed at a complete stranger. Never mind that he'd deserved it.

"Way to feed that old goat some crow." Amusement danced in Mollie's green eyes. "If I had any doubts that you could make it in this business, they just walked away on Updike's back."

The woman had a spitfire way with words, but Mollie was right. Ida couldn't let sour men like that hold her back. She deserved to be here as much as he did, and she was here to stay.

Up in the loft, Tucker stuffed clean straw into one of the four bags he and Otis carried on the wagon. A snort and a stomp drew his gaze to the floor of the barn where Titan and Trojan chomped hay in adjacent stalls.

Tucker tossed the full sack over the edge, watching it land on the canvas over the back of the ice wagon. He grabbed another sack off a sheaf of straw and continued the process. He and Otis had completed the ice deliveries by two o'clock that afternoon. Even after he'd stopped by the livery to order a hay drop and done some shopping at the Blue Front Grocery, he'd still been home by half past three.

If it had been Monday, he would've spent an extra hour on the last delivery, visiting with the warm and wise Miss Hattie and eating shortbread cookies. Yesterday's conversation in the post office with Miss Ida Sinclair had shown him that Miss Hattie wasn't the only woman who possessed a compelling blend of compassion and wisdom. And it was Ida Sinclair he most wanted to see.

"Rushing to her would be my first instinct as well."

Ida had shown wisdom in questioning his initial yearning to rush to Willow's side at the first sign of hope. She was right—perhaps his absence would be better for Willow. For both of them. Perhaps his presence had served to remind her of the tragedy that caused her ailment and helped keep her mired in the depths of melancholia.

"What you're doing here is of great significance to your parents."

Although delivering ice and talking to bankers, lawyers, and brokers didn't seem of great significance, he was doing what he felt God would have him do. His being here, trying to build up the business, honored his father and mother.

But alone in the barn with only horses and mice for company, the urge hit him to go directly into the house, pack his bag, and march straight to the train station and buy a ticket to Stockton. For home.

Tucker tossed the last sack of straw over the edge of the loft and climbed down the rustic wooden ladder.

The parsonage in Stockton had been home to him until nearly four weeks ago. He hadn't felt at ease in his family home since the day he'd told his father he'd chosen to move to San Francisco to attend seminary. A war of words ensued, and he'd stomped out with a saddlebag full of his belongings. That had been his last day in the ice business. He'd bunked at Sam's house for the month before he and his best friend left for seminary. The Lord had blessed him with Sam's friendship, even though their time together was short.

"Taking over your father's business so he can receive the care he needs…is a noble task in and of itself."

For now, this was where he belonged. He would watch and wait, look for God's provision, and praise the Lord for His faithfulness. Even when doubt clouded his vision.

Tucker, his mouth and throat dry, decided he'd done enough chores. He needed a cup of coffee and some psalms. He glanced at the stall, where Titan and Trojan savored the remnants of their supper.

"See you later, fellas." He pulled off his worn work gloves and tossed them on the wagon seat, and then closed the barn door on his way out. Before he headed to the house, he glanced toward the creek and the bench he'd placed on a knoll at the creek's edge.

She wasn't there. Silly to think she would be. For one thing, Miss Ida Sinclair would still be at work. And why would she trust this part of the creek to be any safer, after what had happened to her farther down? Besides, it was better she didn't come. He needed to concentrate on the needs of his own family. Whenever Ida came near, she proved to be a distraction.

Life seemed so much simpler in Stockton. He'd see Willow on Wednesdays and travel by horseback to preach on the weekends. Nothing here had been anything less than complicated since the moment he'd stepped off the train.

Walking back toward the house, Tucker watched Colin Wagner drive a black enamel carriage up the road. He might understand the attorney having business with him on a weekday afternoon, but why would Reverend Taggart accompany the attorney for such a visit?

The reverend stepped out of the buggy and waved. Tucker liked the clergyman, but the verdict was still out on the law counselor. He told himself his uncertainty had nothing to do with the man's obvious attentions to Miss Ida Sinclair.

"Reverend Taggart." Tucker shook his hand then regarded his companion. "Mr. Wagner. Welcome, gentlemen." He shook the spruce attorney's hand as well.

"I hope we haven't come at a bad time." The reverend wore his few strands of hair splayed across the top of his balding head.

"Not at all." Tucker removed his hat and slapped it against his dusty pant leg. "Just finished my chores for the afternoon, and I'm headed into the house for a cup of coffee. Join me."

Once inside, they hung up their coats and hats. After Tucker showed the men to the parlor, he went to the kitchen to pour the coffee. He'd lit the stove and started the pot before going back outside, but he wasn't used to entertaining guests. What else did he need? He drank his coffee black, but not everyone did. Tucker retrieved a bottle of cream from the icebox, a bowl of sugar from the shelf, and a spoon from a cupboard drawer.

When the brew was ready, he filled three mugs and carried the tray to the parlor. He set a steaming cup in front of each of the men and sat on the sofa across from them. "So what brings you two down here on a Thursday afternoon?"

Reverend Taggart glanced at Mr. Wagner and reached for the sugar bowl. "Colin and I have been talking about you."

Tucker couldn't say why, but the thought dried out his mouth even more. He lifted the coffee and let its warmth soothe his throat while he waited for his answer.

"When you first visited the church, you and I chatted afterward." The reverend pushed his round spectacles up on his crooked nose. "You shared with me that you're a preacher."

"I was, yes."

Reverend Taggart nodded, causing his thick neck to bob on his shirt collar. "I've accepted a pastorate in upstate New York, starting after the first of the year. And we wanted to talk to you about—"

"Like Reverend Taggart said, we've been talking about you." Colin Wagner diluted his coffee with a generous dousing of cream and clanged the spoon against the sides of his cup. "I learned about your chosen profession in our interview for the prospectus. Ever since the reverend told the board of deacons his plans to move, we've been praying for a suitable replacement. Someone comfortable living and serving in a rough-and-tumble mining town."

"We'd like you to think about accepting the pastorate, Tucker. Pray about it." The reverend lifted his cup to his mouth, causing his spectacles to fog.

Tucker suddenly felt encased in a fog of his own. His second Sunday at church, he had asked the reverend to call him by his given name, never dreaming he could be asked to take on the man's duties here in Cripple Creek. "I'm not planning on staying in town any longer than is necessary to see that my parents' business is prosperous enough to provide for their needs."

Reverend Taggart glanced up at the ceiling as if receiving a message from God.

Or perhaps it was Tucker who received the message, as a piece of scripture pressed itself into his thoughts. *Trust in the LORD with all thine heart; and lean not unto thine own understanding…and he shall direct thy paths.*

Tucker held back a sigh. "I'll pray about it."

"That's all we ask." Colin set his coffee mug on the sofa table and stood.

Reverend Taggart followed suit. "And that you lead the responsive reading of the Scriptures on Sunday mornings."

Wearily, Tucker agreed. *Lord, You don't plan for me to stay here, do You?*

TWENTY

*F*or his mercy *endureth* for ever."

Ida's voice blended with the others in the congregation. Tucker Raines stood on the platform and led them in a responsive reading from Psalm 136.

"For his mercy *endureth* for ever."

How was it possible to read responsively while thinking of something else entirely?

"For his mercy *endureth* for ever."

Despite her best efforts to think spiritual thoughts, other matters caused her mind to wander. This week had held more ups and downs than the railway through Ute Pass.

"For his mercy *endureth* for ever."

She'd received her first wage. She'd visited the Exchange for the first time and bought stocks. Both wonderful firsts. So why couldn't she just enjoy her new life without impediment from people who didn't know anything about the business?

"For his mercy *endureth* for ever."

Hattie had been the first to step forth as a naysayer. *"I gathered Mollie may have her ducks lined up too tightly."* Her landlady's comments had washed away with the rains. Ida could also write off her brother-in-law's concerns easily enough. She couldn't expect a mine accountant to understand her work with stockbrokers and investors.

"For his mercy *endureth* for ever."

But ignoring a sister's words of caution was nigh to impossible.

"Some people don't agree with the way Mollie obtains information... It sounded like she was buying stock based upon what you'd learned from a client."

"For his mercy *endureth* for ever."

Ida sighed and flexed the hand that supported her Bible. She was only doing her job and seizing opportunities that the Good Lord Himself had set before her.

"For his mercy *endureth* for ever."

And then there was Colin Wagner. The attorney stood in the front pew, directly in front of Tucker. The two men couldn't be more different from one another than a seafaring ship was from an ice wagon. One wore a gray herringbone suit with a navy blue silk tie. The other wore brown trousers, a white shirt with a string tie, and a tweed jacket.

"O give thanks unto the God of heaven: for his mercy *endureth* for ever."

The congregation joined Tucker in reading the final verse of the chapter. Pretending to study the Bible passage further, Ida stole a glance at the ice man as he returned to the back pew and sat down. He read Scripture as if its essence had bubbled up from his heart.

A man who set aside his plans to tend to his family's needs. A man with a sick sister he cared deeply about. A noble man.

The man she needed to avoid. And she would, after today's Sunday supper at Miss Hattie's. Ida's landlady had extended the invitation to Tucker

Raines in the vestibule when they first arrived, and he'd promptly accepted, earning a shy smile from Faith. Perhaps the two fancied one another.

A pang of jealousy tightened Ida's throat and she swallowed hard against it. If those two did care for one another, she could more readily concentrate on more sensible pursuits.

Reverend Taggart was more formal in his preaching style, but Tucker enjoyed hearing him present the Word of God. His current series topic was especially engrossing—the unlikely servants of God. Walking from the church to Miss Hattie's, Tucker viewed Nehemiah's story from a different angle. A cupbearer for the king who became the impetus God used to rebuild the walls of Jerusalem. Tucker rubbed his chin as he dodged a mud puddle.

Was that why he was in Colorado? Had God wooed him here as a means to rebuild the Raines family?

If that were the case, how did Miss Ida Sinclair fit into His plans?

A friend. Certainly, she was a picture of determination and tenacity— a person dedicated to her family. And she'd already given him good counsel.

As he approached the yellow house with white trim on Golden Avenue, Colin Wagner came to mind and Tucker wondered if the attorney had been invited to Sunday supper as well. Wagner hadn't sat with Miss Sinclair during the service, but he'd certainly showered her with attention beforehand.

Scolding himself for caring, Tucker reached for the bell pull. Soon his father's business would be stable enough that he could return to California. To Willow.

Morgan Cutshaw met him at the front door and ushered him inside. "Judson and I are chatting in the parlor."

Tucker hung up his coat and hat.

"It'll be good to have another man in—" A distant burst of giggles interrupted the doctor. He grinned. "Unless you'd prefer to take your chances in the kitchen with five women."

Tucker shook his head with vigor. "Rumors of me achieving such a high standard of bravery are sorely unfounded."

Morgan laughed and clapped him on the shoulder. "We haven't either. You can hide out with us."

Judson waved at him from where he sat in a wingback chair. "Welcome to the men's hideout."

Tucker extended his hand to Judson. "You heard that, did you?"

Nodding, Judson stood and shook Tucker's hand then glanced down at the cup of coffee sitting before him. "You want a cup?"

"No, thanks. I'll wait." Tucker lowered himself onto the sofa across from the two men.

"On a more serious note"—Morgan paused—"have you heard anything from your parents since they left for Colorado Springs?"

Tucker leaned against the cushioned back of the sofa and propped his booted foot on the opposite knee. "I received a letter from my mother at the end of last week. My father is less than pleased with the living arrangements, but he seems to have stabilized. She said he's breathing easier and able to walk the grounds some."

"That's good news." Morgan loosened his tie and unbuttoned his vest.

"Ida said you're staying on to run the ice business." Judson reached for his cup of coffee.

"For a while. If I can build up the business, I'll turn it over to someone who can run it. "

Morgan lifted his coffee cup from the table. "Don't be too surprised when you discover you don't want to leave Cripple Creek."

Tucker brushed his hand through his hair. "I have responsibilities in California. I plan to return there as soon as possible."

Judson tugged the cuffs on his shirtsleeves and met Tucker's gaze. "You mind if I ask you a personal question?"

More matchmaking? Planting both feet on the ground, Tucker drew in a deep breath. "Go ahead."

"You play checkers?"

Tucker laughed. "That's your personal question? Do I play checkers?"

"It's a lot more serious a question than you might realize." Morgan lowered his voice as if being heard would usher in the apocalypse.

"So, do you?" Judson returned his cup to the table.

"I do play checkers, actually."

"You any good at it?"

Tucker leaned forward. "Just the best in seminary."

"I like the sound of that." Morgan gave Judson an exaggerated nod. "I think we might finally have an advantage against the Sinclair sisters."

Light footfalls drew Tucker's attention to the doorway.

"Dinner is served." Miss Faith Dunsmuir was the only person he knew with that small a voice. She stood in the doorframe, rocking on her heels.

All three of the men jumped to their feet, and Tucker followed the others into the dining room.

A feast filled the table. Slices of roasted beef, creamed peas, whipped potatoes, and golden brown dinner rolls.

Ida Sinclair stood behind a chair, facing him. He held her chair out for her and then did the same for the more timid Miss Dunsmuir. As he did, he couldn't help noting the distinct differences between the two young women.

Timid was not a word he'd ever use in describing Miss Ida Sinclair. Instead, he'd use words like *confident* and *deliberate*.

Distracting…

Ida watched her brother-in-law's fingers fly across the piano keyboard while she joined the others in one of Miss Hattie's favorite pastimes—a hymn sing. After supper, she'd followed the crowd into the parlor. Her landlady's phonograph usually provided background music, but not when Morgan Cutshaw was around to play the square grand piano she was storing for him until the couple's home was finished.

"'This is my story, this is my song, praising my Savior all the day long.'"

Kat's alto voice rang out from her position on the bench beside her husband. Nell sang soprano while Judson stood next to her on one side of the piano, singing tenor. Opposite them, Faith stood beside Tucker Raines while Ida and Hattie framed the Cutshaws. The harmony of voices sent chill bumps up and down Ida's arms, but it was the rich timbre of Tucker Raines's baritone that warmed her heart.

Called away from his sick sister and his life as a preacher to deliver ice and build up a neglected business, the ice man had quite the story to tell. He hadn't told her what ailed Willow, but given the man's rejoicing at the post office over even a slight improvement, it had to have been something serious.

Still, he sang praises to his God. An extraordinary man.

All the more reason for Ida to concentrate on the keyboard and Morgan's nimble fingers. She couldn't avoid the warmth of Tucker's voice, but she could and would avoid the tenderness she saw in his eyes—for her sake and for Faith's.

The schoolteacher had managed to sit beside Tucker at supper and stand with him at the piano, and she hadn't been nearly as diligent as Ida at controlling her impulse to stare at him. Positively googly-eyed, that girl.

"'Praising my Savior all the day long.'"

The last note still hung in the air in Judson's deep bass when Hattie began clapping. "A piece of heaven." She looked at each one of her seven guests. "My family gathered 'round in sweet song."

"I agree, Miss Hattie." Tucker's voice drew Ida's gaze upward, to his Adam's apple and his strong jaw. "Good food. Good company. Good music." He stepped around the piano and kissed the older woman on the cheek. "Thank you for including me."

"Anytime, dear." Miss Hattie patted his arm like a mother would. "You're part of our family and welcome here anytime."

Tucker stepped back. "I best make my way home. Titan and Trojan are no doubt convinced by now that I've abandoned them."

Faith followed him to the parlor door. "Mr. Raines," she whispered.

He stopped and looked at her, his brows raised.

"Might I have a word with you before you leave?" She approached him with slow steps.

Tucker glanced up at the rest of them, then nodded. "Of course." He held his arm out to her and Faith laid a thin hand on his shirt sleeve. "We can talk on our way to the door."

They left the room, Faith speaking to him in hushed tones while her calico skirt swayed side to side, and jealousy surged through Ida.

She turned back toward the quiet piano keys. She obviously needed to rein in her interest in Tucker to better align it with the notion of friendship.

Thankfully, her upcoming social engagement with the charismatic Mr. Wagner was just what she needed to help her in that regard.

Twenty-One

*I*da scrutinized the clothes hanging in her wardrobe. She started with the blue chemise gown she planned to wear to the Butte Opera House Saturday night for her outing with the charming Mr. Colin Wagner. And Mollie and Mr. Miller, of course.

That was still two days away. Tomorrow was Friday, and she needed to pay special attention to what she wore to work. An outfit for participating at the stock exchange required a careful mix of femininity and business attire.

Earlier in the week, she'd worn her green serge dress to the Exchange, and her gray floral skirt late last week. For now, she only had five or six others to choose from.

She'd just pulled her black wool skirt off the clothes bar when she heard a timid knock on her bedchamber door. Definitely Faith. Miss Hattie's knocks sounded more like a hammer pounding the head of a stubborn nail.

"Come in."

The door clicked open. Faith took two short steps forward before pausing in the doorway. "I'm sorry to bother you."

"Don't be silly. We're neighbors, and you're not a bother. Maybe you can assist me."

Faith stepped inside, then closed the door behind her. "I'd be happy to try, but I'm not sure how much help I'll be."

She reminded Ida of a skittish bird sitting on a brittle branch in a windstorm. Even when she'd summoned the courage to follow Tucker Raines to Hattie's door last Sunday.

"It's my outfit for work tomorrow. Which one do you think I should wear?"

Faith looked past her at the open wardrobe, her eyes wide.

Ida suddenly felt embarrassed by her comparative affluence. She'd only seen the schoolteacher wear two different skirts and one housedress. "I didn't...wasn't showing off. I didn't mean to—"

"Now who's being silly?" Faith's monotone punctuated her sagging shoulders.

Ida liked the schoolteacher, but she and Faith didn't have much, if anything, in common. Other than their curiosity about Mr. Tucker Raines, though Ida suspected the girl's interest in the ice man ran deeper than mere curiosity.

She couldn't help noticing the way Faith had looked at him in church and again at supper while he told a story about his travels as an itinerate preacher. *Doe-eyed.* As soon as Miss Hattie had announced Tucker would sit opposite her at the table, Faith claimed a chair beside him. Then there was that hushed conversation in the entryway. It seemed Tucker enjoyed the schoolteacher's attentions.

Good.

Was that why Faith had come to her room, to talk about her feelings for the ice man?

Not quite ready for such a conversation, Ida held up the black wool skirt. "Which dress do you think I should wear tomorrow for my visit to the stock exchange?" She pulled a pale blue broadcloth shirtwaist off a hook and paired it with the skirt. "This one?" She returned the outfit to the wardrobe and pulled out a plum-colored linsey-woolsey two-piece. "Or this one?"

"I like the plum dress for a Friday."

"The plum one it is. Thank you."

A tentative smile quirked Faith's mouth on one side. "You're welcome."

Ida returned the clothes to the wardrobe, wondering why Faith had chosen plum specifically for a Friday but even more curious about the girl's reason for wanting to talk to her. Faith didn't even have money enough for a new dress, so stock investment was out of the question. And the business world was far removed from the school yard. They had nothing in common there. That left Mr. Raines and matters of the heart.

Faith's fingers worried the sleeve of her pink floral housedress. "I like your flair for fashion."

"Thank you, but I have to give my sister Vivian credit for much of it. She designed the blue shirtwaist and the plum outfit." Once Ida began making some serious profit from stock dividends and her commissions with Mollie, she'd show them all what real fashion looked like on a Sinclair sister.

"Your sister has good taste, and so do you." If the strength of the teacher's voice was any indication of the strength in her knees, Ida had cause for concern.

She closed the door on the wardrobe and turned the chair in front of her dressing table to face the bed. "Would you like to sit down?"

"Yes, thank you."

Ida sat on the edge of the bed. As nervous as the girl was, a man had to be the subject on her heart. When Faith didn't show any outward signs of beginning the conversation, Ida drew in a deep breath and took the lead.

"Faith, if you're worried about what I think of you and Mr. Raines growing…uh, closer, don't be."

The younger woman's eyes widened while her cheeks out-pinked her dress. She popped up from the chair. "That's not what I want to talk to you about."

"Oh?"

Faith paced from the dressing table to the wardrobe and back. "It's a school matter."

"I see." It was a common expression, but why did people say they saw when they didn't *see* anything at all? Ida certainly couldn't *see* why the teacher would come to her with such a matter.

Faith sat back down and clasped her hands in her lap. "I have a student who is having difficulty with multiplication."

The teacher's intentions were still no clearer than the mud in Colorado's potholes. "You have a business mind," Faith continued. "I've heard you talk at the meal table and during our tea times with Miss Hattie. I hoped you could help him."

Ida moistened her lips. "I'm not a teacher, and I don't—"

"I *need* you to help him." Tears pooled in Faith's blue eyes, and one spilled down her cheek.

"I keep plenty busy with my work and my sis—"

"The banker is on the school board. Eugene Updike."

Ida blinked. On her first visit to the stock exchange, she had engaged Mr. Updike in a hissing match that ended with him welcoming her to the *"snake pit."* Ever since, she'd gone out of her way to avoid him.

"He voted against hiring me but lost to the majority." Faith brushed the tear from her cheek. "I'm sorry. I don't want to cry."

"It's okay. I've been known to shed a few tears myself. But I don't see what—"

"My student, he's the banker's son."

Ida groaned. Now she was beginning to *see*.

"If I can't teach him to calculate multiplication problems, I might lose my job. I need this job, Miss Sinclair."

Something else they had in common—they both had jobs they wanted to keep. "And you think I can help?"

Faith's staccato nod bounced the dark curls on either side of her aqua eyes. "You could tutor Delos Updike. You could help him learn his multiplication tables. You could help me keep my job."

At seventeen, Faith was the same age as Vivian. And if Vivian were in trouble, Ida would want someone to help her. The big-sister blood running through her veins boiled. She had to help Faith stand against the bully banker and hold on to her job.

Ida pulled a handkerchief from her pocket and rose from the edge of the bed. "You're very persuasive."

"I am?"

Nodding, Ida handed the linen kerchief to Faith. "I'll tutor him Saturday mornings at ten o'clock for one hour. Eight Saturdays would put us in the middle of December."

Faith blotted the tears from her face, and a smile chased the cloudy hue from her blue eyes.

Ida returned the teacher's smile. "Delos should well be able to calculate by then."

"That'll be wonderful. Thank you."

Big sisters are such an easy mark. At least I am.

But it felt good to help this girl. And she'd much rather tutor Eugene Updike's son than hear Faith talk about her romantic feelings for Tucker.

TWENTY-TWO

*F*riday morning, Tucker stopped by Charles Miller's office on the way to the depot. Two secretaries worked feverishly at their desks. A stack of certificates occupied the older woman on the left, while the girl on the right was on the phone, placing an ad in the newspaper.

The woman with graying hair waved him back to Mr. Miller's private office. Charles Miller couldn't be any taller than five foot nine, but he was a big man in Cripple Creek business, and well respected. Tucker had received mixed reviews about some of the other men who dealt in the stock exchange.

"I have something for you." The trim broker unlocked a cabinet behind his desk and pulled an envelope out of a folder.

Tucker's pulse jolted at the thought of stocks in his father's ice company having sold. He might actually have capital for growing the business.

"This is the first bank draft. I have several more investors looking at the company, waiting to see what you do with this first influx of cash." The broker smoothed his hand over his thin mustache, holding Tucker's gaze as he held out the envelope. "Spend it wisely and diligently stick to your business plan. Remember, your prospectus is what these people are betting on."

Mr. Miller's counsel hung in the air in sharp contrast to Colin Wagner's. *"What a person does is directed by his own conscience."*

Tucker nodded and opened the envelope. After seeing the number written on the check, he glanced up at Miller. "Have you taken out your fee?"

"I have indeed." Miller smiled, revealing perfectly straight teeth. "More there than you expected?"

"Considerably." Tucker slid the envelope into his coat pocket. "This should be enough to buy another wagon and team and land for the icehouse. And I'd like to have the icehouse built by the time winter hits if more money comes in before then."

"Sounds like a good plan. I'm glad you were pleasantly surprised." Miller tugged his vest straight. "We aim to please our folks on both sides of the quote board."

"I'm pleased."

"Check back with me in two weeks. I hope to have another draft for you by then."

"I will. Thank you." Tucker waved and stepped outside just as the train's shrill whistle echoed through town.

The wind sweeping down from the snowcapped peaks caught his hat. He tugged it tight on his forehead and buttoned his canvas coat. Otis had the wagon that morning, so Tucker walked toward the bank.

From the looks of the clouds gathering and the chill on the wind, he guessed they'd have at least a dusting of snow in the valley before nightfall. But Tucker wasn't worried about the weather hindering his construction plans. Once he and Otis had dug down about six feet and formed the rock lining, there wouldn't much more to do to build the icehouse. They'd have the simple structure finished before the heavy snows came.

God was making a way for him in the wilderness, as He had for Morgan Cutshaw. At supper on Sunday, the doctor had shared how he'd lost his first wife and son in childbirth. How God had given him a second chance with Kat and the child they were expecting. God was doing the same for Tucker. His father still seemed to be in remission. His mother didn't appear to miss her house much and enjoyed spending time with her sister. Willow showed signs of coming out from behind the shadow of sorrow. Both the sanitorium and the asylum had agreed to a sixty-day stay on the bills. God was doing a new thing for him as well.

"Thank You, Lord." Tucker looked around, expecting—maybe even hoping—to see Ida Sinclair watching him as she'd done the last two times he'd prayed aloud on the street. But she wasn't one of the people walking the boardwalk on either side of him, and he continued toward the bank.

After depositing his investment money and a quick stop to see the land agent, Tucker headed to the loading dock at the depot. Otis already had the wagon backed up to the ice car.

"Happy Friday, Otis."

His bear of a friend looked at him from around the back of the wagon. "Well, if you don't look like a mountain lion that done swallowed a marmot."

"Sold some stocks."

Anticipation made Otis's dark eyes shine like a handful of diamonds. "Thank the Lord."

"Indeed. And we have an icehouse to build." Tucker pointed to the four acres of property behind him. "That creekside piece of property now belongs to the Raines Ice Company."

Otis's smile, though still lopsided, enjoyed the full width of his face. "I just know God is blessing you for your faithfulness in the trials."

"Manna in the wilderness?" Tucker removed his hat and held it out to the sky, as if to catch falling bread.

"Yes sir, everything we need."

Tucker nodded. "The next draft should buy us enough lumber to finish up the icehouse and add more stalls to the barn. In the meantime, I have your pay for you." He pulled an envelope of cash from his coat pocket and handed the package to his partner.

"Thank you. I wouldn't take this just now, except—" Otis counted the bills and shoved them and the envelope back at Tucker. "It's too much."

Tucker raised both hands, refusing to accept the return. "Just a small bonus for your faithfulness to my father. And to me. I know you agreed to work for a set pay, but you've been more than just a hired hand to us."

"Thank you." Otis stuffed the offering inside his shirt. "You think when we're done loadin' we could stop outside the Exchange? Boney's been spendin' most of his mornings there lately. Said he'd buy me some stock when I was ready."

"We can do that."

Tucker smiled. Neither Otis nor Boney fit any mold he had ever seen. As a matter of fact, this town was unlike any he'd ever been to, with few people fitting into established patterns. Laborers buying stocks, women running businesses…

And a preacher selling ice.

TWENTY-THREE

*Y*ou've gone beyond an hour, Miss Sinclair." Faith spoke from her desk, where she'd been working through a stack of slates. Ida set her chalk in the tray and glanced up at the clock on the back wall of the classroom. Five minutes past eleven. She looked down at Delos Updike, who stood beside her at the board. "You've done a fine job today."

"I think you're helping me." His smile showcased the freckles that bridged his nose. "Thank you, Miss Sinclair."

The Updike boy wasn't at all what she'd expected. Unlike his father, he had manners and a sweet disposition.

"You're welcome, Delos. You're a hard worker, and I think you'll do fine." Ida retrieved her mantle from a corner desk. "Remember what I told you."

"Yes ma'am. It doesn't matter which number is first, the answer will be the same."

"Very good. I'll see you next Saturday morning then."

He nodded, and his red hair waved like grass in the wind. At the door, he turned to his teacher. "Good-bye, Miss Dunsmuir."

"Good day, Delos. I'll see you Monday."

The boy flew out the door and tromped down the steps.

Faith wore her gray linsey-woolsey dress again today. Ida made a mental note to add a dress for the schoolteacher to her Christmas shopping list.

"You were good with him." Faith's emphasis on the word *good* suggested she'd been just as surprised as Ida by her skill with Delos.

"Thank you." Ida reached for her reticule. "It's been awhile since I contemplated the basics, but I had fun."

"He's a joy to teach, just lacks confidence." Faith could've been speaking of herself, and for the first time, Ida wondered if a lack of confidence contributed to the young schoolteacher's nervousness. Timidity wasn't a trait any of the Sinclair sisters could claim.

Faith lunged forward and enfolded Ida in a tight hug, then let go and swiped at tears that curtained her face. "I'm sorry."

"It's all right." Ida smiled. "My sisters and I hug all the time."

More tears. "That's just it. I've always wanted one. A big sister."

"They're bossy. At least, that's what I've been told." Ida winked, and Faith giggled. Ida felt her own shoulders lift, knowing she still had the magic *big-sister touch*. Self-deprecating humor always worked on Nell and Vivian too.

"You're probably just working too hard." Ida patted her shoulder. "Seventeen seems a young age to strike out on your own and take on the responsibility of teaching other people's children." Especially people like Mr. Updike.

"I like teaching."

"It shows. You'll do just fine." Ida glanced out the window at the cloudless sky. "Would you like to go for a walk?"

"Thank you, but Miss Hattie is expecting me back at the house for lunch, and then she's helping me with my hair. We're going to Dr. Cutshaw's piano concert tonight."

"I'll be there too. I'll see you back at the house this afternoon."

"Yes. Enjoy your walk."

Ida left Faith standing at the blackboard and put on her wool mantle. As she walked out of the schoolhouse, the bright sunlight made her shield her eyes. The sun's warmth had melted the snow from the steps, but the ground still held a thin blanket of white powder, causing a blinding reflection.

She'd decided on a walk, thinking it might be good for Faith, but since the mention of the concert, Ida's thoughts churned with her own plans to visit the opera house that night with Colin Wagner. A walk seemed like a favorable idea for sorting them out, but the idea of strolling the main thoroughfare didn't appeal to her. She did that every workday.

If only the creek were safe. Burbling water seemed the most compelling destination.

Tucker Raines had once invited her to visit the stretch of creek on his parents' property. Did the offer still stand? Did she dare take him up on it? As much as he'd been working lately, he probably wouldn't be home. He wouldn't even have to know she'd been there.

Ida walked down the hill to Bennett Avenue, then turned left on Third Street and crossed over to Second Street on Warren. She approached the Raines property warily. A modest log cabin, a privy, a small barn. The fence was in good repair, with a gate at the corner. The enclosure seemed safe enough.

Solitude.

Nestled between two slender willow saplings, a narrow, pine bench sat on a grassy knoll just above the creek, exposed to enough direct sunlight to keep the early snow melted off. A peaceful setting and a perfect place for thinking. Was that why Tucker had put the bench here? Did he come here to think and pray?

Ida straightened her spine, hoping to realign her thoughts as well. She wasn't here to ponder the ice man.

Tonight's concert would have been a family affair, except Colin Wagner invited her first and she'd accepted, not knowing her brother-in-law would be the entertainment and all of her Cripple Creek family would be there. The evening was simply an outing for a group of business colleagues, but seeing her there with the attorney could add fuel to the matchmakers' fires. And the fact that Ida would also be in the company of the stockbroker and Mollie O'Bryan might not sit well with the family. Judson, in particular.

"Miss Sinclair?"

Ida jumped up from the bench and turned. Tucker Raines approached her, wearing his blue chambray shirt and a smile that rivaled the warmth of the sun. Ida couldn't help noticing that ice delivery apparently did for the body what good preaching did for the soul. "I didn't know you were here," she said.

"I'm glad you took me up on my invitation." He continued walking toward her, and she grasped the back of the bench to steady herself. She wouldn't admit it to anyone else, but the weakness in her knees had less to do with being startled than with who had startled her.

Ida pressed her collar to her neck. "It's a lovely place."

"I'm glad you're here." He stopped directly in front of her.

"Me too." Had she really said that aloud?

The grin on Tucker's face said she had not only spoken aloud, she had also used Nell's dreamy voice in doing so.

He needed to quit looking at her.

When his gaze lingered, hers did too. And looking into his brown eyes, she suddenly craved a tall mug of rich coffee with a hint of fresh cream.

Tucker shifted his weight to pivot toward the bench. "I'd enjoy sitting with you for a few minutes, if you don't mind." He held out his hand.

She wouldn't tell him she liked the idea, but she did. And why not? They could be considered friends. They both attended the same church. They both adored Hattie. They both felt obligations to their respective families. It made perfect sense for them to enjoy visiting with one another, especially with no matchmaking crowd present.

Ida seated herself at the far end of the bench. *Good.* They wouldn't be looking directly at one another anymore.

Tucker sat beside her and leaned back. *Worse.* He was close enough that she could smell Bay Rum on his scrubbed face. Close enough to lay her head against his solid shoulder.

What was the matter with her? She shook her head to rid herself of such thoughts.

"Are you all right?" Concern etched his voice.

Ida peered over at him, conjuring up that refreshing cup of coffee again. When he reached for her face, her breath caught.

"You have something..." He gently slid his finger over the bridge of her nose. "Chalk?" Without looking away, he wiped his finger on his trousers.

She nodded, waiting for the lump in her throat to allow words through. "I'm tutoring one of Faith's students. I was working at the blackboard."

"So you're not all business?"

Ida's back stiffened and she pressed her hands to her skirt. "Why does everyone assume I'm some kind of self-centered moneygrubber? I do have other interests. I spend time with my sisters. Hattie. Church. Tutoring."

Tucker reached into his coat pocket and pulled out a crisp, white handkerchief. Smiling, he waved it. "I surrender. You have other interests."

Ida giggled as much in a nervous response to her outburst as she did to his humorous antics.

"I didn't mean it as a criticism."

"That makes you the only one." Ida hooked a stray tendril of hair behind her ear and drew in a cleansing breath. "I'm sorry I overreacted."

"Apology accepted." He slid the handkerchief back into his pocket. "I gather you've faced some opposition since you've been in town."

Ida relaxed against the back of the bench. "How did you guess?" More giggles spilled out of her. "Any further word from your sister on how she's feeling?"

Tucker gazed out at the water burbling in front of them. "She's been in an institution for nearly two years."

"Oh." She turned and joined him in an unfocused gaze toward the creek. What if one of her sisters required such care? How would she manage? "Is Willow going to be all right?"

"I received a second report today. She's beginning to respond and speak." He drew in a deep breath. "Bereavement melancholia is what the doctor called it. Something happened."

"If you'd rather not talk about it…"

Tucker picked up a rock at his feet. He seemed to study it and then threw it into the creek before looking at her again. "Willow married my best friend. Sam's the one who shared his faith in Christ with me." He cleared his throat. "He and I were in seminary together in San Francisco. When Sam and Willow married, he moved her into a cottage on the school grounds."

Ida gazed back at the house behind them. "Your parents were here by then?"

"No, they were still living in Stockton. The three of us went down for weekend visits. Sometimes Sam and I practiced our preaching at his father's church there. We liked to go to the San Joaquin River on our breaks to picnic and swim. One Saturday in July of '94, I decided to see if I could swim across to the opposite shore. The wind kicked up some waves, but it didn't seem rough enough for me to give up."

The knot in Ida's stomach told her this story wouldn't have a happy ending, and she swallowed hard against the fear.

"Sam lost sight of me and became worried. Went in after me." Tucker stared into her eyes as if he were drawing strength from her. "I didn't know it until I'd returned to shore. He wasn't there, and Willow was hysterical with fear. I looked for him, but I was too late." His shoulders sagged.

Ida resisted the impulse to pull him into an embrace, to comfort him. He'd been carrying far too heavy a load. And a man of God, no less. A man who appeared to walk by faith no matter the path.

"I'm so sorry." Ida leaned toward him. "You have to know his death wasn't your fault."

"One can know something deep down, but on the surface where we tend to live, those things are harder to see and believe." Tucker pulled his handkerchief from his pocket and wiped the tears spilling down his face.

He was deeper than any other man she'd ever met. And she'd guess his faith in the midst of pain had taken him there.

"After the funeral, Willow moved back in with my folks. She withdrew deeper and deeper into herself until finally my father couldn't bear to see her anymore. He was angry at his inability to help her and embarrassed by her irrepressible sorrow."

"He had her committed?"

Tucker nodded.

Ida laid her hand on his arm.

"Thank you." His smile sent shivers up the back of her neck.

Sympathy. Empathy. That would explain her reaction to this multifaceted man.

Except that he'd stirred her heart long before she knew the depth of his pain. Before she'd seen the strength of his character.

And sitting beside him now in comfortable silence, watching two ravens gliding on a wind current, only served to strengthen the stirring in her heart.

TWENTY-FOUR

*T*ucker guided the carriage he'd rented for the evening's festivities down Bennett Avenue. As Titan's and Trojan's hoofs thumped through the thin layer of snow toward the Butte Opera House, his thoughts churned in rhythm with the wagon wheels.

He was escorting two women to Morgan's piano concert. He considered each of them a friend, but neither had administered a soothing salve to his heart at the creek.

"So kind of you to be our escort this evening, Tucker." Miss Hattie sat beside him. He couldn't see her smile in the shadows, but he knew it was there.

"It's my pleasure, Miss Hattie." He glanced at the seat behind her where Faith Dunsmuir sat looking more like a porcelain figurine than a young woman who kept up with children all day. "Miss Dunsmuir. Two lovely ladies to escort."

Tucker looked toward the opera house. Couples heading to the only wholesome evening entertainment available in Cripple Creek that night clogged the streets. Many older couples stood patiently in line, but he was struck by the number of young couples holding hands and finding pleasure in each other's company. He'd certainly enjoyed friendships with women, but he hadn't courted anyone. He'd been too busy the past six years working at his father's icehouse in Stockton, attending seminary, visiting Willow, and then trying to keep things afloat here.

Once Tucker had turned the horses and the carriage over to the attendant, he escorted his two companions up the steps. Miss Hattie stopped just outside the door and her gaze darted toward Faith.

When he realized what Hattie was suggesting, he held his arm out to the schoolteacher. "Miss Dunsmuir." He didn't want to encourage her attentions toward him, but he could be a gentleman. After all, tonight was reserved for friends and fun with the Sinclair sisters and their husbands. He and Ida hadn't talked about her plans for this evening while at the creek, but she'd no doubt be sitting with her sisters.

The moment Tucker stepped into the lobby with Faith on his arm, he knew he'd supposed wrong. Ida was there, looking like his vision of royalty visiting heads of state, with a gloating man stuck to her side. At least it appeared that way to Tucker.

"Mrs. Adams." Wagner held a top hat. "Miss Dunsmuir." Returning his crown to his head, the attorney shifted his gaze to Tucker. "Mr. Raines."

No doubt about it, the man was a peacock, and his feathers were full out.

Tucker lifted his freshly brushed, wide-brimmed hat off his head with his free hand. "Miss Sinclair, it's good to see you again. Quite a transformation from what you wore earlier at the creek." When Ida's thin smile gave way to a glare, he turned his attention to the man dressed like a president. "Mr. Wagner."

He'd just spread his own feathers. He couldn't say why, but Ida Sinclair didn't belong with that man.

Nor could he say she belonged with a traveling preacher. A brother preoccupied with his traumatized sister. A son who would spend the rest of his life trying to make up for a stupid mistake.

Setting his jaw, Tucker led Miss Dunsmuir and Miss Hattie to their seats.

Ida turned away from Miss Hattie, Faith, and the ice man who wore a poorly fitted rented suit and the schoolteacher's hand planted on his arm. The heat Ida felt searing her face had nothing to do with the temperature in the opera house and everything to do with the unpredictable and perturbing Mr. Tucker Raines.

Fanning herself with the printed program, Ida laid her other gloved hand on Colin Wagner's extended arm, allowing him to lead her toward the mahogany staircase. Thankfully, Mollie and Mr. Miller awaited them in the balcony and not on the bottom floor where her sisters, Judson, Miss Hattie, Faith, and Tucker had seats. After learning about Willow's situation, Ida better understood Tucker's sudden melancholic exit from Miss Hattie's parlor that first day. Obviously, seeing her and her sisters had caused him to mourn his own sister's loss anew. But she saw no good reason for his public announcement this evening.

"Quite a transformation from what you wore earlier at the creek."

Faith's jaw had nearly hit her chest.

The nerve of Mr. Raines saying such a thing in front of her escort. What must the urbane man at her side think? Colin wore an evening dress coat with shallow tails and a silk cummerbund, capping it off with a top hat. If she were in the market for a suitor—which she wasn't—the attorney was clearly a much better candidate than Tucker Raines, who was a more likely match for the schoolteacher. And Ida would tell Miss Hattie so if her landlady chose to mention seeing sparks between her and Tucker ever again.

For now, she'd let go of her frustration and enjoy her brother-in-law's concert.

"Are you all right?" Colin's hazel eyes sparkled in the chandelier lighting.

She nodded and ceased her fanning, gripping the polished railing on the staircase instead.

"You seem a mite disturbed."

"As well I should be," she muttered, stomping up the steps. She felt Colin's arm tighten and slowed her pace. "I'm sorry, but that was rude of him." She resisted the urge to look over her shoulder and glare at the man she'd left on the ground floor. "Mr. Raines had no right to mention such a personal matter."

Colin gave her a hand up at the landing and met her gaze. "So you being at the creek with Tucker Raines *was* a personal matter?"

Ida pressed the pointed toes of her new front-lacing shoes into the Oriental rug on the landing. "That's not what I meant." Why was she stumbling over semantics? Looking away, she studied a slight rip at the seam in the velvet wallpaper. "We weren't at the creek *together*. I was alone on the bench and I didn't expect him to join me." She'd been glad that he had at the time, but no longer. And it was no concern of Mr. Wagner's—they were business colleagues. That was all. "It was nothing, and he shouldn't have behaved that way."

"Jealousy can do that to a man."

It felt more like bluster to her, even spite. Jealousy couldn't be the motive behind Tucker's comment, could it?

"I hope you don't mind that I'm fighting a twinge of jealousy myself."

"You're jealous?"

Colin nodded, staring into her eyes without so much as a blink. "I enjoy working with you, but I'd like to see you more on a social level. Supper on Saturday evening, perhaps?"

Ida moistened her lips. "Let me consider it."

Colin nodded and ushered her to her seat. Mollie and Mr. Miller stood as they approached, and Ida focused on greeting her colleagues and participating in conversation.

Once the concert began, she tried to concentrate on Morgan's playing, but her thoughts kept wandering. She felt as if the moment she'd seen Tucker and Faith step into the opera house together she'd stumbled into a mist that fogged her mind.

Had seeing her with Colin done the same to Tucker?

TWENTY-FIVE

*S*unday afternoon, Tucker brushed Titan's mane. The smells of draft horses and hay blended together in an earthy barn scent that Tucker had come to appreciate since the days of childhood chores. This suited him much better than city colognes and perfumes.

Not that he didn't enjoy a little culture. Not that he wouldn't have enjoyed Morgan's concert. But after he'd stuck his foot in his mouth in front of Ida and Mr. Wagner, not to mention Miss Hattie and Miss Dunsmuir, he'd been able to hear little else besides Ida's gasp and think of nothing outside his inappropriate compliment.

"Look out below," Abraham called from the loft. He, his brother Isaac, and their dad began tossing bags of straw over the edge, toward the ice wagon.

"Thanks for the extra help, fellas," Tucker called back.

"Mr. Tucker." A gentle tug pulled at his trouser leg.

Tucker looked down into the round face of Otis's third-born son.

"I do it now, Mr. Tucker? You showed me good."

Tucker handed Noah the pig-bristle brush and lifted him so the lad could reach Titan's mane. "Your turn."

Holding the brush firm, Noah took a long, slow stroke through the mane, from the roots to the tips. "Titan, buddy, you're a real good horse," he whispered, then twisted around to look at Tucker. The toddler's eyes shone. "See, I even talk to 'im nice like you do."

Tucker chuckled and nodded. "Yes. It seems I've become quite the conversationalist. With horses."

Deep laughter echoed off the barn walls as Otis swung a thick leg over the edge of the loft and climbed down the ladder. "That's the most I've heard you say today." Stopping just outside Titan's stall, Otis swatted straw from his flannel shirt.

"I was even worse company before you all showed up." Tucker shifted Noah to rest against his chest while the boy continued brushing the mane and chattering at Titan.

"Something on your mind?"

Someone. Uninvited. Camped in his thoughts like a squatter who refused to leave.

"That Sinclair sister with the hatpin?" Otis grinned.

Tucker raised a brow.

"Just a guess."

"A mighty good one."

"My arm's tired, Mr. Tucker." Noah dropped his arm to his side. "Can I go play?"

Tucker lowered the boy to the ground and retrieved the brush. Noah scampered off to the sacks of straw and began standing them up against the wagon wheels.

Tucker exited the horse's stall and joined Otis. "I went and made a fool of myself in front of Ida Sinclair at the opera house last night."

"Forgot to change out of your mucking trousers, did ya?" Otis's dry humor could cheer a sleepy bear.

"Worse than that." Tucker repositioned the hat on his head. "Yesterday afternoon, I found her on the bench out there"—he tipped his head in the direction of the creek—"and joined her. We had a real good talk about Willow and such."

"Sounds like the two of you are drawing together."

"I thought so too. Then I went to Morgan's concert with Miss Hattie and Miss Dunsmuir."

"I see."

"As a friend. Anyhow, Miss Sinclair was there and she'd changed out of her woolen frock into a bluebird-blue ball gown. With Mr. Wagner at her side."

Otis groaned. Tucker's sentiments exactly, seeing those two together like that.

"I told her it was good to see her again; that she'd had quite a transformation from what she'd been wearing earlier at the creek."

"You didn't."

Tucker hung his head. "I did."

"Naomi would call that crowing from the fencepost at midnight."

"It was supposed to be a compliment."

"Meant to tell Wagner you too were fond of Miss Sinclair."

"It was?" *He was.* Tucker slapped his thigh, causing a cloud of straw dust to encircle him. "What do I do? She wouldn't even look at me at church this morning."

"You could write her a letter. Most women will read a letter, even if they won't hear you out."

"Another good idea." Tucker swished his felt hat to clear the cloud of dust away from his face. "Good thing I plan to keep you around." He smiled. "Now that we've solved all my problems, what do you say we talk about you for a change?"

Otis leaned against a post. "What do ya want to know?"

"You said you were planning to have Boney Hughes invest in some stock for you. How's that going?"

"I did. A little bit. With the extra pay you gave me. But I plan to buy a whole lot more when ol' Boney finds the ripest opportunity, as he puts it."

Tucker plopped his hat on his head as if it could cap his reservations. He wondered which would be the bigger adventure—Otis's stock speculation or his own with Miss Ida Sinclair?

Alone at last.

Ida smoothed out a piece of onionskin stationery on the writing desk in her room. Despite Kat and Nell's objections, she had managed to bow out of the after-church Sinclair family gathering at Nell's. She wasn't in the mood to rehash Judson's or Kat's concerns about her work. Or about her social life, for that matter.

Instead, she'd enjoyed a bowl of sweet potato soup and corn bread in the boardinghouse kitchen with Miss Hattie and Faith. Thankfully, not a word was said about Tucker or Colin or the opera house except that Morgan had played "Home, Sweet Home"—a favorite song of Miss Hattie's and her George. Miss Hattie couldn't help but make a comment about how she wished everyone could have such a home, sweet home.

In Ida's weaker moments, she found herself wondering what that kind of love would be like. The kind that warmed Miss Hattie's heart with fond memories years after her good-byes with George.

When she caught herself thinking like that, Ida drew on her own memory bank and remembered horrid men like Bradley Ditmer, who couldn't be trusted, and puzzling men like Tucker Raines. A man who could endear himself to her one moment and rile her the next.

No, friendship would be challenging enough after last night's fiasco. She had no desire for romance.

Ida dipped her quill in the ink bottle and began to write, content to hide away in her room for a few hours.

Dearest Father,

Thank you for the letter. I was so pleased to hear from you. We all were.

I shared your news with Kat and Nell, and we're already looking forward to your visit in '98.

If only Vivian were here. Summer didn't seem soon enough. But if Ida mentioned her concerns about her youngest sister, Father would just tell her she'd overspent her *big-sister worries*. Ida sighed, breathing a prayer for Vivian.

To answer your question, Father, I am gainfully employed and making splendid progress in the business world. The stock exchange is exciting and quite profitable.

Ida chose to leave his other question unanswered. She'd considered telling him about Colin Wagner escorting her to the opera house and that she'd agreed to see him more on a social basis. She didn't want Father to be concerned that she was all business, like everyone else seemed to be, but saw no reason for them both to wallow in confusion where the men in her life were concerned.

Before Ida could add another sentence, she heard footfalls on the stairs.

"Ida, you still up here, dear?" Miss Hattie called.

So much for solitude.

Ida wiped the quill dry on a piece of felt and returned it to the desktop. She then crossed the room and opened her door to Miss Hattie.

"I apologize for disturbing your peace, dear, but I have a delivery for you."

"The postmaster is working on a Sunday?"

"Otis Bernard brought it by."

She'd seen Otis outside the stockbrokers' building a time or two but hadn't exchanged more than a few words with him in passing. "I think Boney Hughes might be buying stock for him. I've seen them together at the Exchange. He probably wants my advice on a matter."

Hattie held out a small envelope. "He said the letter is from Mr. Raines."

Ida glanced up at her landlady, who merely nodded. Ida sighed and accepted the envelope. *Miss Sinclair* was written in well-practiced penmanship. Flipping it over, she read a brief note on the flap: "Please read."

"So he knew I wouldn't want to read it, and he's right." She hung her arm, letting the message dangle. "I don't want to hear what he has to say."

"Then don't read it aloud." A mischievous grin tugged at her landlady's rounded cheeks, causing her silver-gray eyes to shimmer like the Atlantic in afternoon sunlight.

"You are enjoying this far too much, Hattie."

The older woman tittered.

When Hattie turned toward the door, Ida walked to the window and lifted the envelope to her nose. She breathed in the ice man's earthy scent.

He smelled of the outdoors and fresh air. And ink, most likely from the pages of his Bible.

She shouldn't read his letter. She shouldn't have anything to do with him. Not if she wanted to guard her heart.

She opened the envelope.

Dear Miss Sinclair,

I so enjoyed our visit at the creek yesterday afternoon.

But your change in demeanor last night alerted me that my comment had offended you. That was never my intention.

Apparently, what I meant as a compliment came out as a warning to Mr. Wagner of my fondness for you.

His fondness? What did that mean? Ida sank onto the bed. "The man is impossible."

She hadn't realized she'd said it aloud until Miss Hattie spun around in the doorway and sat on the bed beside her. "They all are, dear." She patted Ida's hand. "Even my George. Without God's grace manifesting itself in amazing ways… Well, let's just say that without God's grace, our marriage wouldn't have lasted a day past the ceremony."

Ida returned her attention to the letter.

I hope you can accept my apologies.

Fondly,

Tucker Raines

She stood and walked back to the window just in time to see a shiny black carriage roll to a stop in front of the walkway below. A carriage Ida recognized. "What is he doing here?"

Hattie rose from the bed and joined her at the window. "Why, it's Mr. Wagner." She clucked her tongue. "I do declare, Ida dear, you're more popular than my peach cobbler at a church picnic."

Ida laid Tucker's letter on her bed. He would have to wait.

Miss Hattie followed her down the stairs but still managed to arrive at the front door first.

Colin Wagner smiled at them over a perfumed bouquet of silk roses. Yellow ones. "Miss Hattie." He doffed his bowler. "Miss Sinclair, I hope you don't mind my stopping by unannounced like this."

"We were just chatting." Hattie opened the door wider. "Won't you come in?"

"Thank you, but I won't keep you, ladies." He handed Ida the flowers and met her gaze. "I hoped you'd agree to have supper with me this Saturday. I'll come for you at five o'clock."

Ida refused to look at Hattie. She didn't need to see her gaiety, nor did she require her permission. "Saturday at five would be fine. And thank you for the roses."

"You're welcome." Colin placed his hat atop his head and turned back to his carriage.

The moment the door clicked shut behind him, Hattie spun around. "Very popular, I'd say."

Yes, well, according to her family and even to Miss Hattie herself, that could all change soon enough due to her career. On her way to the kitchen to fetch a vase, Ida breathed in the sweet scent of perfumed roses. She'd best nurture her relationships in the business world.

Beginning with Mr. Colin Wagner.

TWENTY-SIX

*S*aturday morning, Ida lifted her teacup from the sofa table in
Hattie's parlor. "During my lunch break yesterday I found a new
sofa in Johnson's Quality Furniture that I think would look perfect in here."

The older woman glanced around the parlor, then down at the sofa
beneath her. She rubbed her hand across the burgundy velour fabric as a
mother might stroke her child's forehead, checking for a fever. "You know,
George and I picked this out of a catalog. Had it shipped from
Philadelphia."

That alone dated her furniture. Ida took a sip of peppermint tea and
leaned back in the Queen Anne chair across from her landlady. "I just
thought you might want something a bit more…modern. A yellow settee or
a beige fainting couch could really brighten it up in here."

Hattie stared past Ida at the fireplace, where split pine snapped and
popped in its attempts to warm the room. "I don't know."

"I say if you have the money to purchase new furnishings, you may as
well enjoy it."

"Dear, I'm content with what I have."

Ida couldn't relate to being content with what she had. But then she
hadn't had a chance to even start acquiring things.

"I'll be the first to tell you that the lure of wealth and finery is great with all the new stores here." Hattie glanced toward the window. "Advertisements seem to float in the air as freely as autumn leaves."

It wasn't as if Ida expected to have it all. Or even that she wanted everything she saw. She opened her mouth with a ready reply, but when the door knocker sounded, her words changed midthought. "They're here. You sure you don't want to go shopping with us today? Might do you good to get out."

"I'm sure, dear. You girls enjoy your sister time."

"We will. Might even start a wardrobe for my niece. Or nephew."

~~~

Nell's womb was still empty, and her heart still ached to give Judson a child as she watched Kat swish side to side in a green woolen maternity dress. Ida had seen to it that the clerk at the millinery shop gave them a dressing room large enough to accommodate all three sisters.

You are my fortress, Lord. In You will I trust. I will not be jealous of my sister. I will rejoice in You blessing her and Morgan.

Stopping to face the mirror, Kat ran her hand over the paisley skirt while Ida bent down and brushed the hem straight.

"Which dress do you like better, Kat?" Ida glanced at the golden yellow broadcloth frock Kat had already tried on.

Their second-born sister raised a brow and shrugged her left shoulder.

Nell gripped the bodice of the woolen dress and pulled it, to be sure it would stretch sufficiently for the baby or two who would very soon fill it. "I think my niece or nephew, or perhaps a set of both, would look positively darling in this one. And stay warm too."

All three sisters giggled.

"One infant will surely keep us all busy enough until yours comes along." Kat winked at Nell, and gave her a knowing smile.

"I like both dresses." Ida reached for Kat's hand and looked at the price tag on the hem of the sleeve. "I'll buy them both for you."

Kat shook her head. "I don't need either dress. Morgan can buy me one, and Vivian will probably want to make one for me. I certainly don't need four."

"Don't be silly. Of course you do." Ida opened her reticule. "Besides, what's the point in being a successful businesswoman if I can't share the wealth?"

Nell moved to Kat's back and began unhooking the bodice. She leaned toward her sister's ear. "You know you can't win this battle, right?"

Kat drew in a deep breath. "I can't seem to warm up this winter, so if you insist on buying me a dress, I'll take this green one."

"I do."

"Then thank you."

Nell had just followed her sisters out of the dressing room when Tucker Raines sauntered through the front door of the clothing store.

He removed his felt hat and dipped his squared chin. "Ladies." He may have been speaking to all of them, but it was Ida he seemed to be studying. "Did you receive my note?"

"I did." Ida's words matched the stiffness in her back.

"And?"

"Apology accepted."

"Good. Does that mean you won't be avoiding me at church tomorrow?"

Ida raised her chin a notch while Nell tried not to laugh. "Does it mean you won't embarrass me in front of Mr. Wagner?"

"You intend to see him socially again?"

"I do."

He rubbed his neatly trimmed beard. "Then I'll do my best to behave myself."

Ida's chin quivered as if she were trying not to smile while Kat and Nell covered theirs. "Good enough." She reached out and shook his hand. "Friends."

It could have just been her imagination, but Nell was pretty sure the man's sculpted shoulders sagged. As soon as Tucker let go of Ida's hand, which he seemed reluctant to do, Ida marched to the cash register and began fumbling in her reticule. But her furtive glances toward the glass door as Tucker stepped outside betrayed Ida's declaration of mere friendship. And when the ice man turned back around and caught her looking, his full-face smile said he knew it too.

"And what will you have tonight, Mrs. Cutshaw?"

"Um." Kat looked up from the Third Street Café's paper menu at the feather that stuck out of Maggie's single white braid. "It all looks so good that I'm having trouble deciding what to order."

Across the table, Morgan leaned forward. "You don't feel like the veal cutlet this time?"

Kat felt her nose wrinkle. She shook her head. These days her appetite, at best, was as unpredictable as Colorado's weather patterns.

Maggie pressed her hand to the red gingham apron at her stick-thin middle. "I was like that when I carried my young uns. All five of 'em. Felt like I could eat a whole menu's worth of food, but not all of it sounded appealing."

"Exactly." Kat glanced back down at the listing.

"Me and the mister aim to please, especially where the appetites of growing babies are concerned. He'll make you most anything that sounds good to you."

"Cabbage salad?" Kat asked.

The feather bobbed. "He can do it."

"A sausage patty?"

Maggie pulled a small notepad and stub of a pencil from her apron pocket. "I can tell I best be writing this down. Memory's not what it used to be. So far we have cabbage salad and a sausage patty."

"And pickled beets."

Morgan clapped his hand over his mouth.

"Two buttermilk pancakes." Ignoring Morgan's poor attempt to stifle a chuckle, Kat took one last look at the menu. "And a dish of banana pudding with raisins on top."

Morgan gathered their menus and handed them to Maggie. "I'm sure Fred has a couple of things left in the kitchen." He flashed that dimpled grin she loved. "Perhaps a sponge or a butter dish?"

Feigning annoyance, Kat slapped her husband's shoulder and looked up at Maggie, whose laugh reminded her of a train whistle. "That should be enough to get me started," Kat said, smiling.

Still laughing, their waitress took the menus from Morgan and darted to the kitchen.

Kat smoothed her napkin over her lap. Curiosity ate at her, and her sisters had encouraged her to talk to Morgan about his past, so she drew in a deep breath, trying to bring some order to her questions before opening her mouth. "I was wondering...was Opal like this? Sick, then eating you out of house and home?"

"Eggs and peanut butter with apple slices seemed to be all Opal wanted. She wasn't sick to her stomach but for the first couple of weeks." Morgan reached for his coffee mug and took a drink, never taking his gaze away from Kat. "Our experience—yours and mine—is different. Brand new."

Her eyes brimmed with unbidden tears. "That's good." Barely able to push the words out past the lump in her throat, Kat looked across the table at her beloved husband. "I'm glad to hear it. I wouldn't want you to get bored with me."

Morgan set his cup down and cleared the path between them. "It'll never happen." He reached across the table and, starting at her elbows, slid his hands down her arms until their fingers intertwined. "You're anything but predictable, Mrs. Kat Cutshaw. And you could never be boring."

When Kat heard a familiar throat-clearing, she looked up. Ida approached their table with Colin Wagner at her side. Smiling, the dapper attorney held his hat in his left hand, while her older sister worried her jaw. Nervous, or just uncomfortable? Kat wasn't sure.

Ida smoothed a curl at her ear. "Seems my timing still needs work."

Kat felt her face flush as Morgan let go of her fingers and stood to shake Mr. Wagner's hand.

"Good to see you, Colin." Morgan gave Ida a quick nod. "You too, Sis." Pointing toward their booth, Morgan returned his attention to Ida's escort. "There's plenty of room here at our table, and I wouldn't mind sitting beside my wife. Won't you two join us?"

"A generous offer, but no. Thank you." Colin shifted his gaze to a corner table. "We have a more private table awaiting us."

Ida gawked at him, then she looked at Kat, her blue eyes wide, and her shoulders lifted in a shrug.

Colin glanced down at the bowler in his hand. "Another time, perhaps."

"Of course." Morgan dipped his chin in Kat's direction. "Enjoy your evening."

Ida nodded as Colin hooked her elbow and guided her away from their table.

"That was a bit surprising," Kat whispered. "She mentioned nothing about it during our outing today."

Morgan sat back down across from her. "You don't approve?"

"I don't know what I think." Kat reached for her glass of milk. "He's a nice-enough man."

"A man who brings her to dinner at the Third Street Café. I recall dinner here was our first private dining experience as well."

"He does have good taste in women and in dining establishments." Kat winked at her husband. "I will give him that much credit."

"And he knows of your sister's ambition and doesn't seem intimidated by it."

Kat unfurled her napkin on her slowly shrinking lap. "I still don't know if I like the idea of them. Is there such a thing as a man being too nice?"

Morgan shook his head. "We men can't win with you sisters, can we?"

"I suppose not. We look out for one another. Is that so bad?"

"No. But I'm not so sure Ida appreciates being *looked out* for."

"You're right about that." Kat peeked at the table in the corner.

"Is that Ida's happy laugh, or is she frowning?" Morgan moved his head to block Kat's view.

"Very funny." Kat leaned back against the cushioned seat. "I just thought it'd be Tucker Raines and Ida."

"I like Tucker too, but ultimately—"

"It's up to Ida. Yes, I know."

Hopefully she'll choose the right man.

TWENTY-SEVEN

here had the month of November run to? Ida had been so busy settling into her job and watching her bank account grow that Thanksgiving Day had snuck up on her. Settling into her chair at Hattie's table, she watched Tucker set a roasted turkey in front of Colin Wagner, who sat at the end, opposite their hostess.

"Shall we pray?" Morgan held his hands out to Kat and Hattie, and Ida accepted Colin's hand on one side and Faith's on the other. Then she squeezed her eyes shut and bowed her head.

I know I have much to be thankful for, Lord, but not this.

She knew Miss Hattie had invited Colin to Thanksgiving Dinner. He'd mentioned it during their supper with Mollie and Charles last Friday night. Sunday her landlady told her she had asked Tucker Raines to join them too since he didn't have any family in town either. She'd seen Tucker often at church and around town, but they hadn't really spoken beyond polite greetings—not since she'd accepted his apology. Now sitting across the table from her, he seemed bent on being more than just a friend, whether or not that was his intention.

"Amen."

Faith let go of Ida's hand long before Colin did and slipped a creased piece of paper onto Ida's lap.

The teacher had passed her a note? As discreetly as possible, Ida opened it with one hand and glanced at the writing. Larger, neater penmanship would've been nice. As it was, Ida couldn't make out the words. Did she have sleep in her eye? A rip in her dress? What could be so important that Faith felt she had to share her message right now?

She couldn't read the note here without causing a scene. Not with Colin watching her every move. It would have to wait. She spread her napkin over the note to be sure she didn't spill gravy on the handwriting.

"Land sakes!" Hattie scanned the table. "We can't very well have a turkey supper without my cranberry sauce."

Clutching the napkin, hiding the note, Ida jumped up from her chair. "I'll get it."

Colin stood with her, and his gaze fastened on her napkin. Had he been watching her? "Your napkin was personalized?"

He'd obviously seen the note. When Colin reached for her napkin, Ida pulled it down to her side. "It's nothing." Or something about Faith's fascination with Tucker Raines. Either way, it was none of Colin Wagner's concern.

"If it's nothing, you won't mind if I see it." Colin's voice was soft as a rose petal, in sharp contrast to the severity that hardened his hazel eyes.

Ida nodded. "I do mind." She willed her wobbly legs to move and turned to leave the room. Before she could do so, Colin grabbed a corner of the napkin.

When she didn't let go, Colin peeled the napkin back from the slip of paper and read just above a whisper, *"You're making a mistake."* He yanked the note free and looked down the table at Judson. "Is this some kind of joke? You're responsible for this, aren't you?"

Judson planted his hands on the table's edge. "I don't know anything about a note."

Apparently, her brother-in-law had made enemies of both Mollie O'Bryan *and* her attorney. But what could have possessed the otherwise poised Colin Wagner to be so rude? And why did he suspect the warning had been meant for him?

Faith snatched the napkin from Ida and spread it out on her lap in another display of uncharacteristic courage. "The note wasn't meant for you, Mr. Wagner." She scooped a spoonful of mashed potatoes onto her plate.

Ida stared down at the schoolteacher, trying to hide her surprise. This Faith wasn't the same timid girl who'd come to Ida's bedroom to ask her about tutoring Delos Updike.

Colin drew in a deep breath, his features softening as he turned his attention to the hostess. "I don't know what came over me, Miss Hattie. Perhaps I've heard too many disparaging comments about lawyers lately." He shifted his gaze to Ida. "Please accept my apologies. All of you."

Hattie nodded and took the dish of spiced green beans from Morgan. "Apology accepted."

While the others returned to the meal, Ida dashed out of the room and into the kitchen, stopping just short of the icebox. She bit her lip, trying to quell the tears that threatened to topple her.

If the note had come from Judson or Kat or Miss Hattie, Ida could assume the warning pertained to her work. But she knew Faith referred to her choice of men.

"I agree with her."

Ida jumped at the sound of Tucker's voice. "You would." She didn't bother to turn around. Instead, she opened the icebox, letting its coolness envelope her.

"The question is, do you?"

"I haven't decided yet." Ida retrieved the bowl of cranberry sauce and shut the door. She moved toward the dining room, careful not to meet Tucker's eyes or touch him as she passed, knowing full well that she'd made her decision.

What she didn't know was how she was going to live with it.

TWENTY-EIGHT

he fragrant scent of mulled apple cider hung in the air as Ida studied the dining-room table in Hattie's boardinghouse. She and her sisters had organized an array of baskets, oranges, nuts, and sacks of hard candy in groups. The table was long and the room wide—the perfect place for their Christmas project.

"I can't believe it's the middle of December already." Kat sat sideways at one end of the table. Some women didn't show until late in pregnancy, but Kat wasn't one of them. Everyone had a task, and Kat's job was to string the name tags Hattie had made onto eight-inch pieces of Christmas-plaid ribbon.

"I agree." Faith wrapped the colorful strips of fabric around the basket handles and then passed them to Ida. "Seems like just yesterday we were all gathered here for…"

"Thanksgiving dinner." Ida checked the number of family members noted on the name tag, then added the appropriate number of oranges and hard candies to the package. "I'm not going to wash your mouth out with lye soap for speaking of it."

Tucker had been the last person to mention the note to her. Not even Colin or Miss Hattie had said any more about it. Not that she'd given either of them much opportunity.

She set the basket at the end of the table in front of Nell, who added a handful of walnuts and pecans.

Hattie huffed in her seat at the opposite side of the table. "You think time escapes you now. When you reach my age, time flies by like it's plastered to the front of a speeding train." Their gray-haired friend topped off each basket with Nell's handiwork—a calligraphy printing of a verse from the second chapter of Luke.

Hattie was right. Ida counted out four oranges for the next basket. Time did seem to pass much faster now than it had when she was a girl. She'd already been in Cripple Creek nearly three months, and she'd finished the last of her eight tutoring sessions with Delos that morning.

This would be her best Christmas since her mother's death, even if Vivian and Father wouldn't be here. She had pursued her dream of being a businesswoman and found success. She had money enough to purchase baskets, oranges, nuts, and hard candies for twenty-five needy families, money enough to buy proper gifts for those she loved.

Her insides quivered with anticipation. She couldn't remember being this excited about the prospect of watching friends and family open their gifts since her mother's last Christmas, when Ida had made her first and only lap quilt and wrapped it for her mother.

"Ida."

She looked at Nell. Blond curls framed a look in her sister's blue eyes that always meant she was up to mischief. "Nell?"

"Kat and I saw Tucker in town this morning."

Up to mischief and *matchmaking.*

"Is that so?" Ida counted out six oranges for the Nash family.

"He sent his regards."

Ida refused to give Nell the satisfaction of having piqued her curiosity.

Instead, she added candy to the basket before passing the gift on to Nell, along with a raised brow that normally gave her sister pause.

Hattie cackled like a mother hen. "Isn't that odd." She smiled across the table at Ida, a twinkle in her eyes. "I saw Mr. Wagner in the Cash and Carry this morning. And he too sent his regards."

Hattie was obviously immune to any hints passed through raised brows, frowns, the shaking of one's head. Even words didn't seem to deter the woman.

Since the note incident, they'd all kept quiet about Tucker and Colin, including Faith. Apparently, whatever matchmaking truce Ida had earned had expired that afternoon.

"I'm not the only single woman in the room, I'll have you know." Ida pinned Hattie with her best "got you" grin.

Or so she thought. Hattie waved an arthritic finger at her. "Oh, no you don't. I'm too old."

Huffing, Ida faced Faith.

"Not me either. I'm too young." The teacher tied a fluffy bow at one end of a basket handle. "I thought Tucker might be the one for me…"

Yes, Faith had most certainly stepped outside her shell in the past several weeks.

"Until the concert, that is. Mr. Raines all but came unraveled seeing you with Mr. Wagner. He wasn't too comfortable Thanksgiving Day either."

Imagine what they'd say if they knew what Tucker had said to her in the kitchen. He hadn't said *he* was the right one, only that he believed seeing Colin was a mistake. That was probably the only reason he'd said what he did at the opera house. He didn't approve of Mr. Wagner.

"I suppose that settles it," Kat piped up. "If Hattie is too old for love, and Faith is too young, that only leaves you for us to work on."

Shaking her head, Ida counted out six Tootsie Rolls. She knew something her matchmakers didn't know, and it wasn't her place to tell them they were wasting their time. Tucker wasn't interested in marriage. Not to anyone here. His place was in California, preaching and taking care of his sister. He'd been ready to take off that day she saw him in the post office. According to Miss Hattie, Tucker had finished building the icehouse. Which meant it wouldn't be long before he'd have the business thriving and he'd be free to leave.

A knock on the back door set Hattie in motion. She turned and tossed words over her shoulder. "That would be the extra block of ice I ordered."

Tucker. Ida straightened and smoothed her dress. But it wasn't Tucker's voice she heard in the kitchen. Or his face she saw in the doorway moments later.

"I offered Otis a cup of cider." Hattie cleared a spot for the big man at the table.

Ida looked at Kat, who gave her a knowing gaze and tapped her sealed lips. *As if her not saying anything would make a difference.*

Ida sighed and nodded. She was disappointed Tucker hadn't come, and there was no point in denying it. Especially since she seemed to be the only one avoiding the obvious—he had become much more than a mere curiosity to her.

Faith was right. She'd made a mistake thinking she could avoid developing feelings for the brown-eyed ice man by socializing with Colin Wagner.

TWENTY-NINE

*M*onday morning, Tucker climbed onto the wagon seat and directed Titan and Trojan away from the door of the boxcar. The load was lighter than normal—just ten iceboxes, no ice—but the horses still lurched through the slick, wet gravel.

Tucker drove the company's oldest ice wagon up Bennett Avenue, a much different experience with two feet of snow on the ground. The balmy Decembers in Stockton hadn't given him any experience to draw on when it came to wrangling a team at an elevation of nearly ten thousand feet with snow blowing down his collar.

Having lived in Cripple Creek for three months, Tucker could see why his father had chosen this place for his fresh start. The valley was majestic, with true changes in the seasons—autumns of golden aspens and winters of white nightcaps on the peaks standing guard over it.

When he turned the horses up the hill toward the church, the wagon took a sudden slide to the left, jarring Tucker out of his thoughts. He pulled hard on the reins to keep the rig on the roadbed. How had his father managed last winter while sick? Otis hadn't said how his father coped with the weakness of his health, probably out of respect, but no doubt the faithful employee and family friend had carried the bulk of the business on his shoulders.

The couple who owned the haberdashery on Bennett Avenue greeted Tucker from the boardwalk, and he waved in return. They'd ordered an icebox for their home, and it was scheduled to arrive in next week's shipment. Once Tucker and his crew—he'd hired three new employees—had finished building the icehouse, he'd spent a lot of time in town in the role of salesman. He'd been able to order iceboxes by the boxcar load with the money from the sale of additional stocks, and hoped that his new customers would be able to pay for the boxes and the continued deliveries of ice.

If so, he'd have the accounts at both the asylum and the sanitorium brought up to date by the middle of February.

Thank You, Lord.

The parsonage was Tucker's first delivery stop of the day. He'd no sooner reined the horses in at the hitching rail when Reverend Taggart stepped out the front door, wearing a knit cap that made him look like a sausage wearing spectacles.

"Good morning, Reverend." Tucker waved.

"And to you."

After securing the reins, Tucker shook the reverend's hand. Taggart stood at the side of the wagon while Tucker pulled out a polished oak icebox and steadied it on the hand truck.

"I have something I want to talk to you about." The reverend removed his spectacles. "I hoped you'd have time to sit with a cup of coffee and have a few words."

Tucker knew what the reverend wanted to discuss with him. Two months had passed since he and Colin Wagner had asked him to think about taking the pastor's position in January. He'd agreed to pray about it and to read the Scriptures during the service each week since, but he hadn't given either of the men an answer.

Seven weeks had passed since the scene at the opera house, and Tucker still couldn't erase the image of the attorney in tails and a top hat looking like he owned Ida Sinclair. But it was the man's fixation on Miss Dunsmuir's note to Ida that troubled him the most.

"Tucker?"

"Sorry. A bit distracted today."

Taggart nodded.

"I still don't have an answer for you, but coffee sounds real good." Tucker pushed the hand truck up the slushy walkway and into the kitchen, where the aroma of fresh-brewed coffee was enough to fight the chill in his bones. Once he'd set up the icebox, he and the reverend carried steaming mugs to the parlor. Between the rich warmth of the brew and the heat from the well-stoked parlor stove, Tucker found he wasn't at all anxious to head back outside. He settled into a floral armchair across from the reverend and lifted the mug to his mouth.

"As you know, I've been called to another church." Taggart set his cup on the side table between them. "I understand you're not convinced taking over the church here permanently is in God's plan for you."

Tucker nodded, then took a long drink of coffee.

"But I hoped I could talk you into filling in for me on the twentieth." The pastor sat back in his chair with his fingers intertwined above his belly and looked directly at Tucker. "I need to finalize my housing arrangements in New York this week, and I can't be here for Sunday services."

"This coming Sunday?"

"I realize that's not much time to put together a sermon, but—"

"You haven't even heard me preach."

"But I do know your former landlord in Stockton." A grin lit Taggart's blue eyes.

"You know Pastor Bill?"

"Bill Hutchinson and I went to seminary together at Auburn." The reverend retrieved his cup. "And my sister heard you preach at camp meetings in Watsonville this past spring. The way she raved about you made me a little jealous. She never goes on about my preaching like that."

"I wouldn't feel too bad. Sisters are that way. Willow never seems all that impressed with my oratory skills either."

Tucker realized he'd referred to Willow as if nothing were wrong with her. The three reports he'd received from the asylum had actually convinced him she was on the mend.

"I'll do it." Tucker set his empty mug on the table. He missed preaching much more than he missed the lower elevation, the docile winters, and the traveling from town to town, and filling in for Reverend Taggart this Sunday would give him the opportunity to preach without having to commit to a steady pastorate. He leaned forward, his hands on his knees. "You mind if I ask *you* something?"

"Fire away."

"How long have you known Colin Wagner?"

"First met Colin at the Third Street Café, summer before this last one. That's when I invited him to church. He's been pretty regular ever since. Became a deacon after the first of the year." The reverend drained his cup. "Why do you ask?"

Tucker breathed a prayer and leaned forward, hoping the concerns he was about to share were unfounded.

THIRTY

*I*da tugged the sleeves of her new silk shirtwaist. She had expected to see Tucker behind the pulpit reading Scripture, as he'd been doing every Sunday for the past two months. Hearing him preach that morning was a surprise. At least Colin had made himself easier to avoid by failing to show up at church. Tucker Raines, on the other hand, was front and center.

"I'll be the first to admit failure. I have failed to lean first on my faith in Jesus Christ. Still do fail at it more often than I care to admit." Tucker looked out at the congregation as if they were all sitting in Hattie's parlor, and he'd just told them a sweet story. "But I desire to keep Jesus first in my heart. Until we know Jesus through faith in Him—through a relationship with Him, God is a mere notion to us. Not a personal reality."

His Bible lay open in front of him. He'd read from the book of Matthew about seeking the kingdom of God first. "Losing my brother-in-law to the river and watching my sister suffer in the loss caused me to struggle in my faith. My sister's needs and my preaching at camp meetings competed for first place. Who or what is first in your life?"

Ida swallowed hard, but her answer wasn't so difficult, or terrible.

God had blessed her with a dear family and she worked hard to do right by them. A twinge of concern for Vivian swept over her. She'd add writing a letter to her youngest sister to her list of activities for this afternoon. And God had given her a mind for business, and she was using it. Not many people could say they were using the talents God gave them *and* caring for the people He had placed in their lives.

"Hardships serve to educate our faith and make it real. But First Corinthians 15:57 tells us: 'But thanks be to God, which giveth us the victory through our Lord Jesus Christ.' If you haven't already, you will come to a crossroads that requires you to dig soul-deep and make a deliberate choice to trust God."

As soon as Tucker had finished his sermon and they'd sung the last hymn, Ida stepped out into the aisle and turned toward the door, hoping to rush out before Tucker made his way back.

"Miss Sinclair?"

She'd been listening to that voice for the past hour. She turned toward him. "Mr. Raines. Or do we call you Pastor Raines? Reverend Raines?"

"Reverend Taggart is out of town this week, but he's still the pastor here. And I'm still Tucker."

Morgan stepped out into the aisle and shook hands with Tucker. "Do you have plans for Christmas dinner on Friday?"

The preaching ice man gazed at Ida. Why did he have to look at her that way? Like he'd forgotten about her being with Colin at the opera house and instead remembered their time together at the creek and missed it as much as she did. Or maybe he was still waiting for her to admit that seeing Colin had been a mistake.

"Kat and I would be pleased if you'd join the family at our house for Christmas."

Tucker didn't look at Morgan. Instead he held Ida's gaze. Was he asking her permission to join her family?

"By all means." Ida tucked a curl behind her ear. "Join us. Hattie will be there too, but Faith will be in Denver with her family." She paused. "No note passing."

His smile was too warm. Thankfully, he quickly turned his attention to Morgan. "I'd like that. Thank you." He tugged his jacket straight. "Now if you all will excuse me, I'll go greet the others."

Ida nodded, suddenly aware that her resolve to avoid Tucker was walking away with him, and she looked forward to seeing him again on Christmas Day.

Late Monday morning, Ida watched Colin Wagner walk through the office door with his usual pinstriped swagger. Sighing a long-overdue prayer, she closed the ledger she was working on.

Apparently, she'd come to one of the crossroads Tucker Raines had talked about. Her relationship with Colin hadn't felt like it required a soul-deep search, but it hadn't felt right either. Even before Faith's note. And it wasn't fair to him that she kept letting him believe there could be more between them than friendship. Even the business side of things would need to change.

Colin removed his bowler and glanced at Mollie's closed office door.

"She'll return in a few minutes." Ida swallowed hard against the uneasiness in the pit of her stomach.

Colin took slow steps toward Ida's desk. "I'm not here to see her."

Ida stacked the files and ledgers on her desk. "I'm on my way out soon as well. Mr. Leonard is expecting me and my steno pad at the railroad office."

"I've missed having you come to the office. Mollie just isn't as pleasant to work with." He set his hat on her desk. "You've been avoiding me."

"I've been busy."

"Avoiding me."

Ida forced herself to meet his steadfast gaze. "Yes, I have been avoiding you."

"Because of my little outburst at Miss Hattie's over Thanksgiving dinner? Because of the note? Or because of him?"

Ida stood, but remained behind her desk. "I can't see you anymore. Not socially." She drew in a deep breath. "Nor can I work in your office."

Colin placed his hands on her desk and leaned toward her. "I know your type, Ida Sinclair."

"My type?"

He straightened, his gaze fixed on her and his hazel eyes narrowing. "You can't convince me that you'd prefer to settle for a preaching ice man rather than accept the hand of a successful law counselor."

Ida glanced up at the wall clock. "You should leave before one of us says something we'll regret."

He swept his bowler off the desk. "You'll regret turning me away."

"That sounded like it could be taken as a threat, Mr. Wagner."

"Merely stated a fact. You deserve better." After setting his hat on his head, Colin hooked his thumbs in his jacket lapel. "Good day, Miss Sinclair. Call me when you come to your senses."

The door closing behind him was music to her ears. And if she had any strength in her knocking knees, she'd rush over and lock it. Instead, Ida sank into her leather chair. She laid her head against the back of it and stared up at the embossed tin ceiling.

First, Bradley Ditmer had proven himself untrustworthy, and now she questioned Colin Wagner's integrity. Which brought her own dependability into question. She was apparently a terrible judge of character. At least where men were concerned.

So what did that say about Tucker Raines? Was she wrong about him as well?

THIRTY-ONE

wo days after preaching in Reverend Taggart's church, Tucker
wheeled another icebox into the rock-lined icehouse. He'd just
received another shipment of eight iceboxes on the morning train. Cripple
Creek had grown to include many more doctors, lawyers, mine investors,
and business owners. Word had gotten out about the new icehouse and his
icebox business.

His business.

Tucker rolled the box into its temporary resting place. While he slid it
off the hand truck beside three other boxes, he chuckled at the bittersweet
and ironic thought of this being *his business.* Building an icehouse and selling iceboxes in this Colorado town's boom time had been his father's dream.
Not his. His own ideas for his future had begun and ended with caring for
his sister and serving God as a traveling preacher.

My thoughts are not your thoughts, neither are your ways my ways.

That truth had never felt more real to him than it did now, as he lived
out his father's dream. In thinking about what his father had wanted and
what he would do if he could, Tucker experienced a sense of fulfillment he
hadn't felt since Sam's death. Even when preaching and winning souls to
Christ.

God had blessed his efforts. No, God had blessed his obedience to come and step into his father's shoes, whether his father wanted him here or not. And God had blessed him with more than the sale of stocks, new customers, and a steady income. He'd hoped and prayed for success in the business so he could take care of his family.

He hadn't thought to hope and pray for friends in this new assignment, and yet God had set him down smack in the middle of a community of friends who had embraced him. Otis. Hattie. Mr. and Mrs. Jing-Quo. Reverend Taggart. Morgan Cutshaw and Judson Archer.

And then there were the Sinclair sisters. Although his heart wanted to believe there was hope of more than mere friendship ahead for him and Miss Ida Sinclair, right now it seemed a lot of obstacles stood in their way. He'd seen how well she fit in with the professionals at the opera house, and he'd seen the way she looked at him after Sunday's service. She'd greeted him with more of a glare, not a glad-to-see-you smile.

Only God knew for sure what lay ahead for either of them. After his dizzying time at the creek with her, which had been capped off with a disturbing night at the concert, Tucker had added the matter of their relationship to his prayer list. It remained there. Near the top.

Tucker was on his knees in the back of the wagon, reaching for an icebox, when he heard snow-crunching footsteps approaching. He tugged the box to the edge of the wagon and fought with the canvas flap to climb out.

"Mr. Raines?"

Tucker turned to look at the postmaster's oldest boy. The envelope he clasped in his hand caused Tucker's mind to swirl with possibilities—none of them good. His father's life teetered at the top of a list of reasons for a hand-delivered letter.

"Archie?" Tucker choked out the name.

"Pa sent me. Said you'd want to see this right away." Archie shoved the envelope at him.

Tucker shed his gloves and attempted to set them on the tailgate of the wagon, only to miss and drop them in the snow. He stared at the handwriting on the envelope. The letter hadn't come from a doctor at the sanitorium. The loud sigh escaping his lips seemed to have risen from his feet, gaining strength on its way up.

"Was Pa right?" Archie wobbled back and forth, a telltale sign of his gangly growth-spurt stage. "Is it important?"

Tucker blinked hard against the tears stinging his eyes and nodded. "It's very important. The letter is from my sister." Not taking his eyes off her distinct pre-illness penmanship, Tucker pulled a coin from his pocket and handed it to Archie. "Thank you. Tell your father I said thank you."

"I will." With a smile on his freckled face, the boy fisted the coin and took off toward Bennett Avenue.

His hands shaking, Tucker left the gloves, the hand truck, and the last icebox where they lay and climbed up onto the wagon seat. The work to be done, even the cold air chilling his nose, didn't matter. He carefully opened the envelope as if it were a treasured artifact. Pulling out the thin piece of stationery, Tucker drew in a deep breath before he began to read.

My dear brother,

Willow had actually written him a letter, called him brother. His heart raced.

I know what you did, Tucker.

His heart sank. Did she blame him? Was that why she couldn't speak to him all these many months? Had she finally written only to tell him so? No, she'd called him *dear* brother.

> I know you came every week. You brought me flowers and drawing pencils. You told me stories and sang me songs.

Tucker wiped the icy tears from his face. She knew, even if her attendant had been the one to tell her. Willow knew he'd been there. Knew he cared.

> Even more than that, dear brother, you brought me your love even when I couldn't give you anything in return.

Removing his hat, he lifted his face to sky. "Thank You for the strength to do that, Lord. Thank You."

> Tucker, I'm drawing again. And I'm counting the days until I can come see you in Colorado and I can sketch Pikes Peak.

Would he still be here by the time Willow could make the trip? He remembered Morgan's statement the first time he'd gone to Sunday supper at Hattie's. *"Don't be too surprised when you discover you don't want to leave Cripple Creek."* Almost prophetic.

> With an undying love,
>> Your Big Sis,
>> Willow Grace

"Thank You, Lord. Your mercy endures forever."

"You're praying out loud again."

The angelic voice drew his attention to the woman standing beside the wagon. Ida had been avoiding him. Why was she here? The icehouse was below the depot, not on the way to anywhere. She'd apparently come specifically to speak to him.

That realization sped his pulse as he looked into her royal blue eyes and hoped her reason was more personal than Hattie having a question about her new icebox or needing another block of ice; more personal than delivering a message for his stockbroker, Mr. Miller. More than anything else, though, he hoped she hadn't come to talk about Colin Wagner. It wasn't his place to discuss the man with her.

Unless she asked.

Ida glanced at the envelope. "More good news about Willow?"

"It's a letter from her, in her own handwriting."

"That's wonderful!" Ida's smile could've brightened the darkest night.

"Thank you." Tucker slid the letter into the envelope and put it in his coat pocket. He extended his hand to her, an invitation to join him.

After looking both ways, apparently satisfied no one else was watching, she placed a shiny patent leather–clad foot on the metal step above the wheel and accepted his help onto the seat beside him.

She twisted her gloved hands into a knot on her lap. "I'm on my lunch break, and I don't have much time." She pulled a pendant watch from her reticule and glanced at it. "It took me too long to decide to come talk to you."

"I'm glad you did."

"But I have only a few minutes left."

"May I drive you back to the office? We could talk on the way."

"I'd like that."

"I'll close up the wagon, and we'll go."

At the back of the wagon, Tucker retrieved his work gloves from the ground. He pushed the icebox to the corner, set the hand truck inside, and latched the tailgate closed. His hands shaking, he untied the reins from the hitching rail. He'd grown up in a house with females, but his mom and sister had never made his heart race or his hands shake.

Ida was watching him when he climbed onto the seat beside her, wishing he could read the look in her eyes. It didn't matter—hope took flight inside him anyway as he clicked his tongue and flicked the reins. Having her at his side felt right, even if it only lasted until they arrived at Mollie O'Bryan's Stenography Firm.

"I'm glad you stopped by the icehouse." He was repeating himself.

"I wanted to ask you a question."

He looked over at her and suddenly wished they were walking hand in hand instead of bouncing across Carbonate Street in a squawking wagon. "Anything."

"You're a preacher"—she glanced at the ice tongs at her feet—"and a businessman."

He nodded, without a clue where she was heading with such a statement.

"Judson doesn't approve of my working for Mollie O'Bryan. Kat's not excited about it either. Even Hattie expressed some concerns about the woman before my interview. People on the street shun us. Even a few folks at the church give me disparaging looks." Ida folded her hands in her lap and looked him in the eye. "So tell me, do you think it's wrong for women to be in business?"

Not exactly the topic he'd hoped to discuss with her, especially given her reaction to his business-related question at the bench. He'd need to proceed with caution. *Help me, Lord.*

Tucker guided the team around the corner and onto Bennett Avenue, pulling the reins to slow the horses. "Fundamentally, no."

Her lips pursed, Ida raised a thin eyebrow. "What does that mean?"

"It means I believe, based upon my study of Scripture, that it isn't the work or the money we earn that matters to God. It's the place our ambitions hold in our hearts and in our passions in relation to Jesus Christ." Tucker looked ahead through town, wishing there were more blocks between Fifth and First streets.

"So as a man of the Holy Word"—she watched him closely as if trying to see into his soul—"you don't think I'm doing anything wrong working in the world of business."

"Not in principle, no." He held her gaze. "Many stories in the Bible show God includes both the poor and the rich in His divine purposes."

"And what about women who pursue financial success and find it?"

"Are we talking about women in general? About Mollie O'Bryan? Or about you?"

Ida looked down at her gloved hands then back up at him. "What do you think of *me* making my own money?"

Tucker drew in a long, deep breath, taking time to gather his thoughts. Not an easy thing to do with her undivided attention fixed on him. "Have you read Lydia's story in the book of Acts? She was a seller of purple cloth—a successful businesswoman. A woman Paul found praying at the river with a group of women. She was a woman who followed Jesus." The wagon passed Third Street, and Tucker hoped he'd have enough time to bring this discussion to a satisfying conclusion.

"So God doesn't mind that I work in business and make money if I put Him first."

Tucker nodded. Had he said all that?

"Thank you."

"My pleasure." Tucker brought the wagon to a stop in front of the brick office building that housed Ida's office. He hopped down and hurried to her side of the wagon to offer her a helping hand. Once he let go of her hand, which he was reluctant to do, she hurried to the office door, then turned and waved.

"Good day, Tucker." She'd used his given name. "And thank you for the Sunday school lesson."

"Any time, Ida." Smiling, he watched her disappear into the office. Yes, without a doubt, God's ways were higher than his ways. His thoughts were most certainly higher too.

He could rest in God's ways, even where the mesmerizing Miss Ida Sinclair was concerned.

THIRTY-TWO

*T*he chalk in Mr. Miller's hand moved across the board especially fast today. Wednesday mornings at the stock exchange weren't normally this busy, but then, Ida hadn't had enough experience to rightly judge the ebb and flow. For all she knew, an escalation of buying and selling was a common occurrence the week of Christmas. Or perhaps this being the last trading week of the year spurred the frenzied activity. Mollie had gone to a meeting in Colin Wagner's office, so she wasn't there for Ida to ask. Whatever the cause, an unusually high number of arms reached for the ceiling and an added dissonance of shouts rang out.

"Miss Sinclair."

Ida recognized the gravelly voice. Picturing a short Ebenezer Scrooge with sleeves too long for his arms, Ida turned to face the smaller-than-life banker. "Mr. Updike."

Clearing his throat, he looked down at his feet and then up in her general direction. "Miss Dunsmuir said you were the one who helped my boy Delos with his multiplication tables."

"I was." He would no doubt have plenty to say about his boy not needing tutoring from the likes of *her*. Ida held her breath, anticipating the worst.

"Yes, well, thank you."

She released her breath. "You're welcome. I'm glad I—"

"Don't get me wrong, Miss Sinclair." He crossed his arms. "I still don't believe you or Mollie O'Bryan belongs here." He glanced around the room full of men.

"Good day, Mr. Updike." She'd spoken as softly as she could. The exact Scripture reference escaped her memory, but thanks to all the time spent gathered around the family Bible, the gist of the passage had not. *A soft answer turneth away wrath.*

Now if only she could remember that on a regular basis.

Ida headed for the one empty chair in the back row and watched an old miner walk toward her. She'd seen him here at least twice a week, sporting his usual attire—worn overalls and an equally worn canvas hat. Boney Hughes obviously wasn't intimidated or influenced by the dandies in the room.

"Hello, little lady," he said.

"Hello, Mr. Boney." She smiled, remembering looking up from the mud at his mule's snout.

"I've been watching you and Miss Mollie." He smoothed a leathery hand over his long beard. "You two ladies seem to have a special sense when it comes to buying and selling stocks."

"No, Mr. Boney, we just have a good job and attentive ears."

He chuckled, revealing more gaps in his teeth than a bow saw. "Well, maybe you'll find a ripe opportunity on the board today."

"I hope so. I do have my eye on some mine stock." According to the preliminary assay report she'd heard about, she could be buying her dream house before the end of the year.

"I'll let you get to it." Boney waved his hat at her and turned toward his corner at the back of the room.

Ida watched him go. He was a bit crusty, but fascinating.

Though not nearly as fascinating as the preaching ice man who studied Bible stories about successful women.

Tucker stepped out of the post office, studying the familiar handwriting on the envelope he carried. Another letter from Willow, only this time the envelope wasn't addressed to him.

Mr. and Mrs. William Raines

Not wanting to think about what that meant, he slid the envelope into his coat pocket and climbed up into the wagon beside his business partner.

Otis shifted on the seat and eyed him with his crooked brow raised. "You're not gonna read it?"

"It's not addressed to me."

Otis said nothing as he drove the team down to the end of Bennett Avenue, then up a dirt road toward a stand of pines in the hills.

The list of things Tucker appreciated about his friend was a long one, and the fact that Otis didn't feel a need to speak first and think later was near the top. Since they'd added employees and routes and diversified the company's offerings, they'd both been working on different wagons to train the others. Tucker had set today aside for the two of them to run deliveries together and then find a proper Christmas tree to take home to Abraham and his three younger brothers.

"You wanna talk about it?" Otis's dark eyes brimmed with compassion.

Tucker pulled his collar tight to ward off the chill, drew in a deep breath, and let it out slowly. "It's good news that Willow wrote to me, that she's writing to our parents. They'll be thrilled to hear from her."

Otis nodded and cocked his head. "But..."

"But she sent their letter here."

"You never told her?"

"Only that I had come to help the folks for a while. Not about my father's illness. She doesn't know they're living in Colorado Springs or about the sanitorium."

Otis clucked his tongue to spur the horses up a steep, snowy incline. "Guess you'll just have to take the letter to them."

It wasn't a question, and Tucker had no trouble filling in the blanks he saw on the man's face. *It is Christmas, after all.*

Perhaps his father's last Christmas. The finality in that thought hit Tucker in the pit of his stomach. Glancing up, he caught his friend's knowing gaze and nodded.

An hour later, they'd found the perfect four-footer, and the tree lay secured to the top of the wagon. Otis directed the horses back through town and toward Poverty Gulch, outside the city limits on the east end of Myers Avenue.

They'd just driven under the trestle when Tucker spotted Abraham running toward the wagon. "Mr. Tucker!"

Abraham's younger brothers, Isaac and Noah, followed closely on his heels. Nathaniel brought up the rear of the swarm, squirming in Naomi Bernard's arms. Otis steered the wagon to the front of the canvas tent-cabin. There was little chance the tree would fit inside the cabin and still leave room for anyone to live there. As it was, the home needed some repairs.

"Thought about using that bonus money you gave me to get lumber to make proper walls," Otis whispered, "but I'll be able to do a whole lot more when my mine stock pays off."

Tucker cringed. He didn't have anything against buying and selling stock if one had the extra money. Using money you needed to live on was a whole other matter. An opinion he'd kept to himself, and now he wondered if it had been the right thing to do.

A time to keep silence, and a time to speak.

He still had trouble discerning which was which.

"Welcome to our home." Naomi wore a frayed apron over a brown housedress. "Real nice day. It's warmed a little, and the boys can't stand being cooped up inside."

But they all needed heavier coats.

"Thank you. I feel the same way about being cooped up." Tucker bent down and tickled Noah in the ribs, earning a heartwarming giggle from the boy.

Otis jumped down from the seat and walked around to the back of the wagon. The three older boys scrambled to keep up with him. When he and Tucker had untied the ropes from the hooks at the corners, Otis hoisted the tree down from the top of the wagon. The boys cheered and ran back to their mother.

"Daddy's got a tree!" Isaac pumped his arms in the air.

Otis carried the tree to the center of the yard and set it up.

"Mighty fine tree, Mr. Bernard. Mr. Tucker." Smiling, Naomi shifted Baby Nathaniel to her other hip. "I guess I need to find a decoration." She ducked into the cabin.

The boys skipped and danced around the tree. Pure joy filled their faces as they shouted, "Merry Christmas! Merry Christmas to all!"

Tucker wiped a tear from his cheek. When had he moved so far away from the joy of Christmas? How had Christmas become more of a chore than a wondrous occasion?

My focus keeps getting foggy. Forgive me, Lord.

The neighboring tents and plank cabins emptied out. Children of all colors ran to join the Bernard boys in their impromptu Christmas celebration. Soon familiar tunes with unfamiliar words filled the air as families gathered together.

Naomi stepped out of her home carrying a cup of coffee and some freshly ripped strips of cloth. Looking in her eyes, he could tell she'd just sacrificed a calico dress for the festive occasion. "For you, Mr. Tucker."

He accepted the tin cup. "Thank you, Mrs. Naomi."

"Thank you." She met his gaze, her brown eyes full of gratitude. "I know you've been takin' good care of my Otis. My man likes workin' with you."

They watched as Otis held each one of his boys and six other children up in turn so they could drape the garland around the tree. Cloth striped the tree from trunk to tip. As Tucker drained his coffee cup, he heard the slap of wood and looked down at the ground. At the foot of the tree, a stringy-haired girl stacked four small logs together and then pulled a ragdoll from the pocket in her dress. She laid the baby on the makeshift manger, and patting the cloth doll, she began to sing a familiar refrain, but in Italian.

Away in a manger, no crib for a bed, the little Lord Jesus lay down His sweet head...

I love Thee, Lord Jesus...

Tucker knelt at the community campfire ring with Otis and set up logs for a fire. Christmas in Poverty Gulch wasn't about gifts you could wrap, but about unwrapping the gifts you had awaiting you.

Tucker added another log and glanced at his friend. "Think you could run things tomorrow without me?"

"I'd be happy to." Otis shook hands with Tucker.

"All right, then. It's settled. I'm taking the train to Colorado Springs first thing tomorrow morning."

Otis nodded, then smiled down at the boy who'd wrapped himself around his leg.

Tucker watched them and longed for his father's embrace.

THIRTY-THREE

*T*he tantalizing aroma of fresh coffee and frying bacon wafted up
from Hattie's kitchen and set Ida's stomach growling. The promise of breakfast made it difficult for her to concentrate as she pinned on her
new forest green hat. Or perhaps the real culprit making it so difficult to
focus was the memory of the man who had once been attached to the hatpin by way of his dirty boot.

Finally satisfied that her hat was secure, Ida grabbed her new beaded
reticule from the dressing table. She stepped out of her room a few minutes
early and smiled when she remembered it was the day before Christmas.
The pine-branch garland that spiraled down the banister added festive color
and a competing woodsy scent to the air. At the bottom of the staircase, Ida
went straight to the parlor for a quick peek at the decorations before going
to the kitchen. A tree nearly as tall as Tucker Raines stood in front of the
window, bedecked with a popcorn garland and candles in tin holders.
Boney Hughes and his sons had delivered the evergreen last evening. After
supper, she, Hattie, and Faith had sipped mulled cider while they decorated
the tree.

Faith had taken the early train to Denver that morning for a family
gathering. Ida planned to gather with her sisters that night at Kat's house.

Next year they'd celebrate in her new home with Vivian there. And perhaps with Father in '98.

The closer Ida came to the kitchen, the louder came Hattie's personal off-key rendition of "Joy to the World." Her landlady stood at the stove, wearing a red apron. A matching ribbon held her gray hair off her face.

"Good morning." Ida sniffed. "Sure smells good in here."

Hattie spun around, almost flinging bacon off the plate in her hand.

Ida took the platter from her and set it on the oak table in the corner, then poured two cups of coffee.

Hattie studied Ida's new red plaid dress and her green hat. "From the looks of things, I'd say you've been down at the millinery store again."

"I went on Saturday."

"Very festive."

"Thank you. I thought the outfit might add a little Christmas cheer to the office this morning."

"But you'll want to change into a housedress before *we* all begin our baking this afternoon." Hattie's silver eyes sparkled. The woman was like a mother hen, and Ida and her sisters and Faith, her little chicks. "This time last year, I didn't even know the Sinclair sisters existed." She set two plates full of hot cakes and bacon on the table while Ida grabbed the plate of biscuits from the warming oven.

They both sat down and bowed their heads. Hattie had just added the *Amen* to her blessing when a powerful knock on the front door quieted them both.

Hattie flipped a tartan-print napkin open on her lap. "Who would come calling before eight o'clock in the morning?"

"Perhaps it's Mr. Boney Hughes bearing more gifts."

Hattie swatted the air between them while a girlish grin thinned the wrinkles at her mouth.

"What? You can't swallow your own matchmaking medicine?" Giggling, Ida stood. "I'll tell Mr. Hughes you'll see him in the parlor."

At the front door, Ida pulled the curtain back on a side window, hoping she might see Tucker Raines. But neither Boney nor Tucker stood on the porch, and the woman who did looked every bit as rigid as a soldier marching into battle, except she held a folded newspaper, not a rifle.

Mollie O'Bryan had never come looking for her. Why would she, when Ida was due in the office in an hour's time?

A deep breath helped Ida regain her composure as she opened the door. "Mollie? Is something wrong?"

Her employer didn't wait for an invitation to enter the house. She stomped past Ida and into the entryway. If the wood beneath Mollie's feet had been even a smidgen weaker, Ida was sure she would've broken through the flooring.

"You care to explain this to me?" Mollie snapped the newspaper open and shoved it at her.

Ida closed her gaping mouth and stared at the front page. As incensed as Mollie was, her outburst had to be related to money. Ida scanned the assay reports. Then she saw the headline: "Olive Branch Breaks—New Stope in Blackmer's Mine a Bust."

"This isn't possible."

"So you're saying the report is a misprint?" Mollie's green eyes looked as if they could ignite into a blazing fire at any moment. "Or perhaps you'd rather I believe that a trusted assayer in Colorado Springs got it wrong?"

"I was in Mr. Blackmer's office and heard him say they'd found a rich vein of telluride ore in the new stope in his Olive Branch Mine."

"That's what you said." Mollie snatched the paper from her. "And I believed you."

"I saw the preliminary report myself."

"I had you buy thousands of shares based upon your word."

Ida drew in a deep breath and swallowed her indignation. "I didn't buy as much as you did, but I sank plenty into that stock as well."

Clenching her jaw, Mollie slapped the newspaper against her leg. "And that's supposed to make me feel better when I have to walk into the Exchange next week and dump them for less than I paid?"

Squaring her shoulders, Ida lifted her chin and met her employer's fiery gaze. "This is not my fault." She pointed a tremulous finger at the printed report. "Something isn't right, but it wasn't I who made a mistake." Unless she'd trusted the wrong person. Again.

Mollie huffed a sigh. "I want to believe you. I would if I didn't stand to lose thousands of dollars buying stock you said was going to pay off big."

"It should've."

"Who is it, dear?" Hattie sauntered into the hallway without her apron. "Miss O'Bryan? You're just in time for breakfast. Care to join us?"

"I was just leaving." Mollie marched to the door then spun around and glared at Ida. "Don't bother coming in today. I don't plan on being in a good mood."

"Very well." Ida held the door open for her. "I'll be in Tuesday, and I'll bring answers with me."

Though just how she expected to find answers to restore Mollie's faith in her, she didn't know.

The moment her employer stomped down the steps, Ida clicked the door shut and leaned against it.

Hattie joined her against the door, slid her hand over Ida's, and gave it a gentle squeeze. "Do you really believe you can find answers by Tuesday?"

"I have to. My job depends upon it."

It sounded like the assayer's office in Colorado Springs was a good place to start her search for answers. First thing Monday morning.

THIRTY-FOUR

*T*he day before Christmas, Tucker followed a nurse down the hospital corridor. He'd boarded the train in Cripple Creek that morning before dawn. At the depot in Colorado Springs, he'd taken the horse-drawn trolley to within a few blocks of the Glockner Sanitorium. Walking the last short distance allowed him to stretch his legs and steel himself for the greeting he expected from his father.

The nurse turned down a hallway that led to a glass door. "Our doctors believe fresh air is the best cure for tuberculosis."

He nodded. "My mother's letters said my father was tolerating the treatment well." Just thinking about sitting outside for hours at a time in the last week of December caused Tucker to shiver and button his coat.

She met his gaze. "You're a good son to see for yourself."

And what was he going to see? The scowl that had greeted him at the hospital when he'd first arrived in Cripple Creek, or the resignation he'd witnessed in his father's bedchamber?

When they arrived at the door, Tucker reached for the knob and swung it open. He and the nurse stepped out onto a wide terrace on the south side of the three-story hospital.

Tucker pulled the scarf at his neck tight. Delivering ice in below-freezing temperatures had sped his adjustment to winter in Colorado, but at work he kept moving. He didn't know how long he'd be able to last standing or sitting in one place, especially since he knew he could also expect a chilly reception from his father.

"Mr. Raines has a favorite chair." The nurse shaded her eyes with a fleshy hand. "He's usually easy to find out here."

Men—mostly older—bundled in red wool blankets sat scattered across the portico like terra-cotta flowerpots.

"That's him." The nurse pointed to two men, one of whom was short with silver hair. "Your father is sitting with his friend Mr. Mercer."

Both men sat at the front edge of the terrace with their feet propped on the railing. The bigger man resembled Tucker's father, but he was laughing, not coughing.

Tucker strained to hear what he and Willow used to refer to as the *choo-choo chuckle*. Too much time had passed since he'd heard William Raines laugh, and the sound warmed Tucker's soul, even if his nose was beginning to feel like a chip of ice.

The nurse cleared her throat. "If you'll excuse me, I need to go back inside for a meeting."

"Yes, of course. Thank you for your help."

"You're welcome. Family and visitors are an important part of the healing too." She reached for his hand and shook it. "Merry Christmas, Mr. Tucker Raines."

"Merry Christmas, ma'am."

The nurse bobbed her head and turned to go back inside.

Tucker tightened his spine and drew in a fortifying breath.

Here we go, Lord. Please go before me.

He was halfway to the railing when his father looked up, straight at him. William Raines didn't turn away. Nor did Tucker see a scowl in his father's expression. If he hadn't known better, he'd have thought his father was glad to see him.

"Tucker?" His father turned back toward the silver-haired man beside him. "Frank, I'd like you to meet my son, Tucker Raines."

My son.

Both men stood, his father easily four inches taller than his friend. The shorter man jabbed his hand at Tucker and shook hands with him. "Name is Frank Mercer, and you're the preacher."

Tucker looked at his father, who better resembled the man he'd known as a boy—laughing and looking proud to introduce him as his son.

"He was until three months ago when he came to Colorado to keep the ice business going." His father sounded proud too.

"Your father's been telling me all about you and your sister."

"He has?" Tucker thought his knees would buckle. "You have?"

"Yes, I have. And I'm glad you came."

Tucker was too and he wanted to say so, but the words were stuck in his throat.

Mr. Mercer pulled an empty rocker over from the corner. After all three of them were seated, his father's friend looked up at Tucker, a smile in his eyes. "Folks around here call me Pastor Frank."

"A pastor?" Tucker directed the squeaky question at the larger of the two men.

His father nodded. "Frank lives here in Colorado Springs."

Quick, soft footsteps on the concrete behind them turned their attention back toward the door. His mother fairly raced toward him, a smile owning her face.

Tucker stood and embraced her. She wasn't shaking and his father hadn't coughed once.

"Did you notice?" his mother whispered in his ear. "Your father has changed."

Nodding, Tucker motioned for her to take his chair.

His mother sat down. "I'm so glad you came." She glanced at her husband. "We both are."

"We've been talking about you." His father placed his hand on her knee. "About both of our children."

The word *change* didn't begin to describe what had happened with his father. You could *change* your clothes. *Change* hairstyles. *Change* where you lived. What he saw in his father was a total transformation.

Thank You, Lord.

Pastor Frank stood. "I have some more visiting to do, if you'll excuse me."

Tucker met the man's gaze. His spirit swam in the peace he saw in the blue eyes of his father's new friend. "Thank you."

Pastor Frank nodded. "My pleasure. Hope you can stay long enough for a chat later."

"Tomorrow's Christmas." His mother reached up and squeezed his hand. "I'm taking your father home to your aunt Rosemary's for the night. She'd be thrilled to see you. She has an extra bed in the sewing room. Can you spend the night?"

He hadn't planned on staying more than an hour or two. Hadn't expected to want to stay over, let alone be invited to.

Tucker nodded. "Looks like we'll have that chat, Pastor Frank."

"I'll look forward to seeing you when I've finished my rounds. Perhaps over supper." Pastor Frank regarded Tucker's mother with a slight bow. "Laurel."

Before walking away, he exchanged joyful gazes with Will Raines.

Tucker lowered himself into the chair beside his father. "I received a letter from Willow this week. She wrote it herself."

"She's well enough to write?" His mother scooted her rocker around. Tucker did the same to form a circle.

"She wrote one to you and Father too." Tucker reached into his coat pocket. He pulled out the envelope and handed it to his father. "It came yesterday."

The changed man ran a finger over the swirled penmanship, then brushed a tear from his face. Tucker couldn't remember ever seeing his father cry. Not even a hint of it.

"What did our Willow say?" His mother stacked her hands over her heart. "Open the envelope, Will."

His father pulled out the single piece of stationery and set the envelope on his lap. He cleared his throat, looked from his wife to Tucker, and then began to read.

Dearest Mother and Father,
    Where do I begin?
    I'll begin by saying I love you and I miss you.

Tears streamed down his father's cheeks in rivulets. "How can she ever forgive me?"

"You forgave me." Tucker looked straight into his father's eyes for the first time in more than two years.

"Sam's death wasn't your fault. And neither was Willow's inability to cope with it. I was so wrong. I've treated my"—he clasped his wife's hand, keeping his gaze fixed on Tucker—"our children so badly."

"I forgive you, Father." They weren't just words. He'd had several weeks of hoisting blocks of ice and sitting alone in his father's house to think and pray.

"Thank you, son. Sam was right."

"Sam?" Tucker glanced at his mother, hoping to see an answer written on her face, but he only saw the adoring look she focused on her husband.

"Sam came out to the icehouse the day before he died." His father paused. "Said he knew why I didn't understand about your commitment to the Lord, your wanting to be a preacher."

"He did?" Tucker blotted the fresh tears in his eyes.

His father nodded. "Sam said it wasn't time. Said there is a time for everything—that my understanding would come in time."

A time to weep, and a time for choo-choo chuckles.

His father began to read again, his voice soft with emotion.

I'm sorry. I know I put you through so much with my illness.

That's what the doctors here are calling my acute melancholia— a mental illness.

But I am improving every day.

His mother whimpered and sniffled, her hand on her husband's leg. He continued reading, apparently drawing strength from his wife—and his Lord.

I will see you soon.

Tucker's mother gasped and cupped her face. "Will, she said *soon.*"

His father's eyes glistened again, and he nodded. He trailed his finger down the page as if to find his place.

Tucker said there is much to sketch in Colorado. Majestic mountains. A creek. Birds.

I regret I won't be there in time for Christmas. My doctor says he wants to wait a few more weeks. Then he expects to release me.

In the meantime, please know I love you and I am counting the minutes until we are together again.

Tucker met his father's tender gaze. "Merry Christmas, Father."

"Merry Christmas, son." As the older Mr. Raines stood, his arms open, Tucker knew God had answered prayers he hadn't had the strength to even hope for, let alone utter.

THIRTY-FIVE

*I*da gazed out the parlor window. Her sister's new two-story house sat on a hilltop with generous views of the winter white town and surrounding mountains. Another eight inches of snow that morning had added weight to the tree limbs and thickened the white blanket on the ground. From where Ida stood at the piano, she had an unobstructed view of Carr Avenue and the walkway that led to her sister's front door.

Tucker Raines had accepted Morgan's invitation to join the family on Christmas Day. So where was he?

"Hark! The herald angels sing, 'Glory to the newborn King.'"

Hattie warbled the last sentence while the word *King* resounded in Judson's tenor voice.

Morgan played the final note on his square grand piano and looked up at Ida. "Looking for Mr. Raines, are we?"

Soprano, alto, and bass snickers echoed off the window. Bracing herself, Ida faced her family, counting Hattie among them. She wasn't sure her "big sister" stare would work on Morgan, but it was worth a try.

"Why, you're redder than the berry pie I brought for our supper, dear," Hattie said, her brows arched.

Ida already knew her stare wouldn't work on her landlady. She swallowed her indignation and focused on Morgan. "He accepted your invitation. And since he's not here, I'm merely concerned."

"The lady doth protest too much, methinks." Kat sat beside Morgan on the piano bench, a smirk curling a corner of her mouth.

Ida shook her head. Relentless teasers, every last one of them. Yes, she'd taught her sisters well.

"Tucker stopped by the hospital Wednesday evening." Morgan thumbed through a stack of sheet and pulled a page to the top, no doubt enjoying having her on a hook. "Said he was boarding the train to Colorado Springs the next morning—yesterday—to go see his parents."

"That's good." She looked down at the song sheet, hoping he'd catch her hint and begin playing the next carol. No such luck.

"He expected to be back in town last night," Morgan said, "but he could have decided to stay over."

Ida nodded. "I imagine that's what he did. So we have nothing to be concerned about."

A grin spread the freckles dotting Nell's nose. "*We* weren't concerned."

Her family was in rare form today, which meant it was best the preaching ice man remain in Colorado Springs for the day.

So why did the thought of not seeing him on Christmas Day bother her so?

∽∾

Tucker felt as if he and his valise were floating up Carr Avenue toward Morgan Cutshaw's new home instead of slogging through a fresh layer of snow. He'd spent yesterday visiting with his mother and father, first outside and then in a sitting room. After eating supper with Pastor Frank and learning more about his father's spiritual transformation, Tucker went with his mother and father to his aunt's house three miles from the hospital. He spent the night in the sewing room and awakened on Christmas morning to the sounds of his family stirring in the kitchen. They shared a hearty breakfast of corned beef and eggs with biscuits before he boarded the train bound for Cripple Creek.

On the way back, he wrote a letter to Willow, explaining the depths of his reasons for leaving California. He even told his sister the reasons he might like to stay in this particular mining town in Colorado.

It had been three days since he'd seen Miss Ida Sinclair. What was it she said her father liked to say? Something about missing someone you loved was like a burr in your union suit—a real motivator.

Motivated, he practically raced up the shoveled walkway to the front door of the Cutshaw home.

There, he'd admitted it—he loved Ida Sinclair.

Morgan opened the door. "Merry Christmas, and welcome to our home." He motioned Tucker inside.

"It's good to be here." Tucker looked down at his valise.

"We can put that here by the coat tree." Morgan took the bag and set it on the floor while Tucker shed his coat and hat. "How are your folks?"

"Very well. Thank you." Tucker followed his host down a wide entry hallway toward the sound of chatter and laughter. "I apologize for being late. I decided to stay over."

"I hoped you might."

They stepped into a well-appointed and well-peopled dining room. Thankfully, Colin Wagner wasn't present.

"Look who's here, everyone." Morgan glanced toward Ida, who sat between her two sisters. Tucker watched her turn pink from her pretty neck to her hairline and got the distinct impression they'd been talking about him and teasing her. Willow would have been doing the same thing—and might be, soon.

Morgan returned to his half-empty plate at the head of the table. Judson sat at the opposite end, and when Tucker met his gaze, Judson lifted the red napkin on the plate to his right and held it up in invitation.

Following a round of Christmas greetings, Tucker sat between Judson and Hattie and laid the napkin across his lap. Several hours had passed since breakfast. Seeing this fine meal and the company surrounding it, he realized his intense hunger. A platter of thick-sliced beef led a parade of foods that included whipped potatoes, gravy, cooked carrots, and what he recognized as Hattie's honey-wheat rolls.

"Oh, and you must try Ida's canned-pea salad." Hattie took a fluted bowl from Morgan and passed it to Tucker.

Cold peas with onion wouldn't normally appeal to him, but if Ida made the salad, he'd try it. He spooned a large helping onto his plate, hoping he liked it. "This all looks delicious." After offering a silent prayer of thanks, he took a generous bite of pea salad. Like her, Ida Sinclair's salad was a pleasant surprise.

While he ate and visited with what felt like his second family, he knew he wanted what Morgan enjoyed with Kat and Judson with Nell, and what George had experienced with Hattie in their marriage—the companionship of a woman he loved and who loved him. Although Ida had given him little encouragement in that direction, something inside him believed the oldest Sinclair sister could be *the one*. Swallowing a bite of spiced carrots, he looked across the table at her as if he expected to see the answer written on her face.

The blue eyes staring back at him didn't look away until he dropped his fork and it clanged against his plate.

Tucker managed to avoid further mishaps the remainder of the meal.

By the time he'd had his fill of berry pie with cream and enjoyed a full-bodied coffee, he felt satisfied on many levels.

Morgan tapped the rim of his cup with a spoon. "It's probably time we retire to the parlor for our family gift exchange."

On his way to the parlor, Tucker pulled the sack of gifts he'd brought from his valise. The parlor glowed with homey warmth. Handmade ornaments and strung popcorn added color to the tree, reminding Tucker of his evening at Poverty Gulch. The memories of the migrant families and descendants of freed slaves joining in a community Christmas celebration wasn't all that different from these festivities. Family and friends gathered in Jesus' name to commemorate His perfect gift to all people. However, the polished tin star on top of the tree and the wrapped gifts on a side table reminded him he was counted among the more fortunate, at least financially.

The women took their seats, and Tucker chose to sit at one end of a brocaded silk sofa, opposite Ida.

Once everyone had settled, Morgan opened his Bible. "Kat and I are so honored to have you all here with us for our first Christmas as man and wife." He reached for his wife's hand. "Our union is nothing short of a gift from God."

Tucker witnessed an exchange of intimate winks between Judson and Nell, and he leaned against the back of the sofa. Yes, he wanted a love ordained by God.

"Before we exchange gifts, Kat and I want to read from the second chapter of Luke in celebration of the greatest gift of all."

Jesus.

Following the reading of Scripture, Morgan closed the Bible and set it on a side table. "The greatest gift you can give us is your love and your presence. But I know some of you brought bonus gifts as well, so we'll let you do the distributing."

"I'll begin." Hattie bent over and pulled small fabric bags from a box under the parlor table next to her. "I have a sack of my butter brickle for everyone."

When Tucker received his sack, he peeked inside and sniffed. "You really know how to get to a man's heart, Miss Hattie. Thank you."

Next, Nell handed out scarves she'd knitted. His was a black-and-white herringbone pattern, very distinguished. Kat had written everyone a poem. The subject of his was, not surprisingly, a traveling preacher.

Ida stood. Reaching behind the tree, she lifted out packages wrapped in pieces of red or green velveteen wallpaper.

Kat unwrapped a new portable writing desk, and Nell a sewing box. Hattie received two new cylinders for her Edison phonograph. The gift created a welcome break in the stunned silence, as everyone chided Hattie about not having to listen to the same three songs anymore.

Ida gave Judson an imported ivory pen set, and Morgan a gold pocket watch chain. Even Morgan and Kat's yet-to-be-born baby received a gift—a folding go-cart baby carriage. It alone probably cost close to seven dollars.

They were all store-bought gifts, expensive gifts. Was Ida trying to earn their favor or trying to prove something?

Ida looked straight at him. "I have a gift for you too."

"You shouldn't have." He meant it.

Ida handed him a round box.

"I didn't expect—"

"Please open it." Ida stood at the end of the sofa.

Inside, he found a pure beaver stiff hat with a narrow, curled brim and black satin hatband. Tucker held the suit hat up for all to see, but he couldn't bring his voice to comment. He didn't wear suits as a general rule. She'd bought a hat for a dandy, not for him.

She didn't like his old hat. Of course she didn't. He was a traveling preacher. She was a city businesswoman. He wore chambray. She wore silk. Her hats seemed to flower and command attention. His, while comfortable, apparently didn't make enough of a statement. Or maybe she wasn't comfortable with the statement his hat did make.

"You don't like it." The disappointment in Ida's voice seared his heart.

"It's not that." He returned the hat to the box.

"Then what's the problem?"

Everyone else looked anywhere but at him. He didn't really like being himself at this moment, but she deserved an answer even if it made her mad. "You spent too much." Tucker glanced down at the fancy hat, then back up at her. "I brought you and everyone else an ice pick with the company's name on it."

Ida stiffened. "Oh."

"Oh, I did spend too much?" Or, *"Oh, you're only giving me an ice pick?"* Tucker didn't have to ask. He saw the answer written in the furrow in her brow and in the tightness of her jaw.

Ida Sinclair could never love a man who wore a simple hat and thought an ice pick was an appropriate gift. Colin Wagner was the type of man she'd shopped for. He would have no doubt welcomed such an extravagant gift.

"So God might not have a problem with women earning their own money, but you do." Sadness rather than anger clouded her face.

"It's not the woman, or the money. It's more a question of extravagance."

"I'm sorry."

"No, I'm the one who should be sorry. It's a nice gift. Thank you."

"You're right—the hat isn't appropriate for you. I'll take it back to the store." She took the hatbox and sat down as far from him as possible.

It didn't matter that his heart believed Ida could be the one for him. She would never believe it, especially now.

THIRTY-SIX

*C*hristmas night, Ida lay in the dark and listened to branches crack under their burden of snow. She knew how they felt. She'd been tossing and turning in her bed for two hours. Her past kept colliding with the present, both weighing heavy on her heart and mind.

Ambition had been her close companion since childhood, and now it seemed to have turned on her. At the age of twelve, Ida helped her sick mother as much as she could, and the sacrifice hadn't been enough. Her mother had died anyway, leaving her with Father and three younger sisters to care for. Then she'd done her best at the Alan Merton School of Business in Maine only to have Bradley Ditmer try to take advantage of her. For the past three months, she'd spent most of her time and energy pursuing the business opportunities afforded her here in Cripple Creek and made money in the pursuit.

And for what?

She'd dumped money into a bad investment. Mollie didn't trust her. Monday, she'd take the train to Colorado Springs to find out what had gone wrong with the assay, not knowing whether or not she could or would ever uncover the truth. In the meantime, she wasn't certain she'd have a job next week, even if she did find answers for Mollie. As Ida pulled the quilt tighter under her chin, she wasn't even sure she wanted to work for Mollie O'Bryan anymore. She didn't like the person she was becoming; the power her position afforded her didn't seem to be good for her.

Ida had watched her siblings and her in-laws open their gifts. Nell's eyes lit up when she handed Ida the scarf she'd made. Joy had danced across Kat's face when Ida read the poem Kat had written for her.

In turn, she'd seen the pleasure of self-sacrifice disappear when her sisters and the others opened their extravagant, store-bought gifts. Sadness had even darkened Hattie's eyes for a moment when she'd seen the two music cylinders.

Ida knew her family's and friends' subdued reactions didn't mean they didn't like the gifts she'd given them or even that they wouldn't enjoy them. They'd seen into her heart. They knew she had jumbled her priorities long before she'd realized the love of making money had taken hold of her heart. God hadn't been first in her life, in her decisions.

She'd been able to ignore the truth until the brown-eyed ice man stared at the garish beaver hat and spoke out.

"You spent too much."

"So God might not have a problem with women earning their own money, but you do."

Only with a woman who flaunts it. Not his exact words, but flaunting her success and wealth was exactly what she'd done. Tucker had been brave enough to say what her family apparently wouldn't utter. At least, not on Christmas Day.

He cared about her. She'd seen the affection in his eyes, heard it in the jangle of his fork dropping onto his plate when he'd caught her looking at him. She couldn't help feeling a pull toward him and his ability to see into her heart. For a moment, she'd found herself hoping Tucker could be the person with whom she'd exchange winks and playful jabs next Christmas. The man from whom she'd receive pecks on the cheek.

But Tucker Raines didn't care for her in that way. Especially not after the gift exchange this afternoon. An impervious businesswoman didn't belong with a preacher. She didn't deserve a man with a heart much more valuable than the gold she'd pursued with an unmatched passion.

Yet Tucker wasn't the only person who weighed heavily on her heart that Christmas night. She thought of her employer. Mollie now held a lot of worthless stock because of her misinformation. And God only knew who else might suffer because of the assay debacle.

Boney.

Ida pulled the quilt tight under her chin. The morning she'd bought the Olive Branch stock, the old miner had said she and Mollie seemed to have a special sense when it came to buying and selling stocks. She'd seen him bid on the same stock.

That *feeling* about a stock wasn't a special sense, but secret information. Information she had no right to make use of, even if there were no laws against it. Hattie, Judson, and Kat had all tried to warn her. Greed was spreading through the town like a deadly epidemic, and she'd succumbed to it. No wonder some people shunned her as if she were a leper.

Pride goeth before destruction.

Tears poured down her face and soaked her pillow.

She'd been prideful. She was ashamed of the arrogance with which she'd answered anyone and everyone who had tried to warn her. Why did she always have to be right? She didn't have anything to prove. She didn't have to earn the love that mattered most to her—God's love.

Ida knew she couldn't continue to be the strong one. She couldn't live the rest of her life feeling alone, with nothing but her ambition to keep her company at night.

She had to make this right. But where would she even begin?

Thanks be to God, which giveth us the victory through our Lord Jesus Christ.

This was the crossroads Tucker had talked about in his sermon.

Ida slid down to the rug beside her bed, pulling her quilt with her. She huddled beneath its warmth, on her knees.

Please forgive me, Lord. I've made a mess of my life. I've hurt myself and others in the process. I've hurt You. I never meant to hurt anyone.

Sobbing, Ida rested her head against the bed as if it were God's broad shoulder.

Lord, Tucker said that genuine faith seats You—Jesus Christ—where You belong. First. Above anything or anyone else. I haven't done that. Not for many years. Please forgive me. I will trust You.

Lord, please help me make things right.

Her bedroom door creaked open.

"Ida, dear, are you all right?" Hattie stood in the doorway, holding a lantern.

Nodding, Ida took a swipe at her wet face. "I've made a mess of things. I've been so selfish."

Hattie rushed to her side and stroked her hair. "I'm sure Tucker likes the hat." Her soft voice was full of compassion. "You surprised him, dear. You surprised all of us."

"It's not about the hat." Shuddering, Ida mopped her face with the quilt.

"I know you're having troubles at work too, dear. But you're on your knees and you couldn't have gone to a better Source of help."

Ida nodded and sniffled.

"Let's you and I go downstairs and have us a nice cup of peppermint tea." Hattie placed her forearms on the bed and raised herself up from the floor.

Ida wiped her face again, but before she stood, she turned back to the edge of the bed and whispered, "Amen."

THIRTY-SEVEN

*I*da stepped away from the game table in Nell's parlor and moved to the bookcase, where Judson stood. "I need to speak with you."

Her brother-in-law regarded her with wary blue eyes and a raised brow, then glanced over at his wife. Nell sat engrossed in the checkerboard. Ida had already lost to her. Morgan squirmed while Kat, his coach, sat beside him.

Judson nodded and led her into the kitchen. "Shall we sit down?"

"A good idea." Ida chose a chair and Judson sat across from her, looking much more relaxed than she felt.

He cleared his throat. "This about what I said at the picnic?"

"It's about Colin Wagner. Thanksgiving Day, actually."

Judson leaned forward, his forearms on the table. "Figured you'd get around to asking about that."

"Why did Colin assume you'd written me the note?"

"He didn't."

"What do you mean? He glared at you and asked if you were responsible."

Judson folded and unfolded his hands, then grew still and looked her in the eye. "Colin assumed I meant the message for him, not you."

Jigsaws were easier to put together. Even beating Nell at checkers was less of a challenge. "Colin thought you were telling him he was making a mistake?"

Judson nodded.

"Why would he assume that?" Ida squared the place mat in front of her and looked up at her brother-in-law.

"You think you're ready to hear what I have to say about the man you're seeing?"

"I'm not." She looked away. "Seeing him anymore, that is."

"I'm relieved to hear it."

"But there's other trouble."

Judson met her gaze, showing no sign of being surprised by her news. "The assay report for the Olive Branch Mine?"

"Yes, and I need answers."

"You believe Colin is responsible?"

She frowned. "That's not what I... Is that what you think?"

"I think he's somehow involved. Yes."

Ida pressed her fingers to her forehead, trying to assuage an oncoming headache. "Why would Colin falsify the report? How?"

"Mollie trusts him. The mine owner, Blackmer, does too."

"Yes, so why would he betray their trust and take that kind of a risk?"

"It's all the love of money." Judson stood and leaned on the back of his chair. "A couple of weeks before Thanksgiving, I saw Colin accepting a package from a suspected high-grader who works at the Mary McKinney Mine."

"High-grader?"

"High-grading is stealing valuable ore from the mine. Sneaking it out and selling it on the sly."

Ida pressed her hand against her roiling stomach. "How can you be sure it was Colin?"

"He and his high-grader friend met in the shadows between two buildings. When he saw me, I told him he was making a big mistake."

"And what did he say?"

"He tried explaining away his contact with the man as part of his job as a law counselor." Judson shook his head. "That's not what the high-grader said when I later threatened to expose the deal he had with Colin."

Clearly, Mr. Wagner wasn't who he'd purported to be—an upstanding citizen with concern for his fellow business folk. She heaved a sigh. "Have you told anyone else?"

"Deputy Alwyn and, more recently, Reverend Taggart."

Swallowing the acid burning her throat, Ida rose from her chair. "Colin was only seeing me to get to you?"

"I don't know about that. I just know Colin Wagner is not what or who he professes to be."

"I assumed Faith wrote the note out of her infatuation with Tucker. She was a bit enamored with him at first, and I figured she was just telling me Tucker was a better choice than Colin." She paced between the icebox and the stove. "Do you think Faith knows something more about Colin?"

"You'll have to ask her."

The schoolteacher was due back from Denver that afternoon. "I will."

"I know I can't tell you not to get involved in this mess—you already are—but be careful, will you?" Concern narrowed his blue eyes. "We care about you."

"I'll be careful. Thank you."

Judson smiled. "We'd best return to the tournament. My wife is probably ready for her crown."

Ida laughed and then breathed a prayer of thanksgiving for her family.

◦~◎~◦

An hour later, Ida knocked on Faith's bedroom door.

"Come in," Faith called.

Ida obliged, breathing in the sweet scent of lilac.

Faith pulled a stack of sachets out of the carpetbag on her twin bed and twisted to look at Ida. "A gift from my grandmother."

"So you had a good Christmas with your family?"

Faith nodded and set the sachets on top of her bureau. "It was hard to leave."

"I'm sure it was."

"I can't imagine having a family member off in Paris. Denver is far enough." Faith pointed to an armchair in the corner. "You want to sit down?"

"No, thank you. I won't keep you long. I just wanted to ask you something."

"All right." Faith chewed a fingernail as if anticipating the topic of their conversation.

"Why did you write me that note? Why do you think my seeing Colin was a mistake?"

Faith sat on the foot of her bed. "I saw Mr. Wagner in town one day. He didn't see me."

"And?" Ida sank into the chair.

"He walked out of the tobacco shop with another man."

She'd never seen Colin smoke. Nor had she seen any evidence in his office. Not that buying tobacco or smoking was a crime. "The tobacconist is probably a client."

Faith pulled her bag onto her lap. "I don't know about that, but I think Mr. Wagner might be living two lives."

"There's more?"

Faith nodded. "I heard him talking when I came around the corner. He said women have no place in the business world; that a woman's place is in the"—the schoolteacher looked down at the bed and blushed—"bedroom."

Ida felt her eyes widen and her mouth drop open.

"Said it just as clear as a church bell."

"And about as far removed from his decent deacon image as Cripple Creek is from Paris, France." Ida huffed. "Why didn't you tell me this earlier?"

Faith's gulp of air answered the question.

Ida nodded. "I haven't been real eager to hear the truth. I'm sorry."

"Are you going to quit seeing Mr. Wagner?"

"I already have."

"And what about Tucker? Are you ready to pursue him?"

Ida weighed her answer while she tucked a stray curl behind her ear. "I'm not sure *pursue* is the right word, but I do care about him."

A smile replaced the shadow on Faith's face. "I knew you were a smart woman."

Ida hoped she hadn't gotten smart too late.

THIRTY-EIGHT

*L*ate Monday afternoon, Tucker pitched a forkful of hay down into Titan's stall. He repeated the action for Trojan and the four new horses. The repetition reminded him of his prayers for Miss Ida Sinclair. He'd been praying about her every few hours since Christmas Day, when he'd practically scolded her for her generous gifts to him and the others in Morgan's home. He hated that he'd caused her such disappointment. She'd bought him a nice gift, and he'd let his pride stand in the way of accepting it with grace.

"Mr. Tucker, you in here?" The voice belonged to Otis, but the monotone was foreign.

"Up here." Tucker set the fork against the wall and climbed down the ladder. He hadn't seen Otis much that day, and he hadn't expected to see him here after work.

His co-worker leaned against the back of the wagon. The shine had left his eyes. The perpetual smile was gone. He carried the weight of the world on his slouched shoulders.

"Mrs. Naomi all right?" Tucker asked. "The boys?"

"They're fine." The words came out flat as Otis stared down at the straw covering the barn floor.

Tucker tugged off his work gloves and tossed them on the wagon seat. "You sick?"

Otis shook his head.

"I'll make some coffee. We can sit on the back porch." Tucker escorted his friend out of the barn and latched the door behind him.

Twenty minutes later, the two men occupied the rocking chairs on the porch and stared out at a white blanket of snow. Tucker held his cup of hot coffee up to his face and breathed in its aromatic warmth. The other cup waited untouched on the table between him and the uncharacteristically quiet Otis. Tucker sat with his feet propped on the railing. Otis sat with his hands on his knees, looking as though the world was about to roll off his back and crash to the ground. Tucker could grow old waiting for his friend to speak his mind.

"Otis, I'm not as patient as you are." Tucker set his cup on the table and slid his feet to the wood flooring. "Something's wrong." He straightened and looked his friend in the eye. "I can't help you if I don't know what the problem is."

Otis leaned forward and placed his head in his hands. Tucker heard the snort of a man trying not to cry.

His friend's words from the other night echoed in Tucker's head and soured his stomach. *"I'll be able to do a whole lot more when my mine stock pays off."*

Tucker pressed the heels of his boots into the boards beneath them. "The stock you bought?"

A pained look overtook Otis's face, and he nodded. "I lost it all, and more."

"What do you mean 'more'?"

"Boney said it looks like the certificate is just worthless paper." Otis labored to speak every word. "Stock's not even worth what I paid for it. I thought—"

"You thought it was a good investment. You thought you could earn more to better provide for your family."

"It doesn't matter what I thought." Otis picked up his cup. "I was wrong."

"You sure it's as bad as all that?"

"Boney said the Olive Branch Mine didn't pan out. The ore wasn't high-grade after all. Report says it's not even worth the diggin'."

Tucker rubbed his forehead in frustration. Hattie had known Boney Hughes for nearly a decade. He'd been a friend of her late husband's. Tucker trusted her judgment.

"Boney feels real bad." Otis heaved a sigh. "Said your friend and her boss lady are rarely wrong in choosin' investments."

Tucker straightened. "Ida invested in the same stock?"

Otis nodded. "Boney followed her lead."

Tucker had heard the talk in town. Many people didn't like the tactics she'd learned from her employer, who profited from secrets heard in clients' offices and the ignorance of others. Could he have been that wrong about Ida's heart?

"Your lady friend probably lost a lot too." Otis shook his head. "I know I'm not the only one hurt by this, but…"

Tucker's concern for Ida wasn't whether she'd lost money, but her physical and spiritual well-being. The business was ruining people. Not just financially. It was time Ida knew what Reverend Taggart had told him about Colin.

Tucker drained his cup and stood. "Hold on to the stock certificates for now. Let me look into the situation before you do anything."

∽◦◦∽

Thirty minutes later, Tucker stood in the doorway of Miss O'Bryan's private office.

"Hello, Mr. Raines. How may I help you?" Before he could open his mouth to answer Miss O'Bryan, she raised her hand. "Just know I don't need any ice, and I'm not in the mood for a sermon."

Tucker drew in a deep breath and met her gaze. "Ma'am, people here are being hurt by what you and Miss Sinclair are doing."

"And what exactly are we doing that is your concern?" Miss O'Bryan cocked her head.

"Garnering inside information from your clients and profiting off them and others who don't have the benefit of your foreknowledge."

"If you're riled about the Olive Branch Mine stock, I'll have you know I sank money into it too. I trusted Ida, and we all got hurt because of her mistake."

She'd made a mistake? That didn't sound like Ida. There had to be more to this mine stock calamity.

"Where is she?" he asked.

"She left me a note under the door this morning saying she was taking the train to Colorado Springs. I expect her back at work tomorrow morning."

What he had to say couldn't wait that long. If he didn't find her at the depot, he'd go to the boardinghouse.

"Thank you." Tucker walked out the door and took long, heavy strides toward the depot.

∽◦◦∽

Ida was sure, if given the chance, the nervous energy inside her could enable her to outrun the train she rode, no matter its speed. She'd read and reread the assayer's official report no fewer than five times. She'd spent the better part of the afternoon in Colorado Springs and found the answers she'd promised Mollie O'Bryan. Some of them, at least.

It turned out that the sample the assayer evaluated wasn't the type of ore found in the Olive Branch Mine. Someone had switched the sample. When she and the assayer had realized what had happened, he had telephoned Mr. Blackmer to find out who signed for the sample before it was delivered to Colorado Springs.

Mr. Blackmer had claimed he'd personally handed the chunk of ore to his attorney, Colin Wagner. And according to the assayer, a man with hazel eyes, wearing a pinstripe suit and a bowler hat, had delivered the sample to him.

Colin Wagner. A leader in the church. A deacon. Mollie's friend, whom she had trusted even if she didn't always follow his counsel.

A few weeks ago, Ida wouldn't have believed Colin was capable of re-placing the high-grade sample with a counterfeit. But now her mind seemed set on reliving and analyzing everything he had said and done, starting with his warning to Mollie about one of her clients. Had his concern simply been a ruse to gain her trust?

During Ida's work on the Raines Ice Company prospectus, Colin had told Tucker that what a person did was directed by his own conscience.

Not, necessarily, by what is right.

Judson had seen Colin with a man suspected of stealing valuable ore from the Mary McKinney Mine. Was Faith right? Was Colin living a sec-ond life in the shadows?

If so, why? What did he have to gain in switching the ore? Money, yes, but the attorney had already made a good deal of money. Because of his friendship with Mollie and Charles, Colin had access to the same privileged information they did. Why would the attorney want to sabotage Mr. Blackmer? Why would he want to dupe the stock exchange and hurt Mollie and countless others who had invested in the stock based upon the find in the new stope?

Ida folded the assay report and slipped it back into her reticule. The law would have to dig for those answers. Judson said he'd reported what he'd seen to a deputy. Perhaps with the evidence she'd gathered, the sheriff would have enough to arrest Colin, or at least investigate him more thoroughly.

In the meantime, she could use a little rest. She leaned against the back of the seat and closed her eyes. A few minutes later the train whistle blew, causing Ida to jump.

"Cripple Creek." The conductor made the announcement from the front of the car as the train slowed for the final stretch.

Tomorrow she'd have an opportunity to redeem herself. Hopefully, her news would help them all find more answers. Then, if she still had a job, she'd decide what to do.

In the meantime, she yawned and draped her new silk-lined mantle over her shoulders, ready to hire a ride home and crawl into bed. So much had changed inside her since Christmas Day, since that night when she'd found herself broken at a crossroads, and repentant.

Ida stepped off the train and blinked to adjust her eyes to the post lanterns. The sun was sinking behind the Rocky Mountains and shadows stretched across the valley. Respectable women didn't walk about town after dark. She looked around the platform for a porter who could help her find suitable transportation to the sheriff's office.

Instead of catching the attention of a porter, however, she caught Colin

Wagner's gaze. He strolled toward her like he didn't have a care in the world. Would he be able to do that if he were guilty of the improprieties she was investigating?

Am I looking at a friend or a foe, Lord?

"Good evening." His smooth voice held no hint of guilt.

Ida took a deep breath. "Mr. Wagner." She raised her chin a notch. "Are you taking the evening train?"

"No. Mollie said you were on a business trip and were coming in this evening. I realize you don't want to see me socially—unless, of course, you've changed your mind." A coy smile softened his features.

Ida shook her head.

"At any rate," he continued, "it's dangerous for you to be out alone at night. I was out taking care of some business of my own and thought I could give you a ride to the boardinghouse. Surely that would be permissible."

Was she looking at a mere scoundrel, or someone who was even more of a threat to her than that? Did he know where she'd been and what she'd found out?

"I have other plans. Thank you." Ida pulled her mother's pendant watch from her reticule and turned it toward the light from the post lantern.

Before she could read the time, Colin snatched it out of her hand. His smile wasn't that of a charmer, but the sneer of a snake. "What do you say we call this cat-and-mouse game a wash and get right to my proposition?"

"You're being childish." Ida straightened to her full height, fighting a surge of fear. "I'm not interested in hearing another word you have to say." She held out her hand. "Return the watch."

"I have a better idea." His voice dripped with syrup. "How about you come with me, and I'll see to it that not only do you get the watch back, but that Miss Hattie is released, safe and sound?"

He'd taken Hattie hostage? Ida's knees threatened to buckle. Her arm fell to her side.

"I thought you'd see it my way." Colin reached into Ida's cape and grabbed her upper arm, pulling her off the platform.

Her boots sank into the snow, her spirit taking the plunge with them. Miss Hattie was in danger.

Trust in the Lord. Surely at least one of the many folks milling about outside the depot would notice them.

"Why couldn't you and Mollie just learn your lesson?" Puffs of steam carried Colin's words into the cold night air. "You should've kept your nose in your own business."

As Colin charged up the street toward his buggy with her in tow, Ida's thoughts proved as erratic as her steps. He'd switched the ore to teach her a lesson? Why wasn't anyone helping her? She should call out, but she couldn't. Her determination to get answers had put Hattie in danger.

Please, Lord. Keep Hattie safe. I'm trusting You. Please help me.

At the buggy, Colin stopped abruptly and stared at her, his grip still strong. "Women don't belong in business. You and Mollie don't belong."

"Then why did you represent Mollie? Seek our secretarial services? Put in a good word for me?" Ida sighed. "Pretend?"

"I started out wooing Mollie. She would have eventually realized she needed to give up her business pursuits for me. But then you came along— more my type."

Ida resisted the urge to spit in the despicable man's face. An escape would require more of a distraction than that. She needed to be patient. Wait for the right moment.

"You've had your fun, playing in our world, but it's time you realized your true purpose." His voice softened and so did the lines at his eyes. "Your place is in the home with a man who can provide everything you need.

Who can take care of you properly." His breath hot on her face, Colin shifted his grip on her arm, expecting her to step up into the seat.

Ida rose to her full height and met his gaze. "You're wrong, Mr. Wagner! My place is *not* in your kitchen. And I assure you that my true purpose has nothing to do with you." She stomped the top of his foot and punched him in the gut with her other hand.

Snarling, he lost his hold on her long enough for her to run into the middle of the street. She nearly ran headlong into a young woman, painted up and baring her chest.

"Get the sheriff! Please!" Ida begged her. She recovered her footing and darted around several mules, hoping to see Boney Hughes, hoping the other woman was racing toward the sheriff's office, but she didn't dare turn around and risk losing ground. Clutching her aching side, she willed herself to keep running toward the Third Street Café.

Before she reached the safety of the restaurant, Colin jumped in front of her and grabbed her by the shoulders. "You fool! You could have had it all."

Behind him, a familiar ice wagon rounded the corner. And the man driving it needed only a moment to size up the situation. Ida had seen that look on Tucker's face before, at the mud puddle.

"Wagner!"

Ida relaxed at the sound of Tucker's familiar voice, firm as iron, yet smooth as butter.

Colin jerked around as Tucker jumped from wagon. Her captor shifted his grip to her arm, squeezing her tight to his side. "Raines is your '*other plans*'?"

Ida nodded, unable to take her eyes off the ice man with the perfect timing.

"If you don't let go of Miss Sinclair this moment, your fate could meet you right here, saving you the trouble of a trial." Tucker pointed behind them.

Ida was able to turn her head far enough to see Sheriff Snelling and his deputy standing within ten feet of her and Colin.

The younger man pointed a gun at Colin. "Do as the man said, Mr. Wagner. Let go of the lady."

When he did, Ida felt herself falling. Then tender, strong arms scooped her up.

Thank You, Lord.

THIRTY-NINE

*T*ucker watched Colin Wagner shuffle away with a deputy on either side of him and blew out a deep breath. Ida had given the lawmen enough information to arrest him, and it sounded like Henry Blackmer, Mollie O'Bryan, and many others would have a lot more incriminating evidence to offer them.

Tears trickled down Ida's face. "I've made such a mess of things."

Tucker pulled a handkerchief from his pocket and slipped it into the hand that held her mother's pendant watch.

Staring up at him, she blotted her tears. "You're certain Hattie is safe?"

Tucker nodded. "While you were talking to the sheriff, Deputy Alwyn told me that Judson stopped by their office today and told him you too had reason to suspect Colin of a crime. Alwyn went to the boardinghouse to follow up with you and had just returned from Hattie's when a woman came in and told him and the sheriff what was going on in the street."

A woman from Myers Avenue, to be precise. He intended to thank Felicia for her kindness as soon as he could.

"Colin's threats were just a ploy to scare me? To make me go with him?" The pain in Ida's moist blue eyes tightened Tucker's throat.

"Yes." He choked out the word.

"I trusted him."

A bitter taste rose in his mouth. "Countless people trusted Colin. And many people stood to lose a lot of money because of what he did." Tucker met her tender gaze and brushed a golden brown curl from her face. "What you did today—digging for the truth and standing up to Colin Wagner—took a lot of courage."

Ida drew in a deep breath. "Tucker Raines, you were God's answer to my prayers for help."

Emotion tightened Tucker's throat, and he swallowed hard. He wanted to kiss the woman he loved, but this wasn't the time or the place.

"You've had a long day. I need to take you home." He tucked his arm around her and led her to the wagon. The partial embrace wasn't a kiss, but it felt mighty fine, nonetheless.

Thank You, Lord.

Riding down Bennett Avenue in the ice wagon beside Tucker Raines, Ida felt a contentment she hadn't experienced in the office, the millinery shop, or at the stock exchange. And watching Tucker guide the two draft horses up Hayden to Golden Avenue, she couldn't think of any place she'd rather be.

Tucker wasn't like any man she'd ever met. He never pretended to be something he wasn't. He set his own work and plans aside to follow God's plan for him and to meet the needs of his family. He was a man who had suffered the loss of a dear friend in a tragic drowning. A brother who had watched his sister spiral into a sorrow that took *her* away from him too. Tucker was also an honest example of what it meant to live life and fight battles carrying the shield of faith. His quiet strength had supported her and comforted her whether she'd deserved it or not.

She loved him.

He brushed the brim of his worn hat and tugged it down over one eye. "I think I'm ready for a newer hat. The one you bought me was nice and all, but—"

"It wasn't really you."

He shook his head. "Nope."

"I didn't mean to flaunt my money. I only wanted to give you a nice gift."

"I know."

And if Ida didn't know about his obligations in California, she'd say the two of them belonged like this side by side, forever and always.

FORTY

*T*uesday morning, as Ida made her way down the hill to Mollie O'Bryan's office, her heart relived every moment from the previous evening. When Colin Wagner had met the train and tried to kidnap her, she'd tasted a fear she hadn't experienced since the day the miners found her at the creek. Colin had fooled and betrayed her, as well as everyone in the business district and everyone in the church.

Almost everyone. Early on, she'd sensed Tucker Raines's hesitance to trust the man.

She hadn't paid attention to Tucker's instincts then, but she was now.

Ida paused in front of the familiar brick building. Before opening the door, she reached into her reticule and pulled out the folded envelope she'd addressed to Miss Mollie O'Bryan. No more using privileged information from clients. No more frequenting the stock exchange every day. She'd only been in town three months, but she needed a fresh start. Tucker's frankness with her on Christmas Day and her revelation that night had sparked a new beginning, and her experiences yesterday had prompted her next steps.

Ida opened the door to Mollie O'Bryan's Stenography Firm. The inside resonated with the sound of laughter. Mollie and Mr. Miller were in Mollie's private office with the door open.

"Pardon me, Miss O'Bryan." Ida took slow steps toward it.

"Ida's here!" Mollie rushed through the open doorway with a full-faced smile lighting her green eyes. Mr. Miller joined her. Each of them held a half-empty champagne glass in one hand and a lit cigar in the other.

Miller set his glass down and pulled a piece of paper from the top of the desk. "Thanks to your diligence, Ida, we have answers concerning the questionable assay report."

Ida set her reticule and the envelope on the corner near Miller's glass. "You heard the ore sample from the Olive Branch Mine was switched?"

Mollie nodded, and the ostrich plume on her hat bobbed.

"I know that you and the assayer in Colorado Springs telephoned Blackmer yesterday." Miller handed the sheet of paper to Ida. "As soon as Blackmer hung up the telephone, he hand-carried another ore sample to the local assayer. That's the authentic report."

Ida studied the certificate. Her information had been correct, despite the fact that her methods for procuring it hadn't been.

Mollie set down her glass. "Colin Wagner had us all wearing blinders." She perched a hand on her hip. "He switched the sample. And come to find out…this wasn't the first time he'd pulled the wool over our eyes."

"A young assay trainee here in town worked for him before the assayer suspected something and fired the kid. Seems Wagner had quite an impressive high-grade business." Miller retrieved his glass from the desk. "He bought raw gold and high-grade ore from mine employees and sold it to crooked assayers. Running a regular *den of thieves*."

And she'd walked right into it.

Ida lifted her envelope and held it out to Mollie.

Mollie set her cigar in a tray on the desk. "What's this?" She slid her finger beneath the sealed flap and opened it. "You're resigning?"

"I—"

"You want an apology, is that it? I can apologize." Mollie straightened and cleared her throat. "I was wrong to burst into the boardinghouse in such a foul mood. I'm sorry if you felt like I accused you of wrongdoing."

"I'm not quitting because you were mad." Ida met Mollie's narrowed gaze. "I liked working here. You taught me a lot." *Not all of it good.* "But I didn't know what our *gleaning methods* could do to the broader majority in Cripple Creek. I do now."

"Sounds to me like my protégé has developed scruples."

Miller nodded and tucked the assay report into his herringbone jacket.

"Since that's the case, it won't do either of us any good to have you here for the two weeks you offered me in your resignation." Mollie turned back toward her office. "I'll release you, pay you for the two weeks, and we'll call it even."

The new assay meant she and Mollie hadn't lost their investment but instead had made a considerable sum of money. It meant the same for Boney and Otis, but Ida knew many folks had already sold their stocks, not knowing how valuable they were to people like her—who did know. She'd confessed her wrongdoing and knew God had forgiven her, but she also knew other people hadn't been as fortunate and were a long way south of *even*. She couldn't right all of her wrongs, but she longed to do something good with her windfall.

Lord, what can I do?

Tucker didn't go directly to Taggart's office. He wanted a little time alone in the sanctuary before giving Reverend Taggart his answer.

As Tucker started up the center aisle, he imagined himself waiting at the front while Ida Sinclair sashayed toward him, dressed in white. This time he didn't scold himself for thinking such thoughts.

He loved Ida. Perhaps he had since the day he'd seen her in town after his ill-fated meeting at the bank. He'd asked God aloud what He was doing and Ida had heard him.

"So did He tell you? You asked God what He's doing. Did He tell you?"

"Not yet. Unless you're part of an answer."

Even then, at least deep down, Tucker had known he wanted more than mere friendship with the enigmatic Miss Ida Sinclair. He'd asked her to coffee and she'd refused. At the time, he was thankful she'd had the good sense to turn him down. But after their time in the post office and at the creek, he could no longer deny his feelings. After he'd left Ida alone in Hattie's entryway last night and driven home to an empty house, he knew he'd left part of himself with her.

He'd thought the life of an unattached traveling preacher suited him, but he didn't think that anymore. God no doubt knew it long before Tucker opened that depot door and ended up with a hatpin stuck in the toe of his boot.

Footsteps alerted him to someone else's presence and he turned around, hoping it would be Ida. The reverend had found him instead.

Reverend Taggart shook Tucker's hand. "You have your answer yet?"

"I do."

FORTY-ONE

A twinge of worry slowed Ida's steps up the hill. She didn't know what she would do for work, but she'd figured out what she wouldn't do. For now, that was enough. She'd chosen to trust and obey God. Not knowing what her future held felt foreign and exhilarating. Not having a plan for her every move would be an adventure.

She'd start that adventure first thing tomorrow. Today, she had plans.

From Mollie O'Bryan's office, Ida headed to the church. The First Congregational Church sat on a large corner lot with a parsonage behind it. Staring up at the white steeple, Ida wondered if Tucker would ever tire of traveling. Would he ever want to settle down in a community church and live in a parsonage?

With me?

As Ida climbed the front steps, she wondered what it would be like to walk the same steps hand in hand with Tucker Raines.

Husband and wife.

Whoa, girl.

She couldn't rein Tucker in. He had to follow his heart, even if it took him on the road again. Back to Willow. Back to scattered audiences.

She would trust God's plans for her, which she believed included seeing the reverend.

When Ida stepped into the vestibule, she heard two men conversing inside the sanctuary. She'd just reached the back pew when she heard Tucker speak.

"I'll turn the management of the Raines Ice Company over to Otis Bernard." Wistfulness tinted Tucker's normally smooth voice. "Otis and his family will move into my parents' home."

Ida gasped. Tucker really was leaving, and soon, if he'd already made such arrangements.

Both men noticed her at the same time and fell silent.

"I didn't mean to interrupt." She focused on the reverend for fear that looking into Tucker's brown eyes would flood her own. "Please excuse me."

"Don't mind us. We're just two preachers jawing." Reverend Taggart's smile involved his whole face, wrinkling well up onto his bald head.

Tucker moved toward her. "Were you looking for me?"

"Actually, I came to see Reverend Taggart, but since you're here, I do have good news to share with you."

"Good news?"

Ida nodded, still avoiding his gaze. "Henry Blackmer personally took another ore sample to the assayer here in town. It's authentic and quite valuable."

"Then Otis's certificates are—"

"Once again a good investment." Ida gave her full attention to the shorter man. "Reverend, I have something I want to give you." She set her reticule on the back of the pew and pulled out a folded stock certificate. "I planned to do this in private, but"—she lowered her voice—"you mentioned a great need for funds to help the widows and orphans. I want to donate this. The stock should pay out nicely within a couple of weeks."

Pushing his spectacles up on his nose, the reverend accepted the certificate and studied the sheet of paper. "You're donating five thousand shares of Olive Branch Mine stock?"

"Yes sir."

"This is very generous of you."

"Then you have the Lord to thank for that, sir." She retrieved her reticule.

"I have some news myself," Tucker said. A strand of molasses-brown hair drew her attention to his temple and the memory of him brushing back a stray tendril of her hair last night.

The reverend clapped Tucker on the shoulder. "Miss Sinclair, you're looking at the new pastor of the First Congregational Church."

"I am?" She gazed at him in wonder, then glanced down at her boots to see if they were planted on the ground. "That's great news!"

"Reverend Taggart is moving back to New York next month, taking a church there to be closer to his ailing parents."

"Congratulations."

"Thank you, but I haven't been voted in yet."

"Just a matter of time." The shorter man's smile rippled clear back to his receding hairline again. "I don't expect that'll be a problem in the least."

Ida felt her smile fade. *Unless the congregation doesn't approve of the company he keeps.* She could name at least a handful of influential people in the church who didn't approve of her involvement in business.

"If you'll excuse me…" She took a step back.

Tucker moved toward her. "I'd like to see you later." That strand of hair still pointed to his coffee-brown eyes.

She offered a quick nod and a wave, then took unladylike strides toward the door. She had more stops on her list.

Ida approached the icehouse, remembering her first visit, when she'd found Tucker sitting on a wagon seat, reading a letter from Willow. Today Otis Bernard was sliding an enormous block of ice into the back of a wagon.

He noticed her and stood. "Miss Ida." After removing his hat, the gentle giant then pulled off his gloves. "Good day, ma'am."

"It is a good day, Otis." She shook his hand.

"Mr. Tucker isn't here, ma'am. Expect he'd be here soon though if he knew you was coming." A lopsided smile revealed a dimple in the man's chin.

"Thank you, but I came to see you about the Olive Branch Mine stock Boney bought for you."

"Yes ma'am, he did."

"The sample taken to the assayer was a fake."

His eyes grew wide. "What are you saying, ma'am?"

"I'm saying we have a new report back on the actual sample, and it is good news. Your stock is worth far more than you paid for it."

Otis tossed his gloves into the air and let out a whoop. On the starriest of nights, Ida couldn't expect to see as much light as she witnessed on his face.

A good day, indeed.

Thank You, Lord. For grace and mercy. For redemption. For relationship with You.

And that Tucker Raines plans to remain in Cripple Creek.

Forty-Two

ucker took the long way home from the church. He hadn't intended to, but then, he hadn't expected Ida Sinclair to show up in the sanctuary and then leave as quickly as she arrived.

He thought she'd returned to work, but shortly after his meeting with Reverend Taggart, he disproved the work theory. As he reached for the door at the stenography firm, Miss Q'Bryan and Mr. Miller stepped out of the office.

"You *are* a persistent one, Mr. Raines." Miss O'Bryan clucked her tongue and locked the door behind her. "But you won't find Miss Sinclair here. She quit today."

He felt a jump in his chest and a catch in his throat. Ida was apparently following her heart, and he hoped it would lead her to him.

His second detour didn't prove successful either. At least not where Ida was concerned. Stopping by the boardinghouse had, however, earned him a piece of cherry pie and a chat with Miss Hattie. Amazing how quickly a story could spread and grow arms. He'd assured her there were no brawls in the mud or gunfire involved in last evening's happenings and went on to tell her his plans for the future.

Tucker's other guess as to Ida's whereabouts involved her sisters. But he couldn't be sure she was with them, and since showing up at Kat's or Nell's home unannounced wouldn't be appropriate, he walked toward Warren Avenue and headed toward home instead.

As he cleared the intersection at his property, he glanced toward the creek.

A lone figure sat at one end of the bench beside the small, now leafless willow tree, wearing a navy blue silk turban hat and a wool cape. Her presence set his heart to racing.

"Ida." He called out to her long before she could hear his footfalls. He did not want to startle her.

She stood and watched him walk toward her. "You said you wanted to see me later."

"I did." He stopped directly in front of her. "Thank you." He felt twelve years old again and just as awkward.

Ida pressed her lips together as if to stunt a grin. She looked down at the bench, where a large hatbox lay. "I have something for you."

"Let's sit down, shall we?" Tucker motioned to the bench and then picked up the box.

"Can't take seeing another one of my presents standing up, huh?" Ida giggled and lowered herself onto the bench at the far end.

"You've figured me out." Tucker placed the gift between them and removed the lid. He ran his fingers down the edge and under the wide brim of an austere, handsome black felt hat. He slowly lifted it out of the box and inspected it from every angle. He reached up and removed his old hat and set it in the box. Then he held the new beauty with both hands and lowered it onto his head. "Thank you. It's a perfect fit."

So was she. And he believed with all his heart that God had brought them together.

❧

Tucker cast his big, brown-eyed gaze her way and Ida thought her heart might thump right out of her chest.

He liked the new preacher's hat she'd given him. He wasn't leaving town. He was giving up the life of a traveling preacher to settle down in Cripple Creek. Was it too much to hope they could have a life together?

"My father and mother plan to remain in Colorado Springs." Tucker paused. "Father agreed that Otis can manage the day-to-day operations of the ice company, including caring for the horses and wagons. I'll be moving into the parsonage, if the church votes to call me as their new pastor."

"That makes sense."

"Mind if I ask you a question?"

She nodded, her heart responding favorably to the twinkle in his eyes. "I mean go ahead, ask me."

Tucker switched places with the hatbox and moved to her side. "My question has to do with courtship."

"Courtship?"

When Tucker reached for both of her hands, she wished her gloves were tucked into her pockets so she could feel his tender touch. Clearing his throat, he looked directly into her eyes. So this was what it felt like to swim in a pool of hot chocolate.

"Do you suppose our two creekside talks, a chat at the post office, three buggy rides, Thanksgiving and Christmas suppers with the family, and a showdown in the street could comprise a proper courtship?" There was that sunny smile of his again.

A sudden wave of lightheadedness threatened to overcome her, and she squeezed his hands. If Tucker hadn't been holding on to her, she surely would've slid right off the bench onto the snow. He wasn't asking to court her.

After courtship came marriage.

Ida gulped. "Are you asking if we might forgo a formal courtship?"

"I didn't want to love you, or anyone else. I considered my plate full." He removed his new hat and set it on top of the box. "But I do love you, Miss Ida Sinclair. I love that you are sensitive to God's Spirit."

"A little late."

"I love your no-nonsense approach to life and your determination to be equal to any person, man or woman. And I want to spend the rest of my days on earth—many or few—with you at my side."

Tears streamed down Ida's face. The preaching ice man loved her. And he wanted to spend the rest of his life with her.

She blinked back her tears and looked up into his glistening eyes. "I love you too."

Tucker let go of her hands and reached into his coat pocket. He pulled out a jewelry box. "Miss Ida Sinclair, I would be honored to call you my wife." His voice cracked, and he opened the box. "Will you marry me?"

Ida stared at the delicate gold band. Two leaves flowed outward from the center, joined at the stems by a single diamond.

She so wanted to tell him yes. She wanted to shout it. So why couldn't she so much as whisper her heart's desire?

"I haven't been voted in yet."

"I'll move into the parsonage, if the church votes to call me as their new pastor."

If. The congregation, without a moment's hesitation, would call Tucker Raines—the single man—to be their pastor. They loved him, his heart and his preaching.

But they didn't feel the same way about her. She'd given them no reason to. Her heart had deceived her, and them. She'd seen the raised noses, heard the whispers and the gossip. She'd felt the cold shoulders on the boardwalk and in the pews. The church wouldn't choose her. And if she agreed to marry Tucker, they wouldn't choose him either. They could only see his choice for a wife as bad judgment. An undesirable quality for a spiritual leader.

She wouldn't stand in the way of his calling. Tucker Raines was a preacher from his hat to his boots. Being a pastor coursed through his veins just as freely as being a family man did. But he couldn't form a family with her *and* pastor a church here in Cripple Creek.

"I can't."

She wasn't sure what hurt her most—the reality of those two simple words, or seeing the pain etched in Tucker's eyes.

Tucker blinked hard against the stunned disbelief. When he opened his eyes again, nothing had changed. Ida still sat on the bench beside him, shaking her head. But the tenderness in her royal blue eyes said *yes*.

Had he missed something? He was certain she felt the same.

Just moments ago, she'd said she loved him. He'd seen the joy on her face when he told her he was staying in Cripple Creek. She'd blushed when he mentioned courting.

"*I can't.*"

"If you're worried about my family, don't. My parents and Willow already know how I feel about you." He glanced down at the ring box. "This ring belonged to my grandmother. Christmas morning at my aunt's house, my mother asked about the pretty girl with the flying hatpin and gave me the ring."

"She remembered me from the depot?"

"You're unforgettable, Miss Ida Sinclair." Tucker closed the jewelry box and set it inside his new hat. He was sure God had purposed for him to shepherd the people of the First Congregational Church. Had he been wrong about God's plans for him and Ida? He had if she didn't want to be a pastor's wife.

"You don't want to be married to a preacher?"

Ida stood and moved down toward the creek, and he followed her. Not that there was much to the creek this time of year. It was frozen solid.

"It's not the preacher, Tucker. It's the preacher's church." Ida brushed a curl back from her face. "God has forgiven me for the grief I've caused. But even if the people in the church could forgive me, they won't approve of a businesswoman with connections to scoundrels in the role of the pastor's wife. They won't let you do what you were born to do."

"I think you're wrong."

She bit her bottom lip and turned toward the path that led to the gate.

He drew in a deep breath. "Promise me you'll pray about it."

"I have." She looked at him one last time, then walked away.

He hated to let her go, but he too needed time to think and pray.

FORTY-THREE

*I*da sat with Hattie on one side and Faith on the other in Morgan and Kat's new carriage. She wanted to hear Tucker preach that morning and witness the voting, but she didn't want to distract him from the life of ministry God had set before him here in Cripple Creek.

When Morgan and Kat stopped by the boardinghouse on their way to the church, Hattie rounded up Ida and Faith to ride with her. "What a fine way to start a new year of Sundays," she'd said.

So on this third day of January, the carriage wheels slapped the slushy ground, headed for the house of worship. If Hattie sensed the latest tempest inside Ida, she hadn't let on. And neither had Kat, who sat contentedly in front of them beside her husband. Bright sunlight reflected off a fresh blanket of snow that covered the ground and the trees. The sunny skies overhead mocked the storm churning in her heart.

Five days had passed since Tucker's proposal of marriage. Those five days had felt like five months, despite Hattie doing everything in her power to keep Ida busy since she'd become unemployed. They'd mended aprons and darned socks for the Sisters of Mercy. They'd cleaned all the windows of the boardinghouse, inside and out, and even waxed the hardwood floor. If Ida expected to get any rest, she either needed to find another job or a new place to live. If the latter, she'd definitely miss her landlady's unpredictable company.

In the past few days, she'd talked to Hattie about everything from fashion to furniture, but she hadn't said anything of substance to the older woman. Nothing about her love for Tucker and his love for her.

Perhaps she should have. Sharing such feelings with the motherly landlady had worked out well for Kat and Nell. But Ida hadn't even told her own sisters what had transpired at the creek on Tuesday. She needed to sort out her feelings, and it suited her best to keep her turbulent emotions between her and God.

If things were different...if there was any hope of building a life with Tucker, she'd be the first one to spill the beans.

"It'll all work out, dear." Hattie winked at Ida and patted her knee. "You'll see."

Leaning toward her maternal companion, Ida whispered, "You know?"

"I'm not sure if I know what you think I know, but..." Hattie cupped her mouth as if that might help lower the volume of her speech. "I *know* you and Tucker love one another. Plain as a stick in the snow the night of Morgan's concert."

Ida nodded, remembering. But memories wouldn't help her let go of the preaching ice man. Why would God bring her to the point where she could believe she was part of His plan for Tucker's life, only to lead her and Tucker in different directions?

Hattie tapped Ida's shoulder, bringing Ida's thoughts back to the current carriage ride. "Just remember this, dear—you'd make a fine pastor's wife." Her silver-gray eyes twinkled with dreaminess.

Nearly an hour and a half later, Ida stood in the third row between her sisters while the congregation sang the last stanza of the benediction hymn—"More About Jesus."

More of His love who died for me.

While everyone else sank onto their pews, Reverend Taggart walked toward the pulpit.

Tucker closed his Bible and accepted the balding man's handshake. "Reverend, if you don't mind, I have something I need to say to the good folks of the First Congregational Church before they vote on me as their candidate for pastor."

Nodding, the reverend removed his spectacles and returned to the front row.

Tucker gripped the top of the wooden pulpit and straightened to his full height. "It has been my privilege to bring God's Word to you this morning and in the past. And I count it an honor that you would consider me to follow in Reverend Taggart's footsteps as your shepherd."

When the reverend started to stand to begin the voting, Tucker held up his hand to stop him. "Many of you have come to know me through my ice deliveries to your homes and businesses. But there's something crucially important you need to know about me before you make the decision to call me to be your new pastor. Some folks believe that what I'm about to share with you may sway you to continue your search for a suitable pastor."

Ida's breath caught. This was about her.

Whispers rolled over the pews like waves, and Ida wanted to slip to the ground and crawl out the door. But it was too late. Instead, she sat up straight. She gazed up at Tucker, who looked directly into her soul. Or so it seemed. The twinkle in his eyes hinted her name was on the tip of his tongue.

She reached for Kat's hand on one side and Nell's on the other. Their warmth told her words hadn't been necessary between them. Her sisters knew about the love and the squall bubbling up inside her.

She searched Tucker's brown eyes for any hint that he knew or cared that he was throwing away his opportunity to settle down as the pastor of the First Congregational Church. He held her gaze, and his voice rang out strong and clear while he continued his speech.

"The woman I love and who loves me has refused my proposal of marriage. She admits she loves me, but insists we cannot marry. Apparently, she feels she is a sinner who, while not beyond salvation, is beyond forgiveness or acceptance by this body." He looked out over the assembly. "I know this young woman's heart, and I intend to make her my wife. If you have it in you to believe her sincerity and to embrace her as the wife of your pastor, then I would be proud to serve this church. Otherwise, I have an ice business to run."

Tucker stepped out from behind the pulpit and held his hand out to her. "Miss Ida Sinclair and I will be waiting outside while you vote."

Ida prayed she wouldn't trip as she stepped out of the pew and met him in the aisle. She joined her hand to his, forcing herself to resist her desire to embrace him then and there, in front of God and everybody. She fairly skipped to the rear of the church with him and out the door. On the steps, Ida could only look into Tucker's eyes and wonder if this was all a dream.

Very few minutes passed before the door opened and a hunched man with sprigs of white hair on his head invited them back inside. Ida kept a solid hold on Tucker's forearm as they walked up the center aisle to the front of the church.

Reverend Taggart's voice rose above a flurry of applause. "I know you have backup plans in place, Mr. Raines, but this congregation has asked me to assure you that other plans won't be necessary. We all wish to invite you to be the next pastor and hope to be invited to your wedding."

The relief and longing she glimpsed in Tucker's brown eyes rivaled her own. "That's good news," he declared.

Ida nodded, refusing to divert her attention from the man she loved.

As the congregation paraded by their new pastor at the door, they all stopped to thank him, and the ladies gave Ida hugs.

When the last parishioner had left and Reverend Taggart had bidden them farewell, Tucker looked into Ida's face. "Well, then?"

"Reverend Raines," Ida said, smiling uncontrollably, "it seems to me a proper courtship would include at least one more buggy ride."

"I figured as much. I rented a proper carriage for the occasion, and I know of a perfect destination." He held his arm out to her and she hooked her hand at his elbow, letting him guide her down the church steps, feeling like royalty.

Moments later, Tucker helped Ida up into the seat of the white carriage, then took his place at the reins right beside her.

Before Ida could count all her blessings, she and Tucker passed through the gate onto the Raines property. Tucker directed the horse across the open pasture and up to the highest spot, overlooking the creek. There, he jumped to the ground. He escorted Ida from her perch and down to the plain plank bench between the two dormant willow saplings.

As soon as she was seated, Tucker dropped to one knee in the snow. He reached into his coat pocket and pulled out the familiar little box.

Her breath whooshed out on a sweet sigh.

"Now that we have your concern out of the way, I will ask you again." Tucker opened the box to display the little gold ring with the leaves and the diamond. "Will you, Miss Ida Sinclair, do me the honor of sharing my life as my wife?"

Ida fought for a breath, worried the man she loved would misinterpret the delay as indecision. Even to her, it seemed an eternity before she blurted out, *"Yes!"*

FORTY-FOUR

*N*early one month later, Ida pressed the bodice of the wedding gown she wore against her mother's corset. *Something old.* Spinning like a princess, she backed up to the newest arrival to Hattie's Boardinghouse. "Can you close this up for me?"

"I'd be happy to help." Willow's voice carried a satiny lilt as she began sliding the silk-covered buttons through their loops.

Tucker's sister had arrived on the early train six days ago, just in time for the Sunday morning service—a true vision of God's amazing grace and emotional healing.

"You said your sister designed your gown?" Willow asked.

Ida nodded, taking care not to muss the fine job Kat had done pinning her hair up into a French twist. "Our youngest sister, Vivian, designed the dress, and our aunt Alma did the sewing." Ida drew in a deep breath when Willow reached the buttons at her upper back.

"So Vivian and your aunt are still in Maine?"

"They are, but Vivian will join us here in Cripple Creek in the summer," Nell said from where she sat on the bed, polishing Ida's white boots.

"Four sisters." Willow's fingers stilled. "I've wished for a sister nearly all of my life—since the day I first picked up a doll." She resumed her task. "Not that I haven't grown accustomed to my little brother, mind you."

Turning to face Willow, nearly five years her senior, Ida grasped her hands. Tucker's sister shared the same dark brown hair color, but her eyes were green, not brown. "I'm so glad you're here." She pulled Willow into a tender embrace.

"What Ida didn't tell you is if you are her sister, you're our sister too." Nell's voice was as warm as the kindness filling her eyes.

"And don't forget about me." Faith held up the bouquet of dried roses and a pine bough she'd been arranging.

"Six sisters." Ida glanced at the dressing table where Hattie stood, adding the final touches to Kat's auburn curls. "And a mother hen."

Hattie cackled and all five sisters of the heart joined in.

"And..." Ida pointed a playful finger at Willow. "You're older than I am, so you get to be the *big sister*."

Willow shook her head. "Oh, no you don't. Big sister to one brother is enough of a distinction for me."

The weeks since Tucker's declaration of love in front of the congregation had been feverish and glorious. And today she would wed the man of her dreams—a man who loved God with all his heart and allowed that love to spill over into his affection for her.

"Speaking of my brother, I hear you have a new job."

Kat tugged a ripple out of the top of her skirt. "You're going back to work?"

Ida nodded, taking care not to upset her curls. "As the new office manager for the Raines Ice Company. Otis will manage the deliveries, and I'll keep the books. In the spring, we'll open a showroom where I can sell iceboxes."

A smile lit Nell's aqua blue eyes. "The man does have great taste. A wife and savvy businesswoman in one package." The slap of horse hoofs on the road below drew Nell to the window. She turned back toward Ida. "Your carriage awaits, Fair Princess, and Boney has the reins."

"Boney?" Willow scrunched her forehead.

"Boney Hughes." Kat's voice exuded admiration for the man. "He's an old miner who keeps his wings hidden, but he's always ready for action."

"One of Cripple Creek's many colorful characters." Ida smoothed the lace that covered the skirt of her gown.

"You should stay in town, dear. Cripple Creek offers an abundance to inspire your drawing." Hattie started for the doorway, then flung more words over her shoulder. "And I like having you here."

Ida gently lifted her skirts while her sisters, blood and otherwise, followed her out of the room and down the staircase. Within a few dizzying moments, Ida sat surrounded by women she loved in a carriage that transported them to the First Congregational Church of Cripple Creek.

While Morgan played the piano, Ida stood in the vestibule with her hand resting on Judson's forearm. The doors at the back of the sanctuary opened and the wedding march began.

Judson looked at her and smiled. "Shall we?"

"I thought you'd never ask." Ida made herself take slow steps up the aisle so she could capture every moment of the bedazzling walk toward her future with Tucker Raines.

Will and Laurel Raines stood at a front pew beside Naomi Bernard and her four sons. Hattie, Boney, and Faith crowded the pew on the other side of the aisle.

Ida's attendants—Kat, Nell, and Willow—faced her, beaming warm smiles while Otis Bernard did the same from the other side of the pastor, where he waited for Morgan and Judson to join him. Her preaching ice man stood front and center with Pastor Frank Mercer, his father's friend from the sanitorium.

As soon as Ida and Judson had cleared the front pew, Tucker took two quick steps toward them. He extended his hand to her, and when their hands joined, she gazed up at him. Staring into her beloved's adoring brown eyes, she breathed a prayer of thanksgiving that God had included her in His plans for the Reverend Tucker Raines.

Readers Guide

1. Which of the Sinclair sisters do you identify with most? feisty, stubborn Kat? gentle, romantic Nell? ambitious, determined Ida? What about that sister draws you?

2. One of Ida's defining characteristics—and her defining struggle—is her ambition and drive to succeed as a businesswoman. What is good about Ida's ambition? What's bad about it? How does it lead her into making material wealth her highest goal?

3. If Ida struggles with her ambition, what does Tucker struggle with? guilt over Sam's death and Willow's melancholia? hHis need for his father to forgive him? his purpose in Cripple Creek? What do his particular struggles say about him as a person?

4. Why do the people of Cripple Creek look down on Mollie O'Bryan and, by association, Ida? How does Ida respond to this, and how is she able to convince herself for so long that what she's doing is acceptable?

5. Mollie O'Bryan is a historical figure who lived in Cripple Creek at the time this story takes place. Ignoring her fictionalized personality and behavior, what do you think of Mollie's accomplishments as a businesswoman in an 1896 mining town? What qualities do you imagine she must have possessed in life that made it possible for her to become a successful businesswoman in this era?

6. Ida distrusts most men, assuming they either want something from her or want to put her in her "place." Many of the men she meets, both in Portland and in Cripple Creek, reinforce her distrust. Do you

share her feelings toward men at all? Have you encountered any men like the ones who shattered Ida's trust or been discriminated against because of your gender? How does Ida's distrust cause her to lash out at men who mean her well, like Tucker or Judson?

7. Tucker spends most of his time in Cripple Creek wondering what his purpose is. He feels adrift, unable to decipher what God wants him to do. In what ways was Tucker right where God needed him to be, despite his doubts? When in your life have you shared Tucker's sense of being lost? Did you eventually discover God's will for you in that time?

8. Kat and Nell have very different reactions to Kat's pregnancy, and neither is the expected unconditional joy. How do you think you would have responded in either of their situations?

9. Ida doesn't want to complicate her life with romance, focused as she is on her career. But God brings Tucker into her life, and Ida falls in love with him in spite of her desires. Has God ever brought something— or someone—into your life that you weren't looking for or ready for?

10. How prevalent do you think schools of thought similar to Colin's still are in this day and age? Do you see signs of it anywhere in society or media, or do you think we've moved past a dominantly patriarchal society? What about other parts of the world?

AUTHOR'S NOTE

*P*art of the pleasure in reading and writing historical fiction is the promise of being transported to a distant time and place. While researching *Too Rich for a Bride,* I made several interesting historical discoveries I believe will add delight to your journey.

I like to feature actual events and places in my historical fiction. *Too Rich for a Bride* highlights the rambunctious lot of stockbrokers and investors who flocked to Cripple Creek in its gold mining boom days. While the Butte Opera House was most likely still called the Butte Concert and Beer Hall at the time Ida's story takes place, I opted to adopt its current title. The Glockner Sanitorium, which was one of many tuberculosis or consumption treatment centers in Colorado during the 1800s, is one of the actual places I introduce in the story. You might be tempted to fix the spelling of *Sanitorium* to the more common and modern spelling—*Sanitarium,* but my research shows the historical spelling featured more *o*'s than *a*'s.

Harper's Bazar, the magazine I feature in the series, offers another spelling twist. If you're like me, you wanted to add another *a* after the *z,* but until the November 1929 issue, the magazine was spelled with only two *a*'s.

In each of the Sinclair Sisters of Cripple Creek novels, you'll meet at least one real-life woman from Cripple Creek history. In *Two Brides Too Many,* Sister Mary Claver Coleman of the Catholic Order of the Sisters of Mercy served as the historical woman in my fictional tale. *Too Rich for a Bride* introduces Miss Mollie O'Bryan, the first female member of a prestigious men's club—the Cripple Creek Mining Stock Exchange. Her portrayal in the story is a fictionalization.

I look forward to our time together in these stories.

May God empower you with His strength to trust His ways and His thoughts for you.

MONA HODGSON

ACKNOWLEDGMENTS

*W*riting is a lot like ballroom dancing. You must learn the steps and allow yourself the freedom to move with the rhythm. Along the way, you alternate practicing the steps alone with dancing with partners who can help you master various steps and styles.

In the case of writing, the story world and the song of the characters provide a writing rhythm. But I have not danced the publication dance in isolation. Countless people within the industry as well as many on the outside have swayed to the music with me, teaching me the dance of story.

- Bob, my hubby, who knows when to step up and step back.
- Janet Kobobel Grant of Books & Such Literary Agency, who has a keen ear for the music of fiction.
- Jessica Barnes, editor extraordinaire, who knows the scales of word-songs well and keeps me on pitch.
- Shannon Hill Marchese, who heard the first notes in the songs of the Sinclair Sisters of Cripple Creek and brought them to me.
- The entire WaterBrook Multnomah–Random House team, who step onto the dance floor with precise timing and lead me to the finale.
- DiAnn Mills, my kindred-spirit critique partner and friend, who helps me feel the cadence in the dance of a community of characters, each with their own song.

- Jeanine, June, Shirley, Debbie, Doris, Karen, Lauraine, and Ann—my personal prayer team, and all who prayed for me during the song that became this story.
- Jan Collins, Director, Cripple Creek District Museum, and Chuck Yungkurth, Library Researcher, Colorado Railroad Museum, both generous purveyors of historical facts that added movement to the dance.
- A big thank you to all of these listed, and to all who aren't, who added notes to the rhythm of this novelist and this novel.

Endless gratitude to the Master Choreographer, Jesus—the Way, the Truth, and the Life. Jesus is the Song that sets my feet to dancing.

About the Author

*M*ona Hodgson is the author of *Two Brides Too Many* and *Too Rich for a Bride,* the first two novels in the Sinclair Sisters of Cripple Creek Series. She is also the author of nearly thirty children's books, including *Real Girls of the Bible: A Devotional, Bedtime in the Southwest,* and six Zonderkidz I Can Read books. Mona's writing credits also include hundreds of poems, articles, and short stories in more than fifty different periodicals, including *Focus on the Family, Decision, Clubhouse Jr., Highlights for Children, The Upper Room, The Quiet Hour, Bible Advocate,* and *The Christian Communicator.* Mona speaks at women's retreats, schools, and writers' conferences.

Mona is one of the four Gansberg sisters of Arizona. She and Bob, her husband of thirty-eight years, have two grown daughters, a son-in-law, three grandsons, and one granddaughter.

To learn more about Mona or to find readers' guides for your book club, visit her Web site: www.monahodgson.com. You can also find Mona at www.twitter.com/monahodgson, www.facebook.com/Mona.Hodgson, and on Facebook at the Mona Hodgson Fan Page.